The People's Flag

The People's Flag

The Union of Britain and the Kaiserreich

Volumes I & II

Tom Black

SEA LION PRESS

First published by Sea Lion Press, 2019
ISBN: 9781089141464

Cover artwork by Jack Tindale

Foreword

Tom Black

'The English have all the material requisites for the revolution.
What they lack is the spirit of generalisation and revolutionary ardour.'
Karl Marx

The following counterfactual history book takes place in a universe much like our own. The point of divergence came in 1917, when Woodrow Wilson was unable to convince the US congress to back war with Germany. With America absent from the war, the Germans had more time to defeat Russia and build up their forces in the west, beginning their final offensive in 1919 (rather than the rushed 'Operation Michael' of our universe's 1918).

The French war effort collapsed and German troops marched into Paris; just as it began, the Third Republic ended under German fire and facing revolution from within. Shortly after capitulating, France descended into Syndicalist revolution, creating the Commune of France. Similar events occurred in the defeated Italy, with the south of the country proclaiming the Anarcho-Syndicalist Republic of the Sicilies, and the victorious Austrians proclaiming a loose federation of Italian duchies in the north under the nominal authority of the Pope.

Ironically, as Western Europe collapsed into leftist revolution, the Whites won the Russian Civil War. Kerensky managed to secure the support of the German armed forces in exchange for acceptance of the Treaty of Brest-Litovsk's concessions, and the White Generals, together with the German army, defeated the Reds. Lenin died at Petrograd, Trotsky, Stalin and Molotov at Tsaritsyn, while Bukharin went into hiding.

But Britain did not capitulate as quickly as France and Italy. Ludendorff and Hindenburg saw the folly of invading the British Isles and instead waged an inconclusive war on the seas and in their colonies. After two years without a decisive outcome being reached, Ludendorff proposed a 'Peace with Honour' to Lloyd George. Neither country would cede any colonial holdings to the other, but Britain would recognise German hegemony over Mitteleuropa and pay 'reasonable' reparations. It was this that began the final months of the United Kingdom. Months after the signing of the Peace with Honour in November 1921, the bloody Irish War of Independence was concluded with the cessation of most of Ireland to Michael Collins' 'Republic of Ireland'. In exchange for recognition of the Republic, Britain kept hold of six of the nine counties of Ulster, establishing 'Northern Ireland'. On the mainland, however, things were going from bad to worse. The economy was exhausted from years of war, and Britons felt humiliated – that they had wasted hundreds of thousands of lives for nothing. All it would take for Britain to fall to leftist revolution also was the right sequence of events. It just so happens that what we in our universe call 'the General Strike of 1926' happened a year earlier in this timeline, and was known as 'the British Revolution'.

These ideas may sound familiar. Many of them formed the basis for a modification ('mod') of the popular video game *Hearts of Iron II*, called *Kaiserreich: Legacy of the Weltkrieg* and first created in 2005. The idea of a Syndicalist 'Union of Britain' arising in the aftermath of a Central Powers victory began with the modification's original creator, who used the online handle Sarmatia1871. I am grateful to him, and the mod team that continues to make *Kaiserreich: Legacy of the Weltkrieg* a worldwide phenomenon.

This book began as a project to 'flesh out' the Union of Britain in the *Kaiserreich* setting, and as such features many divergences from the original idea. Some will remain familiar to seasoned players of the *Kaiserreich* mod over the years, including some ideas I incorporated into the mod myself when I was on the development team – the fate of T.E. Lawrence, for example, and the ideology of 'Totalism' were my ideas in the first place. Others may be confusing to players of a mod that is still going strong fourteen years since its birth and has undergone a number of storyline changes over the years. All writing contained within this book is, of course, my own work.

This particular counterfactual is written as if it were a history book from the universe about which it is written. With this in mind, it is important to respect any foibles, biases or otherworldly concerns that its 'authors' (at this time, most principally Comrades Durham, Hobsbawm and Pollitt) may have. Clues and the like about what lies in store for the future of the Union and the world in general can, if one is particularly eagle-eyed, be gleaned from the hindsight deployed by the esteemed authors of each article in the book.

I began writing this for online serialisation back in 2010. I've recently become aware that *Kaiserreich* has exploded in popularity in recent years, and thus my initial fears that this would be too niche a topic for publication were no longer valid. The two volumes contained in this book are the total of the story so far, as it was written and completed back in 2011. However, the first chapter of Volume III, appearing at the end of the book, provides a snapshot of the hypothetical Second Great War that awaits Britain and the world, and was written this year, in 2019. If interest proves sufficient, I will certainly endeavour to complete Volumes III and IV, which should carry the story into the 1950s, and publish them through Sea Lion Press.

I hope you enjoy this book. It was born as a passion project and I hope that shines through. Everything from this point on is by the 'authors' of this collection, so I will turn you over to the safe hands of John Durham, editor of *The People's Flag*.

Introduction

'Imagine our Union stands for a millennium. When our descendants look back on these first fifty years of its history, will there be any man or woman who can say they were not our finest hour?'
Jack Jones, 24 October 1975

It is perhaps an example of our nation's exceptionalism that, until now, no complete history of our Union has ever been attempted. Historians like Taylor and Kershaw found their efforts frustrated and instead focused on different parts of its history, most prominently the Second Great War, while the closest anyone has come to producing a complete history is the former Commissary for Education Eric Hobsbawm, whose death prevented his work ever being completed. Some of his completed essays and notes are present in this collection.

For that is what this is – a collection. Perhaps where Comrades Taylor and Kershaw went wrong was attempting to write an entire history of such a remarkable nation on their own. Here, I serve as both contributor and humble editor, accompanied by many of the finest minds of our scholarly generation. Even so, the task of chronicling such a long period is not without difficulty; the structure of this publication is that of a series of essays, some narrative and some analytical. The hope is that together, my colleagues and I can create an accurate picture of the Union, from the trials and tribulations of the '20s through to the '50s, through the prosperous yet tumultuous '60s and '70s, and into the reformist '80s, '90s and modern age. Here, we hope you will agree, can be found an uncensored and scholarly picture of the entirety of our Union's history, 'warts and all'.

John Durham, Senior Lecturer in History, Ruskin University

Volume I

1925-1935

Ten Years That Shook the World

"I do not for a moment believe that we shall see the Revolution in our lifetime."

John Maclean, 1924

The Violent Death of Illiberal England

John Durham

"Revolution? My dear Rudyard, this is not France."
George V, 20 October 1925

It is hardly necessary to describe the circumstances which led to the proclamation of our Union, for it is the first thing taught to us in school and the subject of a great many works of literature, from the classic novelisation *The Men That Shook The World*, published in 1930, to the 2006 film *Deepest Red*. It is impossible to remain on this island for more than a month and not learn in detail of the brave struggle of the Welsh miners in 1925, the escalation to a General Strike and the failed government's catastrophic miscalculations of how to deal with it.

What is perhaps less well-known, and is only coming to light as the archives of that tumultuous period are being opened to us now, is the political intrigue among the revolutionaries. Far from the 'United Front' that school textbooks expound at length over, different factions, led by men and women who would (in most cases) eventually form a government of compromise, vied for control. The Autonomists of Niclas y Glais started as Welsh nationalists seeking a Commune of Wales. Horner and Snowden's Federationists came from far less Trade Union-friendly roots than their later actions would have you believe. Annie Kenney's Congregationalists began as little more than an even more militant form of the Suffragettes, believed by some historians to have sprung from the 'Women's Shelters' that were quickly established in abandoned churches as the chaos of revolution and the collapse of the rule of law led to fears of mass rape. And the Maximists, so notoriously personified by Oswald Mosley's iron-fisted rule ten years after the Revolution, were by far the most violent of the revolutionaries. Many of the bloodier acts that school textbooks choose to avoid – the Burning of the Ritz, the Covent Garden Massacre[1] – were perpetrated by hard-line Maximists whose experiences in the Russian Bolshevik Rebellion had closed their eyes to such concepts as cruelty.

In addition to the problems among the revolutionaries, there are a number of myths about the Revolution itself that persist to this day. The 'Glorious Six', as the weeks between the proclamation of the General Strike and the storming of Parliament have been known, have entered our Union's mythos and have, as such, gathered a fair few urban legends behind them. One regards the infamous deployment of a platoon of Territorials against a pamphleteers' march on 14 September. The story goes that the pamphleteers, a massed group of about 500 men and women (their political affiliation within the Revolution is never stated in the popular version of the story), were peacefully marching through the streets of Brixton carrying placards and distributing Revolutionary pamphlets. The story goes on to say that the Territorials' commander, the unfortunately-named Lieutenant Scruton, was so enraged by the sight that he ordered his men to open fire. When the smoke had cleared, forty-one lay dead in the street, and many of the Territorial soldiers would desert later that day.

The truth is not so picturesque. Like the Boston Massacre before it, the politics of the occasion eclipsed the facts of it. It is never said, for instance, that those marching were English Autonomists, calling for the proclamation of an English Republic. Nor is it pointed out that the marchers, far from marching peacefully, were armed with clubs and the occasional firearm and were chanting threats to those citizens who did not agree with their position. Finally, the greatest injustice is always done to the Territorials themselves, who, far from obeying unquestioningly the orders of the admittedly ruthless (and jumpy)

---

[1] Still relatively unknown because of the alleged involvement of Mosley himself, the massacre involved a group of Maximist agitators opening fire on a crowd leaving the Covent Garden Opera House, killing 17 and wounding dozens more. Among the dead was the then-recently elected MP for Warwick and Leamington, Anthony Eden.

Scruton, refused to fire until it became clear that, due to a miscommunication (believed to be Scruton firing his revolver at a nearby marcher), the marchers intended to charge them. To say that some of the Territorials deserted later that day is also an understatement – almost all of them defected to the Revolution and Scruton himself was found hanged on a lamppost, a .303 round in his heart. The 'Marching Martyrs', as the rhyme goes, were not quite the victims of reactionary zeal and bloodlust, more the catastrophic consequence of one man's possession of absolute power in a high-pressure situation.

But this article's aim is not to give the reader an impression of revisionism and deliberately controversial history. These are just some facts to bear in mind when studying those that all the Union knows; that in 1925, the Stand of the Miners became the General Strike, and that after six weeks of attempted reaction, including the lamentable (and ultimately self-defeating) decision to deploy troops against pamphleteers, the establishment had no choice but to give in as Parliament itself was stormed by the massed workers of London.[2] With London and all centres of communication in Revolutionary hands, it was only a matter of time before popular proclamation led to the inaugural Congress of the Trade Unions in February of 1926.

---

[2] One verifiable example of the United Front is found here – it is not merely an urban legend that Maximist Eric Blair gave his later foe Niclas y Glais a 'leg-up' over the fences surrounding Parliament Square. Blair documented it in his diaries, but it was removed when they were published; the unedited versions only came into public hands in 2001.

The Inaugural Congress

John Durham

"It was all so easy. It made one wonder why we hadn't had a
revolution before."
Tom Mann, 31 January 1926

The first Congress of the Trade Unions, as it soon became known, was
a turning point in British history. It was here that all thoughts of
Royalist reconciliation were thrown away and that the last vestiges of
so-called 'democratic liberalism' were cast aside. Beginning on 1
February 1926, a date much publicised on pamphlets, posters and by
word-of-mouth across the country since the fall of the government on
24 October 1925, the delegates from Trade Unions across the country
filed into Congress House on Eccleston Square with optimism in the
air. The agenda for the day was as follows:

Apologies for absence
Acclamation of the Union of Britain
Election of Officers
Any other business

While point one resulted in the most wads of paper being passed to
the front of any CTU in history (the process delayed proceedings by a
full two hours), point three is of most interest to the historian. As no
elections among the CTU had been held until this meeting, the
question of who should chair the first meeting itself had led to a bitter
struggle among the organisers of the event. The chairman of the TUC
(Trade Union Congress, the spiritual predecessor of the CTU), Alonzo
Swales, had been elected by that body the previous year and fully
expected to take up the leadership of what he considered to be an
'extraordinary general meeting' of the TUC. Very much representing
the most reactionary segment of the Trade Union movement, he found
his plan deeply unpopular and, as such, his candidacy untenable.

Among the contenders for the chair were lifelong socialist and 'candidate of conciliation' Tom Mann and John Maclean, at this time a famously powerful speaker who had invigorated the dockers of Clydeside into some of the most explosive actions of the General Strike and Revolution. Eventually, it would be Tom Mann who was 'elected' as interim chair, though no election took place. Mann was simply proposed as a candidate to the assembled TUC and Revolutionary heads, and no-one raised an objection. The Congress was to be chaired by Tom Mann, and this would not be the last the Union heard of him.

When the Congress eventually got underway, the factions of the Revolution that had hardly been friends during it now turned upon one another savagely, though admittedly only verbally. There is no question that all of them wanted Socialism for Britain and had their people's interests at heart, but there is equally no question as to how vehemently some of them disagreed over the best way to achieve this. To quote a contemporary edition of *The Chartist* (then a recently established radical pamphlet rather than the state newspaper it would become):

'Of the multitude of factions present on the first day of the Congress, the four largest have been established to be the following:

The Federationists believe in giving local Syndicates and Trade Unions a great deal of power over local policy, similar to the local councils of the recently failed state. However, the key difference is the popular support and membership of the worker in each of these Syndicates. National policy would largely be with reference to overseas matters if these men have their way. They believe industry and all practically all domestic matters (barring the 'Key Aims' of each year of the Union's life) should be decided by these local Syndicates rather than the central government. The key figures within this movement include John Maclean, G.D.H. Cole and Philip Snowden.

The Congregationalists are a feminist-oriented group, headed by Annie Kenney. Economically they are similar to the Federationists, but believe the path to Socialism must be quickened through greater involvement of women in the Revolution. Isolationism is the core of their philosophy, believing Britain suffered enough trying to maintain an Empire and presence overseas. 'Socialism in one country' is their motto.

The Autonomists believe in further decentralising the Union, arguing for the home nations to have greater autonomy, possibly even total independence for England, Scotland and Wales. Instead of the more widely-accepted 'Union of Britain', they believe in establishing a Federation of the British Isles with its capital in Birmingham, while each nation would be a full and independent member of this federation. They are led by the Welsh Poet Niclas y Glais, who has described his plans as 'the independence of the States in the United States of America combined with true Socialist freedom'.

The Maximists favour a strong central government and full state control of the economy. Controversially, they are also heavily nationalist, and support an immediate expansion of the military so that Britain may not only defend herself but also project and expand the Revolution. They are led by Revolutionary hero Arthur James Cook.'

As the experienced student of history will notice, the factions thus remained very similar to the state they would be in by 1936. But the factions would need to form powerful voting blocs if they wanted to achieve anything at the Congress, something they immediately set about doing.

The second point on the agenda, planned by Tom Mann himself, was a very careful piece of wording. The Union of Britain itself had already been 'proclaimed' *per se* by the red-banner waving revolutionaries on top of the Houses of Parliament. The new constitution – drawn up by, among others, GDH Cole, Victor Gollancz and John Maclean – had been widely circulated as a pamphlet for the last two months. To proclaim the Union again, therefore, would be irrelevant and potentially dangerous. What Mann proposed instead was that the assembled members would, on behalf of those local people they represented, show their support for the Union of Britain through acclamation and thereby cement its status as the accepted way forward for Britain. Unsurprisingly, the motion was met with great enthusiasm. Margaret Cole wrote in her diary: 'There were whoops and cheers and goodness knows what else. All around me were men and women stamping their feet and throwing their hands into the air. Gradually, a chant began to emerge, and as soon as I heard what it was I too felt compelled to join in. "Onwards Britain!" we cried, "Onwards Britain!"[3]

This successfully set the mood for the Congress to be highly jubilant and assuaged any fears of a bitter or violent contest. Point three of the agenda could now be advanced to. The election of officers had been accepted as the turning point of the Congress already. Whichever faction got its people elected would be in *de facto* control of the Union already, given the Chairman and General Secretary's power to decide the agenda of the Congress, and the simple fact that whoever won a majority in this election was likely to do the same on the matters of policy that the constitution required voting on over the coming days.

The four candidates who gained the sufficient nominations for Chairman were, unsurprisingly, all representatives of a major faction. Representing the Maximists was coal miner and union leader Arthur James Cook. The Congregationalists put forward Victor Gollancz as their candidate, apparently believing (with perhaps some accuracy) that at this stage in the Revolution a woman stood no chance of being elected. Niclas y Glais, a poet and natural orator, stood for the Autonomists. The Federationists nominated John Maclean, seen by many as the natural leader.

The candidates were each permitted to give a six-minute speech on why they sought this office. Many memoirs of those present have thought it important to note that Victor Gollancz spoke somewhat quietly and in a far more subdued manner than his opponents, with one delegate noting that 'he could have been proposing the finest implementation of Marxist theory ever put forward by man or beast, I just couldn't bloody well hear him'. Cook chose to give a fiery speech (he is said to have been trained in oratory by his close ally, Oswald Mosley) about the need for 'Permanent Revolution', using examples from his time leading miners against the army in the Revolution. It was a strong speech, but contained few sustainable ideas, according to those

---

[3] Margaret Cole, *Living for Britain: My Diaries* (London: Penguin Publishing Cpv., 1945) p.73

present. Niclas y Glais, arguing for by far the most complex of the four factional proposals, found his audience uninterested and even appeared to detect that his views were not widely shared, declaring at the end of his speech 'and if my message is not heeded here in the towns and cities, I shall take it to the hills and valleys, where it might be better understood!'[4]

The final speech came from John Maclean of the Federationists. Cutting a massive figure as he strode towards the podium, he spoke without notes for the full six minutes, promising a small central government that acted in the interests of local Syndicates and Trade Unions, the right to local autonomy for workers' groups, and socialist reform of the armed forces. His conclusion was greeted with thunderous applause from all sides of the chamber, notably a great number of women and Congregationalist supporters. When the voting took place, there was already a clear idea of who would be the first elected Chairman.

As expected, Maclean won the Chair by 'a clear majority', believed to have been achieved through the support of Congregationalists who supported many of his views while sensing Gollanz's inability to win. In his acceptance speech, he urged his assembled comrades to elect his choice of General Secretary, Philip Snowden, something they promptly did (the closest competitor was Arthur Cook, who stood again in an attempt to create a 'balanced government').

With the two major offices elected, the first day of the inaugural Congress drew to a close. The 'any other business' almost turned into a lengthy debate on the exact role of the CTU and its officers in running the country, until Tom Mann, in his final act as interim Chairman, banged his gavel and declared such discussions were for the following days of the Congress, not now. As the delegates parted ways for the first time, there was still a feeling of optimism in the air. The

---

[4] Though a poetic phrase and one he is much-remembered for, y Glais' hopes never came true. His politics were not much more popular in the valleys of Wales than they were in the town halls of England. That he and the Autonomists survived as a political entity for so long is an historical oddity that is examined later in this book in an article by Terry Pollitt.

Federationists were arguably the least controversial choice, and Maclean was personally popular with almost all the delegates. It would remain to be seen how effective this unofficial 'Federationist majority' would be in deciding the major questions of the coming days – the role of the constitution, the army and the other officers (now named 'Commissaries') that would serve as the equivalent of 'ministers in cabinet' under the old regime. The only tension detectable in the atmosphere of the departing delegates was how much of a split would occur if some choices proved unpopular, or there were serious disagreements over how important the 'federal authority' should be. As they left, Oswald Mosley is said to have remarked to a young Eric Blair, who was by his side, 'Today we have seen the end of the beginning. Let us hope tomorrow is not the beginning of the end.'

The Royalist Exodus

Eric Hobsbawm

'I shall return.'
Winston Churchill, near Plymouth, 5 November 1925

It is a favourite pastime of Royalist intellectuals to wistfully speculate on the futures of those men and women who, either through untimely death or flight from the British Isles, left the British public sphere forever after 1925. A recent bestseller is Mr Windsor and Mrs Simpson *by Australasian-born Philippa Gregory. The novel is a racy counterfactual loosely based on the brief courtship between Edward VIII and an American divorcée. Where the courtship broke up in the face of the exiled King's national duty in 'OTL' ('Our TimeLine' as I believe the 'counterfactual community' refer to it), the novel pictures a world where a cockier Edward finds himself on the British throne, the Revolution having been averted, but abdicates out of mad love for Mrs Simpson. It was remarked by critic and Chartist culture editor Polly Toynbee that 'only the poor prose and paper-thin characters can make the absurdity of the plot seem true-to-life.'*

But such speculation is not limited to 'aerodrome fiction'. A more dated example, published in the German Empire in the 1930s, is 'Fuhrerreich'. Banned by Von Papen in 1938 for its 'exceedingly dark moral tone',[5] the work portrayed a world created by Entente victory in the First Great War. Casting Imperialist martyr of the Russian Civil War Adolf Hitler instead as a disgruntled dictator, what is more interesting to note is its treatment of Britain. Its author, Otto Strasser, predicted a Britain led by the relatively obscure (and disgraced by Gallipoli) former First Lord of the Admiralty, Winston Churchill, with the equally obscure deceased MP Anthony Eden somehow finding his way into the cabinet. More mainstream Royalist thought has speculated on who among the 'lost political generation' of 1925

---

[5] It became available in all four German states after the Second Great War, and has since been translated into English, French, Italian and Spanish.

would have done great things for reactionary Britain. Stanley Baldwin, Harold Macmillan, Austen Chamberlain and many others are often mourned as having been forced to waste their talents in political isolation during Exile. There is also something of a habit among Royalists to figuratively beat their breasts like mourning Persians over those rising stars killed during their attempts to leave Britain.

It is with this background in mind that we come to the first of a number of articles in this book by the late Eric Hobsbawm. It was first printed in 1981 in 'History Today', and follows in its unedited entirety.

*

The Exodus, as it became known, saw the flight from Britain of thousands of men, women and children. This article shall examine the facts of the matter. Who 'escaped' from Britain, and why? What were the conditions on the way to Canada? And, perhaps most crucially, what became of those members of the 'ancien regime', particularly the large number of aristocrats, who could not get away?

The Exodus began on 26 October 1925. Two days after the collapse of the government and the proclamation of the Union of Britain, Margaret Cole wrote in her diaries that 'a procession of motorcars, some battered and scratched, some even with bulletholes in them, was speeding down the road towards the docks. Their horns were a cacophony of panic. As we lined the streets to watch them go by, a man next to me cried "and good riddance, too!" I later heard that in one of the cars had been our MP. He was a Conservative, and an agreeable MP as Conservatives went. I do not know if he made it to Canada; one heard such terrible things about the overcrowded ships.'[6]

Cole's experience was far from unique. All across the country, local aristocrats, reactionary MPs and members of the wealthy middle classes were racing towards the coast. Some even tried to buy their way onto aircraft at Croydon Airport, without success. The 'terrible things' Cole referred to is something of a euphemism. Those that survived the

---

[6] Margaret Cole, *Living for Britain: My Diaries* (London: Penguin Publishing Cpv., 1945) p.60

'exodus ships' have, in their own memoirs, detailed the level of squalor they experienced. Former Sea Lord Winston Churchill, who travelled to Canada on board RMS *Antonia*, wrote that 'military-issue sleeping mats were spread across the ballroom, its chandelier and wall furnishings now the only thing that distinguished it from an inner-city church hall. Upon entering the room it was impossible not to recoil at the stench. The indignity that some of the society women who were now huddled with their children next to a few tins of corned beef was too much to bear. I found myself standing on the freezing and sea-blasted deck whenever possible.'[7]

Churchill's entry, although published in Royalist Canada, was seized upon by the British press when it was made known to them as a gleefully-upheld example of how the Reactionaries had suffered when they tried to begin their fight against the people's Revolution. It just one of many such examples, so it is quite reasonable to conclude that the conditions aboard the ships were truly awful. Churchill was lucky enough to get onto an ocean liner – many of the Royalists had to buy their way onto cramped destroyers, and be content with sharing a tiny billet with a dozen others for the entire journey.

But let us not make too much of the conditions of the 'escape' itself. The real question is 'who escaped, and why?' The most famous and most obvious group to escape was the Royal Family. The King, for reasons obvious to the reactionary authorities, was given absolute priority to escape the country. He and his wife, along with the Prince of Wales who had joined them on the way, boarded the humble minesweeper HMS *Bagshot*[8] and set sail for Montreal on the morning of the 26th. The rest of the immediate Royal Family – the 'Princess Royal', Prince Albert, Prince Henry and Prince George – were to board a similar craft the following day. While Princess Mary, Prince George and Prince Albert made it to Plymouth in time for their evacuation, Henry elected, for reasons that died with him, to lead a

---

[7] Winston Churchill, *The Empire in Crisis* (Ottawa: Britannia Books, 1931) p.42

[8] Cpt. Eric Edwards, *The King had my Cabin* (Ottawa: Britannia Books, 1949) p.12

battalion of die-hard Army troops (from the King's Rifles, aptly enough) who had volunteered to defend the outskirts of Plymouth's harbour district from the approaching 'mob' of Revolutionary forces. Armed only with his Sandringham training and a Webley revolver, he announced to his tearful brother and sister that he would 'rather die in merry old England than live to see it turn rotten'. His body was recovered a few days after the fighting ended, a Webley round in his skull (it is believed he committed suicide to avoid capture). It was buried, like all the bodies of soldiers who chose to side with the Royalists during the revolution, in a simple grave with his name, rank and unit. There was no publicised funeral.

The more minor members of the Royal Family found themselves in the same boat (the pun is, I must confess, intended) as the aristocracy. The Dukes and Earls of Reactionary Britain, some of whom with ancestors that could be traced back to the Battle of Hastings, suddenly found themselves in a world where their birth meant nothing. Many of them tried to 'escape', too, most famously George Bingham, 6th Earl of Lucan, who was rescued from drowning by local 'Cheapside Militia' in the early hours of 8 November, having become extremely drunk and tried to get to the Thames Estuary in 'what looked like a child's rowing boat – the type you see at the fair'.[9] Bingham was far from alone as a member of the aristocracy that failed to escape. There were dozens more like him across the country who, once the window of opportunity to escape had passed (all docks came under the control of the CTU and Britain was declared a 'closed port' on an interim basis), found themselves increasingly worried as to what would happen to them. It is, and remains to this day, a credit to the spirit of our Revolution that not one aristocrat was hanged, or even tried, on grounds of his or her title alone. Of course, those who had served in treacherous Tory, Liberal or 'Labour' governments were tried, and some sentenced to hard labour. The only aristocrats who were executed were members of the armed forces who had been found guilty of 'crimes against the people' for their part in various massacres. Of the four death sentences

[9] Derek Hobbs, *Onwards, Cheapside: My time in the militia* (London: Macmillan, 1955) p.56

handed out by People's Courts in late 1926, two were commuted to life imprisonment on appeal.

But what for those men like Bingham who had lived a fairly harmless life but had hardly sought to change the country for the benefit of their 'social inferiors' either? The answer to that came in the opening days of the Inaugural Congress. Setting a precedent that would remain for decades, the CTU unanimously voted to 'extend a hand of comradeship' to the former aristocracy, and welcome them into the working community. Bingham himself was welcomed into a farming collective in Gloucestershire after he had been declared 'de-Bourgeoised' by the CTU's re-education centres in early 1928. Others, including Charles Wood, 2nd Viscount Halifax, travelled with his son to Newcastle, where they took jobs in the accounting office of the local Mining Syndicate.[10]

The 'hand of comradeship' movement was by and large a resounding success, allowing for the peaceful and (generally) unresented incorporation of the former aristocracy – and numerous members of the upper middle class whose workers had brought them to trial for Reaction, as well as numerous remaining MPs – into Britain's new society. Some were easier than others; the more radical of Labour's MPs were far more willing to take jobs in their local Syndicates than some of the more 'refined' Ladies and Duchesses of Kent. But it managed to deal with an exceptionally difficult situation in a largely satisfactory manner – for the popular majority at least. The problems that it untangled, however, were a mere triviality compared to the issue that was most pressing for the new state: how to defend our Island while ensuring the removal of any malignant or reactionary elements within our own Armed Forces.

The Armed Forces were, thanks to the decadence of the past few centuries, plagued with reactionary elements and dyed-in-the-wool aristocrats. The response of 'the mob', therefore, was swift and just. Earl Haig, so inconceivably granted a peerage after slaughtering

---

[10] Their story was not entirely a happy one; Charles' son, Edward Wood, found himself unable to cope with what he called his 'fall from gwace' and committed suicide in 1930.

Britain's best against the German guns, was arrested and put before a 'people's court martial', presided over by none other than Tom Wintringham. After being sentenced to death by firing squad, the ageing Field Marshall spluttered in protest, declaring 'I fought for Britain's honour like a lion fights for its pride!' Wintringham's famous reply – 'Nay, sir! Your men fought like lions. You led them like a donkey!' – has entered the common lexicon. Haig was executed at the Tower of London after his death sentence was carried by a narrow vote at the Inaugural Congress.[11]

But, in a statement commonly said at the time, 'the lieutenants of the last war will be the generals in the next'. Men like Bernard Montgomery and John Gort, who had fought and bled alongside their men in the trenches, were treated with far less distaste. In a lengthy process beginning in July 1926 (ironically the 10th anniversary of the bloody Battle of the Somme), the Army, Navy and fledgling Air Force had their officer corps entirely examined, one by one, in the dock before people's courts. Though few would swear under oath that they were radical socialists, there were many who sympathised with the common man and, perhaps still angry from the loss of the Great War, agreed that the previous regime had let the people of Britain down. The overwhelming consensus from those who stood before the people and testified their support was that they had sworn to serve and defend Britain – to them, defending their 'king' meant nothing compared to that. This was given additional credence by their very presence on the mainland – particularly the naval officers, who would have been free to leave for Canada if they had a ship under their command. Bernard Montgomery, later hero of the Second Great War, captured the mood of the times when he declared 'A socialist I am not. But a Reactionary am I neither. I entered the Army with no interest in politics, but with an interest in the continued wellbeing of the people of this nation. The Union can provide that wellbeing, and I shall strive to defend it!'

Of course, this was not universally popular. Wintringham in particular wanted to purge the officer corps of all members who were not 100% committed to leftist revolution. But John Maclean himself

---

[11] He would not be the last to die there.

stepped in and prevented this, arguing (quite correctly) that Britain needed soldiers as its defenders more than it needed ideologues – the Armed Forces would, of course, over time be gradually brought into line with the politics of the Union, but with a large section of the Fleet now rumoured to be rearming in Canada, and the Kaiser's armies allegedly sharpening their bayonets in Kiel, the decision was made to keep on all who would swear simply to uphold the Union and defend its people. The period of an 'Apolitical Army', as Kershaw calls it, had begun.

In conclusion, then, what defined the Exodus? It is perhaps best considered to be the flight of the 'old regime' and its replacement by the new. As Margaret Cole's fellow bystander remarked, there was an element of 'good riddance' to many who fled the Union during those tumultuous days. The reorganisation of the Armed Forces would probably not have been possible had its truly reactionary and rabidly rightist elements remained within. All in all, then, the Exodus was highly beneficial to the Union – many who escaped spared the Union the trouble of a messy trial and potential execution. The fate of Field Marshall Haig was, if one believes contemporary sources, desired for many other members of the 'old regime' by the more bloodthirsty members of the new.

Carving out a place in the world: public decisions and diplomatic undertones in the British foreign policy of 1926

Terry Pollitt

'I don't quite know what they've created over there, but I think I like it.'

Jim Larkin, 12 February 1926

It is apparently too great a task for the common historian to worry his- or herself with the complexities of political theory. It is therefore the duty of myself, your humble political analyst, to recount the hum-drums of the processes that have shaped our Union throughout the last nine decades. The first of my articles in this book will focus on the real meaning behind the opening plays of Union foreign policy, particularly the decisions made at the Inaugural Congress.

The second week of the congress had been set aside for foreign affairs. Faith in Britain's military strength was still faltering at this point, so the first item on the agenda was the importance of securing the Union's independent status. There was fear on all sides – some panicking elements of the congress feared that the Royalist 'Exodus fleet' was simply going to refuel and rearm then turn right back round again to reconquer the British Isles.[12] Others expected Germany to take military action against yet another emerging Socialist state. The priority was therefore to establish diplomatic relations with all

---

[12] A ludicrous idea, for the 'Exodus fleet' was little more than a flotilla of under-fuelled and -armed warships and a string of dilapidated ocean liners. See Comrade Hobsbawm's article earlier in this book for more details.

necessary parties, while maintaining an element of isolationism. Germany was deemed the biggest and most immediate threat, and Ernest Bevin was dispatched to the coast with a delegation of negotiators and a CTU-granted overseas travel permit. So what did the dispatch of this physically huge former Baptist minister mean politically? The message that Britain was sending to Germany was 'we're here and we're not going anywhere, but we don't mean any trouble'. Bevin captured the essence of this mentality perfectly in his stoic attitude and presence, grand speaking style (he sounded like a statesman even in casual conversation) and peaceful demeanour. Arriving at Kiel on board a Republican Navy frigate on 9 February 1926, it took the German coast guard four hours to permit him to land. Once there, he was met not by diplomats or ministers, but by the Kaiser's police, who threatened to lock him up if he did not state exactly what his purpose was. Never a man to mince his words, the West Country docker stated that 'my purpose is something far greater than anything you will achieve in your officious, bourgeois little lives – to secure peace and freedom for my people. Now, take me to your Kaiser!' Within minutes he was on a train to Hamburg, where he was met by an undersecretary to 'Chancellor' Tirpitz. The diplomatic wranglings and niceties that ensued are not, to be blunt, particularly interesting – unlike some modern writers I take no interest in what vintage of wine was offered by either party or whether any symbolism of intent can be drawn from the colour of Bevin's handkerchief that day.[13] The outcome is what interests us.

And what an outcome it was! Both countries stopped short of mutual diplomatic recognition,[14] but Tirpitz (who personally arrived at the meeting as it came to a close) gave Bevin an assurance that Germany 'held no interests regarding the British Isles provided those ruling it acted within the boundaries of the Peace with Honour'. Bevin, in return, assured Tirpitz that the Union was content to build socialism

---

[13] It was white. Unlike a certain AJP Taylor, I don't consider that a sign that he sought to 'surrender Britain's integrity'.

[14] Germany continued to recognise the exiled King as rightful ruler of Britain until the fall of the Second Reich.

for its people, and had no interest in any overseas affairs. Bevin returned to the Congress on 11 February to a hero's welcome, but the celebrations were cut short by troubling news from the West – at midnight, Irish troops under military dictator 'President' Michael Collins had flooded over the border into the 'six counties of Ulster' that had made up Northern Ireland after the Irish War of Independence. As the Union had claimed sovereignty over all areas in 'northwest Europe' controlled by previously by the United Kingdom, this was technically the first incursion by foreign military forces into Union territory. So how should Britain respond?

The answers came from all sides. Arthur James Cook and his Maximists called for immediate war with Ireland, in the name of 'preserving territorial unity'. This claim was ridiculed by Niclas y Glais' Autonomists, who argued that the Irish were doing just that by subsuming a missing part of their nation into the whole. More to the point, said Victor Gollancz on behalf of the Congregationalists, the Union was in no way ready for war, not even against a 'priest-infested backwater like Ireland'. But it was the calm-seeking John Maclean who appealed for pragmatic realism to be brought to the forefront of the discussion. Pointing out the total lack of representatives from Ulster at the CTU itself, and indeed the extremely lukewarm reception that socialism had always received there (even in the previous few explosive months), Maclean asked the assembled delegates whether letting the Ulstermen go would be such a bad thing. The 'Irish question' had plagued imperialists for generations, and to hold on to a people who simply did not wish to be one with the Socialist British – many of the rabidly pro-British leaders in Northern Ireland found their extreme Protestantism incompatible with Socialist support, and instead, in one documentable case even at this early stage, had turned to Canada's exiles for support – would surely be reactionary and counter-revolutionary. Nevertheless, Maclean was quick to assure the delegates that he was not taking the matter of an unauthorised military incursion lightly. To demonstrate his seriousness, he turned to Bevin – whose place at the lectern he had taken just minutes before – and asked him on behalf of the Congress to travel immediately to Dublin to meet with 'President' Collins and make clear where the Union stood.

The above is one of the finest political performances John Maclean ever gave. While privately a fiery ideologue, he had always been respected for being able to put pragmatism first in his leadership of the Union. In this case he did just that. His diaries indicate that every fibre of his being wanted to hang on to Ulster so that socialism could be properly spread there, but it was really the vast military superiority of Collins' forces over those in the area, and the disarray in the Republican Navy, that made him think twice. One thing that he truly meant when he said it, though, was the belief that the Ulstermen did not really wish to be one with a Socialist Britain. That much was clear. The final act of his performance came when he asked Bevin – minutes ago proclaimed a hero of the Revolution for seeing off the German threat with such dignity – to deal with the situation personally. There was no way that any hard-line proponent of maintaining a grip on Ulster could have questioned this, and when Maclean so 'humbly' offered to sit on a Extraordinary Steering Committee that Bevin himself would chair about the matter that evening, no-one suspected that it was his intention to 'steer' the committee towards his exact way of thinking. Therefore it is no surprise that Bevin's meeting with Collins at the Four Courts (after first visiting the Dublin Post Office to pay his respects to James Connolly[15]) culminated in exactly what Maclean proposed – Collins agreed to an apology for not informing the Union of his intentions, and issued a full and frank assurance that no further territorial incursions onto Union soil would take place. This point was somewhat moot – what else were the Irish going to want? Cornwall? In exchange, Bevin, on behalf of the workers of the Congress of the Trade Unions of the Union of Britain, formally recognised the Irish Republic's sovereignty over the entirety of Ulster. Collins also requested the right to an Irish representative in London, putting forward Jim Larkin as his candidate for this

---

[15] According to an Irish observer, Bevin directly addressed the name engraved into the stone when he said 'Had you lived, Comrade, my mission would be a far happier one'.

'subambassadorship'.[16] Diplomatic recognition was still a long way off, but both Collins and Bevin recognised the value of such representatives. From this, the idea of a 'Special Representative' was born, and Larkin was granted permission to travel back to London with the Bevin delegation (the eccentric William Joyce remained in Ireland to take up the equivalent post in Dublin).[17]

Maclean had played a masterstroke. Domestically, his reputation was secure and a war had been averted. Internationally, the Union had come across as reasonable and true to its principles of self-determination by abandoning imperialist holdings. While relations with Ireland were destined to always be somewhat frosty on ideological grounds, there was genuine respect for the integrity of Maclean and Bevin in the eyes of Collins and the Irish people. Popular at home and tolerated abroad, it was on this high that Maclean began the most controversial stage of the Week For Discussion And Votes Regarding International Policy – whether Britain should seek friends as well as assurances of neutrality.

The most obvious candidates for friendship were the Commune of France and Republic of the Sicilies. Already maintaining close relations with each other, the two countries were in dire need of friends. Maclean, wary of getting entangled in some sort of alliance, proposed to invite representatives from both republics to speak on the final day

---

[16] The decision to send Larkin was largely a selfish one. Collins hated the man for his radical socialist beliefs and had wanted to put him somewhere where he could not influence Irish politics anymore, but could not afford to arrest or execute him because of his populist support.

[17] Joyce, despite his appearances and 'posh voice', had been a die-hard leftist ever since his attempt to address a group of Labour Party members in 1924 had ended with him being mobbed by a gang of 'Honourists' (reactionary ex-Tommies who took it upon themselves to break up what they saw as 'revolutionary' meetings), who slashed his face with a razor. Calling those responsible 'reactionary heathen', he became involved with leftist militia groups and played an active role in overcoming the Royalist barricades in West London during the Revolution. Nevertheless, his somewhat wild temperament made him unsuitable for serious public service in Britain, so Bevin recommended him as their Special Representative for many of the same reasons that Collins recommended Larkin.

of the 'International Week'. The motion was cautiously carried, and telegrams were sent to both Naples and Paris. Pietro Nenni and Pierre Brossolette (of the Sicilies and France respectively) were apparently only too happy to attend and welcome another socialist state to Europe, for they both arrived with speeches already written. Nenni spoke in passable English but with a fiery Italian passion behind his words. Comparing 'the righteous anger of the British people against their reactionary masters' with the struggles his own people had undergone against the 'Papists and Germans' in the North, he extended a hearty offer of friendship from the central government in Naples, with full diplomatic recognition very much on the table. Brossolette offered much the same thing, while praising the speed with which the British had achieved socialism (in perfect English, he joked that 'my people went through three republics before they saw the light – you managed it with one'). Both men were given a standing ovation as they left the chamber.

As soon as they had left the building, however, the debate began in earnest. Annie Kenney, speaking for the first time at length before her comrades, argued fiercely against any kind of formal link with either state, saying they were both likely to drag Britain into a war, as France had done in 1914. Oswald Mosley, speaking on behalf of Cook's Maximists, argued instead that the links should be nurtured and improved, and that all three nations should work together to improve their military strength. GDH Cole put forward the idea that Britain needed friends, but not allies, so perhaps a compromise could be reached. Maclean seized upon this idea and argued that their offers of diplomatic recognition should be accepted, not least for the trading relationships they would bring. Cleverly turning the extreme isolationists' arguments against them, he 'agreed' that war and alliance was not what the Union needed, but pointed out that Britain lacked many resources of its own, particularly foodstuffs that did not grow naturally upon our island. 'Is a mineworker not entitled to a glass of Sicilian orange juice upon his return home?' he asked, 'May our Syndicates not toast their success with a fine Bordeaux? Are we, as a people, not entitled to the money, grain and vital oil that such a trading system would allow?' Thanks to Maclean's public speaking skills, the day had been won. The motion to open up full diplomatic relations with Sicily and France was passed.

And so ended the so-called 'International Week'. Its public statements had been of co-operation, joy and fierce defense of Britain and her socialist principles. Its undertones had been those of continuity in British politics – the stoical, 'love me or hate me, I'm here to stay' attitude of Elizabeth I, Oliver Cromwell and Queen Victoria lived on in the practices of John Maclean and Ernest Bevin. I am pleased to note that their reactionary beliefs did not.

The Congress Concludes

John Durham

'Comrades! The spirits of Tom Paine, William Lovett, George
Loveless, and all those who suffered for this day can rest easy knowing
that we have achieved the remarkable – some said the impossible.
Some will call it compromise. I call it Congress.'

*John Maclean, hailing the passing of The Motion for Limited Federal
Control and Authority Combined with Regional Autonomy, 1 March 1926*

The foreign policy of the Inaugural Congress having been discussed in
the previous chapter of this volume, it now falls to me to conclude this
book's analysis of the Congress as a whole. What did it conclude in
those crucial final days? Who were the winners and losers, both
individually and factionally? And, perhaps most crucially, how well-
received were the reforms that the Congress voted on, and did they get
put into practice properly?

The final two weeks of the Congress had been designated as
'Matters regarding infrastructure and domestic matters' – a term so
broad it might as well have been 'any other business'. The first item on
the agenda (drawn up by General Secretary Philip Snowden) was the
determination of the exact role that individual workers, Syndicates and
Unions, and the 'central government' would take in shaping Union
policy and practice. The Federationists having a clear majority as a
voting bloc by this stage, it was expected that their way of thinking was
going to triumph. It was therefore of no surprise to anybody when a
nine-thousand-word document titled 'The Motion for Limited Federal
Control and Authority Combined with Regional Autonomy'[18] was
presented by a steering committee chaired by administrative genius and
former miner Arthur Horner. Representatives involved in its

---

[18] Hardly a catchy title, it quickly became known as the 'Limited Federation'
motion.

authorship included Tom Mann, James Maxton (former radical Labour MP[19]) and Jimmy Thomas, the Railway Union leader. The document was both radical and uncontroversial – a theme that runs throughout the years that gave birth to our Union. It was radical in the level of power it gave to local Syndicates and Unions (several Unions made up a local Syndicate, each with their own Congress House), yet uncontroversial in how much power it presented to the Federal Council – effectively the new 'cabinet'. The Council would act only in cross-Syndicate matters as a mediator, and would determine national 'goals' each year that were to be voted on at each national Congress (held every September). The only other matters that the Federal Council would involve itself it were international affairs and matters of infrastructure – railways, electricity and so on – that crossed the boundaries of each Syndicated region. All other matters – the organisation of trades and prices between unions, law enforcement (the police unions were re-educated along the same lines as the army, and elected Commissioners introduced), local transport, utilities and more – fell to the authority of local Syndicates. It was this that was most offensive to the Maximists. Eric Blair called it 'a blueprint for underachievement', while Mosley and Cook both made speeches railing against the lack of a centralised industrial body. There were also those who considered the whole Motion 'utterly unconstitutional', but it was pointed out that the Constitution, proclaimed a few months ago, had always left provision for a proper administrative structure 'to be determined during a Congress of the Trade Unions'.[20]

The Motion was put to the vote in an atmosphere of extreme tension. Oswald Mosley nonchalantly remarked to anyone who would

---

[19] Maxton had foregone the post-Revolution 'examination process' his parliamentary colleagues underwent by personally joining a Popular Militia during the early days of the Revolution, and helping plan the attack on the Houses of Parliament using his own knowledge of the building. A close friend and ally of both John Maclean and Arthur James Cook, he had served as a principled socialist politician for his entire career, and as such was under little scrutiny anyway.

[20] Article iia, line 23, *The Constitution of the Union of Britain*, original pamphlet from November 1925

listen that 'if we splinter here, the whole bloody structure could come crashing down'. It took over four hours of debate and numerous amendments to the Motion (which had already spent ten days in the hands of the steering committee), but eventually it passed by a majority of 355 to 280 – enough, under the Constitution, to make it lawful. There was a great collective sigh of relief as now, finally, it was clear how the country would actually be run. Britain's future, at least for the short term, was secure.

The other major area of policy that had to be defined (and voted on for the first time) was the Armed Forces. As Comrade Hobsbawm's article earlier in this volume pointed out, the 'apolitical army' was the consensus of the day. Maclean, as usual, gave a passionate speech explaining the need for this move. Using a typically Macleanian technique, he gave just enough ground to appear impeccably socialist while at the same time making sure the only conclusion that could be reached was his own. In this instance, he declared that it was indeed a sad state of affairs if Britain had to rely on the remaining members of a 'once royalist army', but it would be sadder state if she had no military minds at all defending her from German bayonets or Royalist shells. Seizing on the spirit of compromise, he proposed that Tom Wintringham, the fiercest proponent of hanging or imprisoning all former army officers and rebuilding the whole service from scratch, be placed in overall command of the operation to ensure socialist values became entrenched in the existing armed forces. Wintringham appears to have accepted this compromise – other than those army, navy or RAF officers who would not swear to protect the people of the Union rather than 'that decadent crown', no officers came to any harm (either prison or the noose) under his command. All this was the result of the general vote on the matter, the motion being 'To preserve the officer corps of Britain's armed services, with provisos for their political re-education, for reasons in the National Interest'. It passed by a reasonable majority, with Cook's Maximists being the only faction encouraging its members to vote 'Nay'.[21]

---

[21] The Congregationalists were also initially uneasy about the militaristic tone of the motion, but gave it their support after Annie Kenney negotiated an

With these and other administrative questions answered (some of which will be expanded upon in later chapters covering the development of the Union in the 1920s), the Congress now turned to the matter of electing those of its members who would oversee their putting into practice. While the election of Syndicate chairmen was a matter to be decided locally, the 'Federal Council' that would meet each week in Congress house was to fill the role of the cabinet under the failed state. The people who sat on this council would have briefs and, in some cases, Commissions (based largely on the old system of 'ministries'). The Commissary for the Exchequer, for instance, would be based out of the old treasury building for the time being, keeping control of inflation through careful mediation of price control among the regional Syndicates. The old 'Foreign and Colonial Office' was stripped of its paintings of foreign dignitaries and Emperors (notably a disgustingly large picture of Napoleon III that Queen Victoria had allegedly refused to keep in any of her homes, and so given to the Foreign Office) and re-opened as the 'People's Commission for Foreign Affairs'. The election of the men to fill these posts, then, was to be the final stage of cementing the government of the Union of Britain.

Philip Snowden had already been elected as General Secretary of the Congress of the Trade Unions (CTU),[22] so the major roles that remained to be filled were the Exchequer, Foreign Affairs, Home Infrastructure and Industrial Relations. Several candidates had each put together a manifesto for why they should be considered for these posts, but there were clear frontrunners in each category. Arthur Horner was a close ally of John Maclean and well-known as a superb

---

amendment to the Motion which placed the emphasis on Britain's defence rather than any overseas operations.

[22] The role of General Secretary was a powerful administrative one that involved the planning of all Union Congresses and the maintenance of the very structure of the state itself. Snowden would have found it easy to set a precedent for the General Secretary outshining the Chairman and eventually overtaking him as the *de facto* head of state and take his crucial 'casting vote', but this never took place, to our Union's benefit. The General Secretary remained the role it was supposed to be.

mathematician, so easily took the job in the Exchequer, despite strong opposition from Oswald Mosley, beginning their decade-long feud. Ernest Bevin, given his recent escapades abroad, was the obvious choice for Foreign Affairs. Jimmy Thomas, head of the National Union of Railwaymen who had successfully crippled the Reactionary efforts to keep the country moving during the Revolution[23], made his case for being the Commissary for Home Infrastructure by arguing for a strong system of railways, bolstered by popular support and Union involvement, carrying more freight and passengers around the country to help underdeveloped sections grow. He was elected to little opposition. Finally, the eccentric James Maxton was elected as Commissary for Industrial Relations after much recommendation by his old friend John Maclean. Maxton was, in many ways, the ideal candidate as a mediator between Syndicates and Unions (this being what the job entailed). His experience in parliament made him one of few Revolutionaries who had spoken with real power behind his words before now, and his fiery manner was well-respected by tough-talking Union leaders. The first ever Federal Council, therefore, was thus:

Chairman of the CTU John Maclean
General Secretary of the CTU Philip Snowden
Commissary for the Exchequer Arthur Horner
Commissary for Foreign Affairs Ernest Bevin
Commissary for Home Infrastructure Jimmy Thomas
Commissary for Industrial Relations James Maxton
Chairman of the Committee for Reformation of the Armed Forces Tom Wintringham

And so the Congress entered its closing stages. John Maclean praised the work that had been done thus far, and talked positively of

---

[23] One amusing incident saw students at Oxford University offer to fire and run steam locomotives from their local depot in an attempt to undermine the strike. When desperate bosses put the manicured scabs to work, they found that all the students were capable of doing was ruining fireboxes and, in one case, permanently warping a boiler. So laughable was the attempt that, after the Revolution, the students responsible's punishment was simply to be named and shamed on pamphlets around the city.

the change that lay ahead. However apprehensive people like Mosley had been about the Congress, the outcome was clear – the people of Britain, through their representatives, were genuinely prepared to 'give it a go', as Comrade Hobsbawm once said. On the other hand, there were certainly 'winners and losers' in the debate – the Maximists had had their centralised views rejected (for now) and had been opposed to a number of Federationist measures that were passed successfully. But the implementation of the policies would be undertaken in a local, regional and fundamentally decentralised manner, and this is what made the process so popular and easy for local administrators. So what conclusions can be drawn from the end of the Congress? A sense of optimism, no doubt inspired by the Revolution itself and the decadence of the previous regime, played a large part in the congeniality of this first Congress. A degree of British openness and fairness resulted in the free debate that carried on almost without interruption over every issue. The most important conclusion, then, in the mind of this author, is that the Inaugural Congress symbolises the very essence of where our Union came from. A Revolution with very little bloodshed, compromise abounding and a hand of brotherhood being extended to those who, under the Bolshevik Rebellion, for instance, would have been executed. The Congress was, therefore, the perfect microcosm of what Tony Benn would later call 'our unique brand of a very British Socialism'.

The End of Empire

Eric Hobsbawm

'Where the devil is Valletta?'
Ernest Bevin, 14 April 1926

The following article was written as part of Comrade Hobsbawm's planned book on the transition of the United Kingdom into the Union of Britain. It was never completed, and we are indebted to his wife Marlene for presenting the manuscript to us.

*

It is perhaps unsurprising that in Royalist literature regarding the collapse of the British Empire, parallels are freely and viciously drawn between it and the end of the Western Roman Empire. Most popular among these flawed ideas is that one that, like the barbarians who brought down Rome, the Revolutionaries who marched on London were to blame for the 'catastrophic loss' of the Empire's overseas holdings. This is something I am only too happy to discuss, for just as scholarship on the fall of Rome has recently shifted the blame away from the generally harmonic barbarian peoples (themselves fleeing oppression under the Huns, just as we Britons fought our oppression under the Bourgeoisie) and onto the corrupt 'magister militum' – the cabal of military leaders who were essentially running the Roman Empire for their own personal gain – real scholarship regarding the end of the *British* Empire has also shifted the blame onto a far more culpable set of individuals – the exiled colonialists themselves.

The reasoning for this is clear. If, as all now accept, an Empire was a morally bankrupt drain on Britain's manpower in exchange for resources that were being denied to those proletarians who harvested them in their homelands, what interest was the 'new government' of the Congress of the Trade Unions meant to have in preserving the Empire of the failed state? The loudest argument for keeping hold of as much of the Empire as possible came from the young Eric Blair, who at just 23 had made a name for himself as a pamphleteer, militiaman and ally of Oswald Mosley. 'Letting the Empire collapse is not an option,' Blair argued in his pamphlet 'The Lion and the Unicorn'[24] (although he conceded that a more socialist name than 'Empire' needed to be found[25]); 'the alternative is to throw our holdings overboard and reduce the Union to a cold and unimportant little island where we shall all live on herring and potatoes!' While Blair stressed that it was also the duty of the Revolutionaries to ensure quality of life and peaceful Socialism for the workers of the Empire rather than just 'cutting and running', some naturally decried this as reactionary snobbery. The economic thrust of his points, however, was accepted by John Maclean, and matters regarding how to deal with the Empire in a manner least economically damaging to the Union were sent to the top of the agenda in the first meetings of the Federal Council.

Matters had been taken out of the Council's hands in some parts of the Empire, notably India. The already fragile Raj had splintered into three factions in a short but catastrophic war that broke out almost immediately after the Royal Family fled mainland Britain. An uneasy stalemate had set in across the borders of the subcontinent's three new states – the Raj (though it had little claim to this title, and was more popularly called 'Delhi' after its capital), the Princely Federation (made up of the 'gun-salute' Princes who had so loyally served the British and now found themselves having to oppress their people themselves) and the People's Republic of Bengal. Both the exiles, desperately trying to create some level of bureaucracy in Ottawa by which to rule the Empire, and the Federal Council in London were at a loss as to how to make any reclamation of what was once the jewel in Britain's crown.

---

[24] In a somewhat flimsy analogy, the Lion represented British will, and the Unicorn the colonies of the failed state that were now, like the elusive mythical creature itself, seeking independence.

[25] Blair himself proposed 'Commonwealth of Nations'.

The exiles had some luck on their side – the 'Raj', or Delhi, pledged support to the Royal Family but made it clear that Governor-General Linlithgow was the man in charge of all matters Indian, not the King. The British troops (essentially what was left of 'The British Army In India') running the country had pledged allegiance to the Governor-General rather than the King 'until a more stable circumstance should arise'. The Canadian and exile response was to refuse military support for a 'reclaiming of lost territory', allowing the country to descend into further chaos. The Princely Federation naturally wanted nothing to do with either the exiles or the Revolutionaries, being more interested in preserving their wealth on their own terms. Britain's eyes, then, fell on Bengal. Bengal had become a Socialist Republic, much like Britain had, and many of its leading lights had learned their Marx and Engels at British universities – James Maxton claimed to remember a young Mohandas Gandhi during the former's visit to Oxford (now Ruskin) University.

Ernest Bevin, therefore, in his first act as Commissary for Foreign Affairs, dispatched a delegation led by R.H. Tawney to Calcutta to broker friendship with the Bengali state, as well as give assurances that the new Britain had no interest in recolonisation. Tawney was by all accounts the ideal man to send, having been born in Calcutta and, during his time in the Fabians, a strong advocate of Indian independence. The results of the delegation were good, and it bore fruit within months – a telegram from Tawney himself arrived back in London in October 1926.

'THEY LOVE US STOP SEE US AS AN EXAMPLE STOP CAN WE SEND THEM SOME RAILWAY ENGINEERS STOP'

Whether the request was motivated by the demands of the Bengali government or by Tawney's own experience of the dilapidated Indian rail network, it was granted and a team of railway engineers was sent out to reorganise and build up the collapsing Bengali infrastructure. It was headed by none other than Clement Attlee, who had only a month before satisfied the 'Commission for Determination of Socialist Belief in Former Members of Parliament' of his intentions and, in particular, his extraordinary planning ability.

For the Union and its interests in India, the best had been made out of a decidedly bad lot. In exchange for the railway engineers (who themselves were instructed to take notes on how to restructure such a system so they could oversee the same thing in Britain on their return), Bengal offered a series of trade agreements brokered by Tawney. Britain's supply of Indian tea, certain rare materials and rubber (through the deals the Bengalis themselves had reached with the emerging Burmese state to their East) appeared safe.

Other parts of the former Empire were more definitely lost to Britain's inhabitants. In the Caribbean, local governors banded together to form the Caribbean Federation with its capital at Kingston. Though little more than an economic union that heavily depended on Canada for its protection, its unsurprising refusal to trade with Britain hurt sugar supplies greatly. Even until the 1930s and the Maximisation programmes, it was said that 'nobody ever asks "how many sugars" anymore, for they are afraid that the answer will be more than one'.[26] Similar failure was found in the South Pacific, where Britain's Pacific holdings were quietly annexed by the Japanese and, to some consternation in London and Ottawa, the Germans. Australia and New Zealand, evidently becoming highly aware of their position many thousands of miles away from both London and Ottawa, rejected the Revolutionary government and formed the Australasian Confederation, immediately swearing loyalty to the King and exiled government of the Empire in Ottawa while, like Delhi, elevating their Governor-General to the post of Governor and transferring some powers reserved for royalty to him. There was nothing the Union could do to stop them, and the exiles were too paranoid about further mutiny in the navy to deploy it in the South Pacific.

The final nail in the wretched, rotten and long-awaited coffin of the British Empire came from, ironically enough, the rising star of its usurper – the German Empire. Chancellor Tirpitz, having apparently

---

[26] Shirley McKitterick, *The Revolutionary Housewife: Liberation and stagnation in British feminism, 1925-1941*, (London: Macmillan, 1989) p.146.

spent every waking moment since Ernest Bevin's initial visit scrutinising the agreements they had signed, had satisfied himself that when the Union said it had no interests outside the British Isles (with special dispensation added for the Channel Islands, which were occupied by Revolutionary forces in the Navy and turned into Communes), it meant just that. With this in mind, on the morning of 13 April 1926 ships, submersibles and zeppelins began docking in major ports and aerodromes around what was left of the British Empire's African and Mediterranean holdings. They flew the flag of truce alongside the war ensign of Germany, but aircraft dropped leaflets announcing these territories' incorporation into the German Empire. The British garrisons, torn between a useless Ottawa and a polluted London and certain of annihilation if they opposed, handed over the territories.

The Congress had been over for a month when the news broke, so there would be no frantic speechmaking or votes *en masse* to decide this particular piece of foreign response. The news officially came through when the Governor of Malta requested assistance from London, as per protocol (ignoring the obvious change of government given the desperation of the situation, as his and others' pleas for help had already been rejected by Ottawa) on the morning of the fourteenth of April. Ernest Bevin, being informed of the call by his assistant, famously remarked 'where the hell is Valletta?' The seriousness of the situation quickly became clear. Unlike far-off parts of the Empire like Guadalcanal or Kingston, the key ports of Malta, Cyprus,[27] Gibraltar (which had been marched upon from Spanish territory on the understanding it would be returned to Spain by Germany after a five year lease) and Suez were a very important part of Britain's naval supremacy and, arguably, continued existence. The unenviable task of deciding what, if anything, to do now fell to the emergency meeting of the Federal Council, chaired as always by John Maclean.

---

[27] Germany held Cyprus for two years before selling it to the Ottoman Empire as an 'act of friendship'. The real reason was they had only really needed it as a stop-off point for their fleets on their way to Suez, and once the canal had been refitted to German standards they had no use for Cyprus.

In his capacity as Commissary for Foreign Affairs, Ernest Bevin admitted that the agreement signed with Germany in February made these actions entirely legal. Arthur Horner, speaking on behalf of the Exchequer, nonchalantly remarked that he had been leaving overseas ports out of his calculations on how to plan the economy anyway. Tom Wintringham, acting head of the armed forces at this point, was adamant that aggressive war with Germany was completely out of the question, and a defensive one would be of dubious outcome. It quickly became clear that the Union could do nothing. The Germans offered no payment for the islands, nor indeed did they contact London directly it what was clearly a calculated insult. Maclean proposed that the assembled council vote on a motion to protest the Germans' decision not to ask London's permission but accept their sovereignty over the islands and African territories[28] they had now acquired. Arguing, as ever, for pragmatism, he pointed out that the Union's navy would be stretched out beyond its capabilities if it had to constantly defend these valuable ports that, to an isolationist power like the Union, were ultimately useless. The vote passed unanimously, with only Philip Snowden abstaining on the grounds that he could not 'in good conscience hand over the residents of these lands to German Imperialism, but equally cannot turn the wrath of the Hun towards Britain herself'.[29]

In summary, then, the Empire collapsed around the Revolution not because of the villainous intent of the revolutionaries, but the incompetence and corruption of the self-serving exiles. Their narrow-mindedness was what led to their own failure to properly mend the disintegrating Raj, or keep Australasian nationalism at bay. The Union can only be blamed for, if anything, not having the resources to properly foster and export revolution in these collapsing states. The loss of naval ports overseas was ultimately of no import to the isolationist

---

[28] All of pre-Revolutionary 'British Africa' fell into German hands, though they would lose control of Egypt by 1931 due to nationalist rebellion. A deal struck with the new government ensured Suez and Port Said remained German.

[29] Philip Snowden et al, *Selected Extracts from the Minutes of the Federal Council, 1926-1931* (London: Red State Publishing, 1993)

early governments of the Union, and the Second Great War and Congress of Trier vindicated early British inaction when the German Empire occupied and oppressed the peoples of Malta, Suez and Cyprus. Trier would see these lands and peoples finally granted true independence and the right to pursue their own socialist destiny – for better or worse.

Staying on track

Jeremy Clarkson

'Oh, Mr Thomas, what am I to do?
Your Restruct'ring Committee
Has sent my train to Crewe
I need to get to Highbury, to see them win the cup,
Oh, Mr Thomas, I do wish you'd hurry up!'
Oh! Mr Thomas, *music hall song regarding Jimmy Thomas'*
Restructuring Committee's perceived slowness and inefficiencies, dated
1928

In an attempt to make this book more 'accessible' to those less scholarly
members of society, this and a number of other chapters in this book are
kindly provided by members of the broadcast and journalistic media. We
thank Mr Clarkson for his frank and amusing writing style.

*

I'll make no bones about it – I'm no historian. You won't find any
pieces of chalk in the pockets of my jacket, or my neck to be crooked
from years of staring down into dusty volumes about the Roman
Empire. The contents of my pockets are more likely to be my car keys,
a notebook containing the latest numbers I've jotted down from the
side of trains, and a plane ticket to Iberia. On a good day, that is. As
you can probably tell, my interests lie more in British engineering than
in British exceptionalism (when Richard Hammond first told me that
phrase in the studio I asked if it was some sort of real ale). So naturally,
when Professor Durham wrote to me to ask if I would contribute to
this book of his, I was more than a little sceptical. So sceptical, in fact,
that you could probably have cut glass on the stiffness of my raised
right eyebrow. But when he told me what he wanted me to write about
– 'something about engineering. The railways, design industry, that
sort of thing' – I was sold. As a railway enthusiast (cars have always

been a secondary passion for me) since my dad first took me on the Brighton Belle when I was four, I consider it a great honour to be able to put down in writing an account of the great railways of this great country.

So, despite me not being much of a historian in general, I'm not ashamed to say that like any self-respecting gricer I know the history of the railways of this fair isle of ours pretty much off by heart. The bit I've been asked to recount first is the initial stage of the plans that the Union put in place when it took over from the UK in the 1920s. Basically, the 'grouping' plan that had been instituted in 1922 after the Great War ended the chaos (or so it seemed) of all the different railway companies in the country by combining them all into four part-state owned but operationally independent companies: the Southern Railway, the London and North Eastern Railway, the London, Midland and Scotland Railway and the Great Western Railway. These groupings, while a marked improvement on the cripplingly inefficient (and horribly exploitative of their workers) companies that were running things all over the country before the Great War, were themselves severely lacking in the efficiency and workers' rights department. It's not surprising that Jimmy Thomas and his railway union were leading lights in the General Strike that led to the Revolution, given how unpopular the bosses of the railway companies were. Working conditions were appalling, and there was widespread concern among the railwaymen that the railway network itself was not helping the most needy sections of the country that it needed to. In short – it wasn't that great, it was too expensive for the poor, and poorer areas were woefully under-serviced.

So that was the lie of the land on the eve of the Revolution. Flash forward a couple of years and Jimmy Thomas (the same bloke) has been put in charge of reorganising the railway network along socialist lines. Complete nationalisation was talked about, but rejected as too expensive and potentially taking too much control away from local Syndicates. Thomas' commission decided instead on two key plans. First, it would work closely with the railwaymen of the Union to improve working conditions and hours, while increasing services in underrepresented and poorer areas. Second, it was to work with both the Federal Committee and the local Syndicates (regional groupings of local Unions, each with their own Chairpersons) to establish a new, freight-focused (there was little call for moving around the country at time) rail network. The track would be the responsibility of both the regional rail operator (there were four, like under Grouping, but they had been given a thoroughly socialist structure now) and the Federal Committee. Timetables, rolling stock and so on would be the sole responsibility of the individual railway operators. Sounds simple enough, doesn't it? Well, I don't blame you if it doesn't sound that simple, because it wasn't.

Thomas and his committee had their work cut out for them. The UK's system of grouping had begun the job of restructuring the network, but focused it more on passenger work. Local Syndicates really had no interest in their own workers deserting them for a more industrially rich area, and the focus that the Union required was very much freight-based. New parts, building materials and so on needed to be able to get across the country with high priority to allow the plans made by the country's Syndicates to take shape – for instance, the lads in Sheffield wanted to triple the city's steel output by 1930. That meant coal from Newcastle, blast furnace materials from Kent and increased supplies of iron from Cornwall. The Sheffield Syndicate (affectionately nicknamed 'the People's Republic of South Yorkshire' thanks to the ballsiness of the men in charge) had successfully struck deals with all the other appropriate Syndicates and were on track (pun intended) to make this happen. The trouble was, the railways weren't up to it. The Sheffield Syndicate was demanding at least five full trainloads every hour until noon, and the network wasn't kitted out for that sort of load. Junctions got clogged up, passing loops had queues stretching back miles and large sections of the line in rural areas were still in single track thanks to the bonkers era of 'railway mania' in the 19th century.

This wasn't the only problem they faced, but it represents all the chaotic redevelopment that the railways had to supply throughout the 1920s. Couple with this (another pun, sorry) the problem of passenger traffic having to exist on the same lines – unemployment might not have existed any more [*Debatable – J. Durham*] but some people still had a gran in Scotland they had to visit, and football fans still had away games to go to – and Thomas and his committee had an absolute nightmare on their hands. By 1929, industry had started improving but not at the rate people wanted, and John Maclean himself was breathing down Thomas' neck like a lorry driver in a queue behind a 19-year-old blonde.

Luckily for poor Jimmy, his saviour was about to arrive. Balding but tanned, healthy yet pipe-smoking (take that, anti-smoking culture) and arguably the greatest administrator this country has ever produced, Clement Attlee arrived home from Bengal on 11 June 1929. He'd been exceptionally highly praised by the locals in Bengal for the work he'd done for their railways, and learned a fair few tricks of the trade while he was at it. His plan for the Union's railways was simple but ambitious, and combined with Thomas' command of the Unions it had a chance of working. Clem is said to have entered Thomas' office without any sense of grandeur, sat down opposite him when invited to do so, and looked him dead in the eyes. 'So, what's your big idea, Comrade?' Thomas asked. Attlee's reply was characteristically subdued and simple, while making a massive statement at the same time.

'Four tracks good. Two tracks bad.'[30]

This simple formula would be applied and extended to every trunk line (and some branches) in the country. The problem had always been the railways choking on the amount of freight they now had to take on. Clem had proposed to, wherever possible, double the amount of track currently in use. It was an incredibly ambitious idea, not least because of the amount of land the railway syndicates were going to have to buy up to accomplish it. Thankfully, regionalisation[31] meant that instead of convincing local landowners acre by acre, once the local Syndicates were convinced (and when their committees had taken one look at the

---

[30] Eric Blair, *Clem: The Man Who Rebuilt Britain* (London: The Book Club, 1955) p.42.

[31] As opposed to nationalisation. A shorthand term used to describe the regional Syndicates' ownership of all formerly private land – Ed.

number of jobs that would be created for local men, they were convinced pretty quickly, I tell you) there were no more administrative hurdles. As a result, the glorious stretches of eight-track line that run on the major northern industrial routes that survive to this day (there is a bridge a short walk from Wakefield Westgate that provides, in my humble opinion, the best spot to photograph large numbers of trains from on the whole network) were underway by 1930 and completed by 1934. The load on all lines was lightened and jobs were created in areas particularly hard hit by the departure of capitalist bosses who left with their workers' rightful wages stuffed in a grandfather clock and set off for Canada. The restructuring, after looking in its early stages like it would fail, had achieved great success. In helping him, Clement Attlee had saved Jimmy Thomas' skin – but not for long. Thomas knew his star was falling as Attlee's was rising, and Attlee found himself elected Commissary for Home Infrastructure after Thomas' resignation at the Congress of 1932.

There was one other piece of business that Thomas' committee had to attend to, although it was usually handed off to the more idealistic and less administratively-talented members. A number of locomotives on the rails and about to be completed were of classes and names most unsuitable for a republican railway network. Thomas' committee's most lasting legacy aside from the increasing of the numbers of tracks is the set of guidelines they published for all future namings of locomotives, as well as the names they gave the particularly reactionary locos running at the time. Here are a few of my favourites:

*Proposed GWR **King Class** (became AWR Visionary Class)*
'King George V' renamed 'John Maclean'
'King William IV' renamed 'George Loveless'
'King Charles I' renamed 'Oliver Cromwell'
'King George IV' renamed 'William Blake'
*Proposed LMS **Royal Scot Class** (became FMR Defender Class)*
'Royal Ulster Rifleman' renamed 'South Wales Territorial'
'Royal Engineer' renamed 'Chief Builder'
'Royal Scots Grey' renamed 'Ironside Cavalry'
'Queen's Westminster Rifleman' renamed 'Cheapside Militiaman'

*Proposed SR **Schools Class** (had focus shifted from now-defunct Public Schools)*

'Eton' renamed 'Slough Middle School'

'Whitgift' renamed 'Croydon High School'

'Repton' renamed 'Milton Keynes School for Boys' (my alma mater!)

'Charterhouse' renamed 'Broadwater School'

*Proposed LMS **Coronation Class** (became FMR Heroine Class)*

'Queen Elizabeth' renamed 'Florence Nightingale'

'Queen Mary' renamed 'Emmeline Pankhurst'

'Duchess of Devonshire' renamed 'Emily Davison'

'Coronation' renamed 'Clara Zetkin'

So there we have it. I hope this summary hasn't been too jarring, stuffed in here between pages and pages of waffle from some men who are no doubt a billion times cleverer than me. What I wanted to convey to you is the beauty of the British camaraderie and ingenuity that was displayed in the restructuring of our railways in the 1920s and 1930s. Organisers like Attlee and Thomas, engineers like Bulleid, Stanier and Gresley (all of whom had turned down places on the Exile ships – they loved their railway more than any king, those fine men) and union men and leaders across the country pulled together to produce the right lines, the right freight plans and the right locomotives for the situation. And in true British style, they did a fantastic job, for our railway system was up to scratch and handled everything we threw at it.

Until the war.

Red Clyde Rising: John Maclean 1879-1931

Shirley McKitterick

'Don't you dare let them put me in Westminster Abbey.'
John Maclean's last words

Any student embarking on a degree in Political Biography will tell you that the first essay they will ever be told to write is about John Maclean. The man known as 'The Great Compromiser', 'The Father of the Republic', 'The Red Giant', and, according to Hugh McDiarmid, 'Beautiful' has, perhaps more than any other leader of our Union, been immune from real criticism or serious evaluation. Perhaps it is his status as the first Chair of the Congress of the Trade Unions, or his death at the relatively young age of 51, that has created this air of an invulnerable historical opinion around him. But one thing should be made clear about this article – I neither come to bury Maclean nor to praise him. There is no agenda here, no attempt to undermine the years of veneration that Maclean has been subject to. What there will be, however, is some investigation into what failings he may have had – notably the 'collapse of compromise' that took place at the end of the 1920s and nearly sent the Union into a spiraling nosedive to anarchy. So here, in the spirit of this volume, is a picture of John Maclean – warts and all.

John Maclean was born in 1879 to Calvinist parents in Pollokshaws on the outskirts of Glasgow. A bright boy, he trained as a teacher under the Free Church and gained a Master of Arts degree in 1904 from the University of Glasgow. It was here that he met James Maxton, forging a friendship and partnership that would last until Maclean's death. Both were fiery orators who engaged heavily with University politics, but Maclean's background in politics had come about through his involvement in the Pollokshaws Progressive Union and the local co-operative movement. His experiences there led him to the conclusion that the conditions of the working classes would only be improved by social revolution, and this in turn led him to Marxism. He joined the Social Democratic Federation, which then became part of the British Socialist Party.

As the First Great War broke out across Europe, Maclean found himself utterly at odds with the imperialist conflict that was separating workers from one another because of 'dented reactionary pride'. Fuelled by a revolutionary spirit, he worked with his comrade Maxton to agitate against the war. His fiery speeches attracted great attention among the dockers of Clydeside, and he along with Maxton is credited with radicalising that generation of workers who became known as the 'Red Clydeside' movement. In 1915, however, he was arrested under the hated Defence of the Realm Act and sacked from his teaching post. Though not imprisoned, he was stripped of official standing within 'society' and consequently turned to Marxist lectures and organization, continuing his hard work as an educator of the workers in Glasgow, eventually founding the Scottish Labour College, which survives to this day as the Maclean Institute. In 1916 he was arrested once again and imprisoned – but released in 1917 following agitation by loyal socialists inspired by the ultimately doomed rebellion underway in Russia. This freedom was short-lived, however, for upon continuing his anti-war organising and speeches he found himself arrested for 'sedition'. On 9 May, he conducted his own defence when his trial began. He refused to plead and, in a confrontational style typical of his early career, replied 'I object to the whole lot of them' when asked if he objected to any members of the jury. The trial was a sham, with sections of speeches and notes being quoted completely out of context to make it seem like Maclean wanted to bring some bloody harm upon the British people, when his quarrel had always been with 'the trickery of the British government'.

As the trial drew to a close, Maclean addressed the jury in an impassioned speech lasting 75 minutes, which he used to attack the capitalist system:

'I had a lecture, the principal heading of which was "Thou shalt not steal; thou shalt not kill", and I pointed out that as a consequence of the robbery that goes on in all civilised countries today, our respective countries have had to keep armies, and that inevitably our armies must clash together. On that and on other grounds, I consider capitalism the most infamous, bloody and evil system that mankind has ever witnessed. My language is regarded as extravagant language, but the events of the past four years have proved my contention! I wish no harm to any human being, but I, as one man, am going to exercise my freedom of speech. No human being on the face of the earth, no government is going to take from me my right to speak, my right to protest against wrong, my right to do everything that is for the benefit of mankind. I am not here, then, as the accused; I am here as the accuser of capitalism dripping with blood from head to foot.'[32]

He was sentenced to five years' penal servitude, and imprisoned in Peterhead prison near Aberdeen. However, a militant campaign was launched for his release:

'The call "Release John Maclean" was never silent. Every week the socialist papers kept up the barrage and reminded their readers that in Germany Karl Liebknecht was already free, while in 'democratic' Britain John Maclean was lying in a prison cell being forcibly fed twice a day by an India rubber tube forced down his gullet or up his nose. "Is the Scottish Office," asked Forward, "to be stained with a crime in some respects even more horrible and revolting, more callous and cruel, than that which the Governors of Ireland perpetrated on the shattered body of James Connolly?"'[33]

The call, surprisingly, was heeded. After being told that continued force-feeding would result in 'irreparable damage to the prisoner's health', the authorities presented Maclean with a bargain that he initially refused: leave prison without charge but on the understanding that no further agitation will be made against the war. This changed,

[32] Max Hastings, *The Long Walk to Revolution: John Maclean's Story* (London: Penguin Publishing Cpv., 1994) p.89.

[33] James G. Brown, *Maxton: A Biography* (Edinburgh: October Books, 2002) p.153.

however, when news of the French capitulation reached Britain. The authorities, terrified that the mobs gathering around the prison would resort to violence to free their hero, freed Maclean that same day.

Maclean immediately rejoined the anti-war movement and wreaked havoc for the government. In the final months of the war before the 'Peace with Honour' he was pushing for a General Strike to cripple the economy – only loyalty to British workers who would face violence kept the TUC from complying. Maclean had established himself, through links with the leaders of dockworking Unions in Glasgow, as a respected figure among Trade Unions, while his friend James Maxton had begun a campaign to enter Parliament as a radical Labour MP. By 1923, Maclean was seen as the spiritual leader of workers across the country, offering lukewarm support for the Labour Party (except when introducing Maxton as a speaker) and appearing at rallies to encourage actual revolution. The security services, knowing that arrest would simply result in all-out rioting, plotted to kill him; on 11 January 1924 an 'unknown assailant' fired a pistol at him from the window of a moving car as he left a working men's club in Leeds. The bullet completely missed him, but struck a companion in the shoulder. Maclean, in a rage, wrote an open letter to *The Times* (a daily newspaper of the day) and challenged those who wanted him dead to explain why 'in broad daylight, before their peers – the workers and poorest of this country – to see how their argument for my demise is received'. *The Times* published it, demonstrating quite how seriously the establishment was taking Maclean by this time. There were no more attempts on his life, but his wife Agnes wrote in her diary that since that day he had seemed 'a little more worried, and, oddly enough, a little more interested in what other people had to say'.[34] It is likely that this assassination attempt is what made Maclean so suitable as the 'champion of compromise' that the Union needed in those early years.

My colleague John Durham has already enlightened readers of this book on the events of the Revolution and Maclean's role in the Inaugural Congress, so I shall add no more on that subject. However, the real business of evaluation requires a careful inspection of

---

[34] Agnes Maclean, *John* (Glasgow: Red Flag Publishing, 1945) p.231.

Maclean's actions as Chair at the end, not the beginning, of his tenure. It was in 1928 that the first cracks in the Union's 'utopian' structure began to emerge. It started a minor disagreement between two Syndicates – those of Devon and Cornwall, to be precise. Devon was home the thriving port of Plymouth, upon which Cornwall relied for much of its overseas tin sales – its main product. The Republic of the Sicilies and the Commune of France both had great need for cheap tin, but Cornish ports lacked the capacity to take the strain of large freighters moving freely day-by-day. The dispute emerged when Devon wanted to limit Cornish Mining Unions' access to the port, saying that Devon, too, had goods to export. Cornwall, led by the charismatic John Spargo, respectfully stated that Devon was not a different country to Cornwall, and under the Constitution of the Union of Britain all resources were to be shared and provided where needed. Devon's reply to Spargo was that a port was not a resource. Spargo's reply was that, actually, it was.

This argument over semantics was in danger of boiling over into something far more dangerous, thanks to Sunderland-based Unions in the Tyne and Wear Syndicate deciding to take umbrage with Newcastle's dockers restricting their own access for similar reasons. The Federal Council watched with alarm, and John Maclean decided to exercise his impeccable compromising ability by calling a meeting between all the affected parties. The meeting was a disaster. Spargo accused Maclean of being 'an irrelevant Scotsman' who had no moral authority to 'dictate on Cornish matters'.[35] The Sunderland Unions believed they were being underrepresented and patronised, comparing Maclean to 'a nice man from the government' that the old regime would have sent up to assuage their fears. To compound this, their leader Joseph Havelock Wilson threatened to strike indefinitely until access to Newcastle's ports was completely open to them as well as any other Union in the country. Maclean was rapidly losing control, and by

---

[35] This quotation made it into *The Chartist*, further embarrassing Maclean and calling into question his very authority outside of Scotland to some more prejudiced Autonomists.

the time the Congress of 1929 came around he was faced with the first seriously contested Chairman's election of his political life.[36]

The candidate who challenged him, with real regional support, was none other than John Spargo. Highly popular in Cornwall and, ironically, Devon after his stance against the meddling of 'an irrelevant Scotsman' in local matters, he appealed to a great many Autonomists at the Congress and was privately endorsed by Arthur James Cook and Oswald Mosley as 'the perfect ferret to get rid of that soft rabbit Maclean', with the intention that Cook would easily take the Chair from Spargo at the 1930 Congress. Spargo gave a powerful speech before the election, promising to reform the 'utterly non-regionally sensitive' Federal Council and 'never again permit spurious meddling' into the affairs of local Syndicates and Unions. He was met with rapturous applause, with some Congress delegates rising to their feet. Maclean sat in his Chair, the blood draining from his face and looking like a broken man. Where was the fire of his youth now? Had he tried to compromise too much? James Maxton, sitting nearby, leant over to him and looked him straight in the face. Allegedly pausing to flick a strand of his unruly fringe out of his right eye, Maxton spoke a simple sentence to Maclean.

'Are you going to let that Sassenach[37] do this to you?'

Maclean's response is famous. Saying nothing to Maxton, he rose to his feet and clapped Spargo himself, before striding to the podium to make his own speech. Clearing his throat with a characteristic return to form, he raised his hands to the Congress. 'Comrades,' he began, 'my Comrade here makes a number of very good points.' The rest of the speech was not quite so pleasant to Spargo. Maclean highlighted the problems with what Spargo proposed, and viciously attacked what he perceived as the man's hypocrisy – he had wanted to force a deal through with Devon yet objected to the elected mediators on the Federal Council helping him do so. Maclean pointed out Spargo's

---

[36] The Maximists, Autonomists and Congregationists had all declined to back candidates against Maclean in the previous two years, in light of his enduring popularity and success.

[37] Pejorative term for an Englishman in Scottish slang.

other faults – his lack of real Union credentials, and how he had allegedly been elected as Chair of the Cornwall Syndicate because each Union leader voted for themselves with Spargo as a second choice. True or not, the comment led to a ripple of laughter around the room, which was said to create a glint in Maclean's eye as he continued to lambast the man while playing up his own successes and plans for the future. 'As we approach a new decade, Comrades, now is not the time for a novice!' he cried, banging his fist into the lectern. 'I may have faltered, but I put to you that I have not failed! If re-elected, my first action will be to meet with Comrade Wilson and thrash out an agreement that is suitable for all – and I promise you now that I will not *sleep* until it is written in the law of this Union that ports are open to all, and no longer under the direct jurisdiction of whichever Syndicate they happen to be in!'[38] The Congress Hall erupted – for the most part. The election was still closer than it could have been, with Maclean winning by just 13% of the votes cast,[39] a far cry from his 97% of the previous year.

Nevertheless, evaluating Maclean requires not only a report of his actions, but an analysis of them. His true motivation for that powerful speech is called into question by Maxton's words just before it – was it heartfelt, or brought on by a genuine Scottish dislike for this arrogant Cornish man who threatened Maclean's personal popularity? We cannot know for sure, but it does not bode well for the picture of Maclean as a constant unwavering and committed socialist who always put the Union before his own ambitions. Similarly, the whole affair damages Maclean's credibility as a great compromiser, for it was here that compromise failed. The Sunderland strikes were averted, yes, but through luck rather than Maclean's work – Joseph Havelock Wilson died in April 1929, and the movement for striking fell apart without his leadership. Maclean also did not put in as much work as he said he would on introducing greater legislation to free ports from local authority, instead passing this duty to Jimmy Thomas and Arthur

---

[38] Margaret Cole, *Living for Britain: My Diaries* (London: Penguin Publishing Cpv., 1945) p.73.

[39] Eric Hobsbawm, *The Ports Crisis* (London: Forward Books, 1967) p.432.

Horner, the latter of which added 'Commissary for the Independent Port Authority' to his ever-expanding list of titles when the work was completed. Maclean was, above all, a tired man. He was elected unopposed one final time in 1930, and appeared 'visibly older' to all present. The strain of the Ports Crisis had taken its toll on him, and he fell sick with influenza at the end of 1930, with most work now being done behind the scenes by the triumvirate of Maxton, Snowden and Horner. On 15 January 1931, aged 51 years, John Maclean took to his bed somehow knowing it would be for the last time. It is said that he turned to Agnes before he closed his eyes and muttered 'Don't you dare let them put me in Westminster Abbey.'

True to her word, Agnes ensured that his instructions were followed to the letter. Tom Mann (taking over as interim Chair until the Congress the following month) and Maxton agreed to have a State Memorial Service rather than a State Funeral, and the casket itself traveled by train overnight to Scotland, where it was eventually carried through Pollokshaw to the graveyard Maclean's home had overlooked as a child. He is buried there to this day, although a plaque commemorating him also sits in Chairs' Corner in Westminster Abbey.

In conclusion, then, John Maclean is in many ways an enigma to evaluate. A decisive, defiant agitator in his youth, and apparently morally upright for his entire life. But a closer look at his actions in his final years tells a different story – a story of a man potentially more motivated by personal ambition and pride, a man whose complacency with his abilities as a compromiser nearly wrecked the fabric of the Union during the Ports Crisis of 1928-29. However, it would be all too easy to reach the incorrect conclusion that his zeal for socialism disappeared during this time – it did not. Even when suffering in his final months, he would answer letters and attend factory openings as much as he could, always seeming genuine and full of pride with what the workers of this country had and would continue to accomplish. Flawed? Yes. Disingenuous? Perhaps. A failure? Never.

The Congress of 1931

John Durham

'Comrade, I knew John Maclean. John Maclean was a friend of
mine. Comrade, you're no John Maclean.'
James Maxton to Philip Snowden, 3 February 1931

With the death of John Maclean in January 1931, what was expected
to be another run-of-the-mill Congress with little debate or
confrontation was turned overnight into a tooth and nail fight for
control of the Union. The Maximists in particular were caught off-
guard – Arthur James Cook was not in good health (he would die later
that year) but remained the unquestioned head of the faction thanks to
the loyal support of his eventual successor, Oswald Mosley.[40] While
support for Cook remained strong within the faction (it is important to
remember that as all political parties were banned, the Maximists were
just an unofficial faction that was perfectly tolerated like any other), the
Maximists had failed to make the ground they had hoped to among the
key voters at the Congress – namely the Syndicate and Union leaders

---

[40] [1] It has been argued that Mosley's attachment to Cook and his close
association with him from the beginning of the Revolution until Cook's death
was intended by Mosley as a means of purging his own aristocratic background
from the public mind. With Mosley seen time and time again at the side of
this plain-speaking proletarian, and using his own eloquent speaking style to
compliment and praise his and his movement's efforts, it certainly had the
successful result of making people think of 'Mosley, the man of the people'
rather than 'Mosley the Baronet'. For more on this subject, see 'Reinventing a
tyrant' by Eric Hobsbawm, available in the JSTOR online archives for *History
Today*.

they believed would by now be disillusioned with the lack of progress being made by Federationist policies.

The difference between Federationism and Maximism at this point could not have been greater. Where Federationists supported the status quo of a somewhat powerful Federal Council that had reasonable power to mediate debate between Syndicates and dictate on national issues, the Maximists wanted to turn this into an all-powerful 'Central Bureau' that would dictate to each Syndicate exactly what it needed to build, produce or harvest. Federationists accused the Maximists of being 'state socialists', while Maximists themselves said Federationism was 'the school of half-measures'. Maximism called for an end to 'wasted production' and the replacement of the Yearly Aims of early Federationism (targets dictated but not enforced or rewarded by the Federal Council) with 'Six Year Plans' that would see carefully calculated construction of industry and management of the eventual output become paramount over local concerns or regional differences. The Federationists, quickly rallying behind the unlikely leader Philip Snowden because of his experience in the second highest office in the land, began to lobby the attending delegates on a platform of preserving regional autonomy in the face of expanding the central power that the Maximists sought to produce.

Where the Maximists had had no trouble selecting their candidate – despite concerns about Arthur James Cook's health – the heir-apparent to the Federationist crown had a fight on his hands. Snowden, while popularly seen as competent and a capable administrator, was believed by some of the more radical elements of the Federationist movement to be 'too soft' and incapable of holding out against the pressure being put upon the Federal Council to implement some Maximist reforms by some of the most influential Unions in the country. It was this, along with his perceived 'improper background' (he had a relatively privileged youth and was the victim of some classism as a result), that lost Snowden the confidence of a section of the Federationist bloc. Seizing his chance, James Maxton announced his intention to stand for the Chair as a 'Radical Federationist four days after John Maclean's death. Radical

Federationism was, for all intents and purposes, Federationism with more fire in its belly.[41] Domestic policy was almost exactly the same, with only a 'greater emphasis to be placed upon regional authority' being the doctrine's self-professed departure from Federationism proper. Foreign policy, however, was a call for 'an end to isolationism' and a promise to rebuild the Armed Forces as an offensive, rather than defensive, force. 'As our Comrades in Russia once said,' Maxton wrote, 'we must seek permanent, world revolution to share our prosperity and ensure our own survival.'

While extremely alarming to the pacifistic Congregationalists (who traditionally voted with the Federationists on policy issues), this rhetoric appealed to many Maximists disgruntled that Mosley, seen as the man who stood a much better chance of winning than Cook, was not standing. The result was a shift in allegiance from some less extreme Maximist Unions to Maxton by the time of the Congress, and the emergence of a new Congregationalist candidate – the arch-pacifist George Lansbury. A former Labour MP with strong Christian values, he seemingly personified everything about the Congregationalist platform – except feminism. A supporter of women's rights he most certainly was, but ultimately, as a man, he was an acknowledgment by Annie Kenney, Christabel Pankhurst and Beatrice Webb that there was no chance of anyone being addressed as 'Chairwoman' any time soon. He was, however, the strongest candidate the Congregationalists had yet fielded, as he was very well-respected in all quarters of the leftist movement. His candidacy was not so much a threat to Snowden and Cook in the sense that Maxton was, but he would certainly take a number of votes away from both candidates, particularly Snowden himself. With the Congress looming and more and more Unions defecting to either Maximism or Maxton (the opportunity for poetry was not lost on satirists of the time), Snowden needed to think fast. Tom Mann, called in as acting Chair, had no love for the warmongering Maxton or the extremist Maximists. It is believed that

---

[41] Maxton wrote and circulated 'The Radical Federationist Manifesto' a week before the Congress, explaining his platform.

he suggested to Snowden the move that would tip the balance in his favour.

On 1 February, 1931, Tom Mann called the Congress of Trade Unions to order. It was a lengthy task, as a verbal altercation had broken out towards the back of the chamber and almost come to blows – a young Maximist Union representative from Southport had objected to a particularly confrontational Congregationalist (they did exist) calling him a 'Bolshie traitor'. Once order had been restored, Mann got through the business at the top of the agenda relatively swiftly, accurately gauging the atmosphere of the Congress as one that wanted to get to the elections as quickly as possible. Therefore, without much delay, Mann began by opening the floor to candidates who wished to stand for election, beginning with those standing for Chair.[42] For the first time since 1926, all the unofficial factions backed a separate candidate, and there were even some plucky independents standing on various local platforms. Here follows a list of the main candidates, along with a choice quotation from each of their speeches to the Congress.

Philip Snowden (Federationist)

'Having worked with the late, great John Maclean for five years in the construction and administration of our Union, I believe I share his vision, skills and ability – I therefore feel that I am best placed to continue his legacy of co-operation and improvement.'

James Maxton (Radical Federationist)

'Philip Snowden said he "shares John Maclean's skills and ability". Comrade, I knew John Maclean. John Maclean was a friend of mine. Comrade, you're no John Maclean. John's radical spirit lives on in Radical Federationism, with greater power for local workers and the ability to look our foreign foes square in the eye, not avoid their gaze for fear of starting a conflict we cannot win.'

Arthur James Cook (Maximist)

---

[42] The Constitution stipulated that the Chair is always the first post to be elected, followed by General Secretary, Exchequer, Foreign Affairs and Home Infrastructure. Other, or newly created posts, could be appointed by the Chair and passed by a simple majority in whatever order the Congress agreed on.

'The workers of this country today have a choice – carry on the stagnation we are subjecting our industry to by maintaining the hamstrung and compromising policies of Federationism, or move into a new age of mass construction to ensure better living conditions for each and every citizen of our republic!'

George Lansbury (Congregationalist)

'I am here to show you that the rhetoric of these men is not the only choice you have. This country deserves peace and prosperity, yet all candidates here apart from myself support the maintenance of our Armed Forces. I say to you now that, if elected, I would abolish the whole dreadful equipment of war and say to the world "do your worst."'

Niclas y Glais (Autonomist)

'Here we are again, Comrades. The same promises, the same plans and the same old Union. Comrade Maxton talks about greater power for workers within their own region – something I applaud. But where Comrade Maxton falls short is the idea of real freedom for the minorities in this country oppressed from London – the freedom that can only be achieved through independence for Scotland and Wales!'

It was impossible to gauge who had swung the delegates the most with their speech. In accordance with the Constitution, Tom Mann then opened the floor to questions and speeches from individual delegates and representatives. It was among these that Philip Snowden's 'secret weapon' was deployed. Just after a planted question from Oswald Mosley had allowed Cook to tear into the 'inefficiencies of the diversified state', Tom Mann gestured to an elderly-looking man towards the back of the chamber. The man rose, and began to speak. 'My name is Ramsay MacDonald, and I used to be leader of the Labour Party,' he began. MacDonald continued with a reflection on how far the socialist movement had come since the Revolution. There was some consternation at his presence, as he had been a controversial figure to many trade unionists because of his alleged commitment to private ownership – something that was never to be tested after the Conservatives narrowly won the 1924 election on a platform of 'Maintain Britain's Honour' – and association with the 'failed' Labour Party. However, men like Attlee and, of course, Maxton himself had proved that former Labour MPs could make more than capable Socialists of the new regime. MacDonald, sensing the crowd had been won over somewhat by his words, turned to the matter of his endorsement for Snowden. 'Accusing' him of being too modest, MacDonald described the time he and Snowden had spent in Opposition, planning budgets and the like, declaring that Snowden was 'the finest economist I have ever known' and that he was indeed well-placed to continue the building of our Union that was begun under Maclean. 'He has,' MacDonald concluded, 'all the credentials this country dearly needs at this time of consolidation. That is my take on this matter, Comrades – I now invite another to speak.'

MacDonald's impact on the election has been debated in many circles since the Congress, but the general consensus is probably that he did not actually win over any Maximists but instead shored up Snowden's support among the Federationists, some of whom were drifting towards James Maxton. It is because of this, combined with Maxton's perceived inappropriate hawkishness, that the results of the final count of the votes for Chair were as follows:

Total Votes Cast – 1203
Abstentions – 97
Arthur James Cook – 433 (36%)
George Lansbury – 91 (7.7%)
James Maxton – 153 (12.7%)
Philip Snowden – 475 (38.49%)
Niclas y Glais – 51 (4.3%)

The result was not met with cheers of adoration, but instead sighs of relief and shouts of anger[43] from different parts of the chamber. Mann invited Snowden to the Chairman's box where he duly sat, without much ceremony (his small frame never gave him much gravitas). Addressing the assembled and still uproarious Congress, he thanked his voters while acknowledging he did not have the mandate his illustrious predecessor had usually enjoyed. Eager to move the work of government onwards, he announced his plans to make good on the Federationists' claims to be more interested in regional issues by

---

[43] Nye Bevan, *Diaries* (Cardiff: Cymru Publications, 1971) p.461.

proposing a set of new posts for the Federal Council, including Commissary for Education and a number of Commissaries for Regional Relations. Gradually the tumult died down and voting on these posts being added to the Constitution could begin. James Maxton, angry and bitter at his loss, made much of declaring the posts to be 'needless platitudes' that hid the real 'contempt' for regionalisation felt by Snowden. Arthur James Cook, looking very pale and flustered, made an angry speech opposing the creation of the post of 'Commissary for Regional Relations', saying it was a 'continuation of the crippling kowtowing that has held progress back in this country for too long', but his fellow Maximist Sidney Webb was happy to speak in favour of the post of Commissary for Education; as a lifelong educator of workers, he believed that the centralisation of the school curriculum and authority was an excellent move. Webb would later win the post when the elections were held.

The elections took place across the period of the Congress, with most candidates elected without a serious contest. There were some surprises – Ernest Bevin declined to run again for Foreign Affairs, saying he wanted a 'well-earned rest' from the business of front-line government, and pledging to return to the docksides of Gloucestershire where he intended to serve his comrades as a Union organiser. This opened the way for G.D.H. Cole, an unassuming but highly intelligent statistician who was known as an excellent diplomatic mediator between Syndicates, to become the new Commissary for Foreign Affairs. The other surprises came from Birmingham – little-known Tom Roberts, who had gained a powerful local reputation for his similar mediatory role since the Revolution, became the Regional Relations Commissary for the Midlands. His friend Jesse Eden, after much campaigning and support from the Feminist wing of the Congregationalists, became the first female member of the National Council through her bid to create and fill the post of Commissary for Female Workers. Eden had led and organised a 10,000-woman strike in the early 1920s against the car manufacturers of Birmingham to nationwide aplomb. The only post that saw a serious contest take place was that of Commissary for the Exchequer, the Union's chief economic post. Arthur Horner vacated the post when he was unanimously elected as General Secretary.[44] Oswald Mosley of the Maximists stood and gained much support. Ramsay MacDonald nominated old Comrade J.R. Clynes to stand, gaining him Snowden (who had been struggling to find a suitable replacement for Horner from his own ranks) and the Federationists' support. MacDonald's support, as well as Snowden's declaration that the Congress should not 'let Maximism in the back door', meant Clynes won with 54.3% of the vote. The final area that saw reform of the elections was the military – Tom Wintringham made much of declaring that the Armed Forces were now ready to operate independently from his Commission and proposed individual heads of each branch to be elected. Military men who had either pledged 'apoliticism' or socialist support themselves led the Army and Navy, but Oswald Mosley, although a civilian, had served in the 'Royal' Air Force during the Great War and put himself forward as a candidate of reconstruction for the Republican Air Force position.

To the consternation of Snowden, he defeated his opponent and announced he would seek to use the post to show what Maximism could really achieve, through the development and construction of new aircraft to defend the Union. After all the elections had been settled, the new Federal Council of the Union of Britain looked like this:

Chairman of the Congress of Trade Unions Philip Snowden

General Secretary of the Congress of Trade Unions Arthur Horner

Commissary for the Exchequer J.R. Clynes

Commissary for Foreign Affairs G.D.H. Cole

Commissary for Home Infrastructure Jimmy Thomas[45]

Commissary for Industrial Relations Harry Pollitt

Commissary for Education Sidney Webb

Commissary for Regional Relations (Scotland) William Gallacher

---

[44] According to Tom Mann, an agreement was reached between Horner and Snowden that saw the former allow the latter to stand unopposed for the Federationists. If true, this adds greater meaning to Snowden's pledge (that he kept) to stand down after five years.

[45] Replaced in 1932 by Clement Attlee.

Commissary for Regional Relations (Wales) Niclas y Glais

Commissary for Regional Relations (Northern England) J.B. Priestley

Commissary for Regional Relations (Midlands) Tom Roberts

Commissary for Regional Relations (Southwest England) John Spargo

Commissary for Regional Relations (Southeast England) William Wedgwood Benn

Commissary for Female Workers Jesse Eden

Chairman of the Home Defence Committee Tom Wintringham

Chief of Staff (Army) Walter Kirke

Chief of Staff (Navy) Ernle Chatfield

Chief of Staff (Air Force) Oswald Mosley

There was some other business to attend to, of course – various new infrastructure agreements were signed (as a sign of the rising star of Clement Attlee, it was he who chaired the discussion) and the Congress voted to maintain the Ports Independence Motion put forward by Maclean in his final months (see previous chapter). William Wedgwood Benn made a potentially controversial suggestion that was surprisingly voted for with little opposition. The Congress, Benn said, should be held in September around the date of the Revolution, as February was not the best time for some parts of the country to attend. Results of the harvest would also be ready, and so on, and the current date of February had only been chosen because the first Congress had been held as soon as possible after the Revolution. The motion passed, with an addendum that this did indeed mean there would be longer than a year until the next Congress. Another proposal came from James Maxton, who spoke with genuine passion and without a hint of prior bitterness as he proposed that the Union's first airship, under construction in Kent under the name 'Revolution', should instead be named 'John Maclean' in honour of the great man. The motion passed unanimously.

On the final day of the Congress, Snowden attempted to bring together all the quarrelling factions for what he thought would be a politically-neutral discussion – the matter of a new flag for the Union.

In the only countries where Britain had formal representation (the Sicilies, France and Bengal), the old Union Flag was used. In Britain itself, the Red Flag was flown at Congress and at official Syndicate events across the country. Since 1926, the workers of Britain had been debating among themselves whether a new national flag should be adopted. John Maclean had thought the idea frivolous and never granted it time at Congress, even going so far as crossing it off Snowden's (in his capacity as General Secretary) draft agenda for the Congress of 1929. Snowden, now in control of a Congress that looked like it might rip itself apart if it had to elect one more controversial new official, turned to the matter as a means of seeking unity.

As it happened, the Congress was more than happy to continue arguing with itself over this new issue. Some die-hard Revolutionaries like Maxton (who was at this point an exceptionally bitter man) opposed the incorporation of any British symbols onto 'the people's flag', and put forward the case for retaining the existing pain red design. Eric Blair of the Maximists argued that the Union was a fundamentally British undertaking and its flag should display this. As a compromise, he tabled a joint motion with John Spargo to include the emblem of the Congress on the flag as well, in traditional gold on the existing red background. Snowden kept out of the negotiations, maintaining his role as Chair meant he would take responsibility for commissioning an artist, but would seek no input in the design itself. The question of, if depicting the Union flag, including the cross of St Patrick on it given the departure of Ulster from British jurisdiction was raised. Mosley and Cook both argued vigorously for the maintenance of the cross, saying to remove it was to remove 'this Union's link with our forefathers who lived under imperial yoke – did they not have good ideas?'[46] A more convincing argument was put forward by Niclas y Glais – back from the political wilderness after his election as Regional Commissary for Wales – who said that such a move should be embraced and applauded. 'To remove those two archaic crossed lines from our country's flag would be to remove our claim to a people we

---

[46] Oswald Mosley, *The Sayings of Arthur Cook* (London: Forward Books, 1935) p.93.

never rightfully ruled,' he declared during the debate. It was quickly accepted that he was attempting to make a link between the withdrawal of British rule over Ireland and his own Autonomist agenda, which called for the same thing in Wales and Scotland.[47] While the gist of his latter intention was not embraced by the Congress, his initial proposal was. It was agreed that a designer should be selected by the Federal Council and given a brief to 'produce a flag that incorporates the following three elements:

i)   the Union Flag as it appeared between 1707 and 1801

ii) the emblem of the Congress of the Trade Unions

iii) the current unofficial Red Flag of the Union of Britain'

The motion passed by a heavy majority, with even the most loyal of Cook's Maximist supports agreeing to the idea. A designer named Charles Perrion, known for his progressive and groundbreaking designs of patterns and furniture, drew up a flag for the Federal Council which, finding the flag to its liking, voted to adopt it.

The Congress ended, therefore, on something of a high note. These were not the halcyon days of 1926 by any stretch of the imagination, but the vote and debate on the flag had been considerably more cordial and collaborative than the previous days' frantic and bitter struggles. The pervading mood was not one of optimism, but of acceptance that the outcome had been the best of a bad bunch – the frightening centralisation plans of Arthur James Cook had been marginally rejected, the fiery and 'dangerous' James Maxton's radical ideas had been exposed as somewhat poorly thought out, and the uninspiring but proven-to-be capable Philip Snowden now held the reins, taking the unprecedented step of declaring he would only hold the post for five years of what he called 'consolidation' before acknowledging the need for a 'new, younger and more dynamic' Chair to take his place. The Union's representatives returned to their home towns and Syndicates and prepared for five years of ennui and more of the same. It was better this, they thought, than a venture into the

---

[47] Ian Kershaw, *Struggle Unending: The Autonomism Question* (Sheffield: Blade Publishing, 1991) p.42.

unknown. By 1936, they would be more than ready for the latter.

How did Federationism work?

Terry Pollitt

'They say a camel is a horse designed by a committee. The trouble with Federationists is that they can't even agree on whether they want a horse in the first place.'

Oswald Mosley

Any self-respecting political theorist will tell you that the title of this article should really be 'how did Federationism fail?' Its failings are far easier to list than its positive aspects, and history has vindicated those who believed its inefficiencies would one day be rejected by the Union as a whole. Nevertheless, it is important to grasp the workings of Federationism, for without it the resulting systems that came to dominate the Union, from Maximism to Democratism, would not have taken the shape they did. Many aspects of Federationism became more than simply tenets of a political faction – they entered the written (and unwritten) constitution of the Union itself. Some of the ideas of Maclean, Snowden and Maxton survive to this day. Others could not withstand the tide of history.

As Federationism is often described as 'a very British flirtation with Syndicalism', it will be necessary to outline the three units by which it governed, the most famous of which being the Syndicate. Syndicates filled the role held before the Revolution by the various Local Authorities of the old regime – county and district councils and so on. Like their predecessors, they handled local issues like road maintenance and infrastructure in addition to their negotiating role with other Syndicates for supplies and transport links. Taxation was also agreed on an entirely local basis, with the Syndicates themselves voting individually on the percentage they would pay into the national coffers.

The main difference was that instead of being a directly elected body, Syndicates at this time were a sort of 'micro-congress'[48] of the local Trade Unions. Each Union elected delegates within itself to sit upon the Syndicate Council, and the chairmen and -women of each Union also gained an automatic seat on this body. Trade Unions themselves underwent radical change in the period between 1925 and 1930 – within a few months of the Revolution the emerging need for Unions to take control and have direct authority over the country meant that the national and regional Unions that spoke for workers across their profession were becoming too unwieldy to effectively administer each individual coal mine, branch line or dockyard. In response, reforming 'Localist' Trade Union leaders began to take charge of local branches of the national Unions and form transform them into Unions that specifically dealt with the surrounding area. The local Unions remained part of their national equivalents and worked with them to improve working conditions and pay nationally, but regionally began to work in the interests of local workers. For example, the Dover office of the National Union of Railwaymen formed the Dover and Ashford Railwaymen's Union, with its Chairman Bernard Browning sitting on the committee of the National Union of Railwaymen itself. The DRU worked with other local Unions such as the Union of Channel Coast Dockers (itself a local offshoot of the Transport and General Workers Union) through the meetings held within the East Kent Syndicate to rebuild the dilapidated docks of the town after the Royalist Exodus had left the port partly sabotaged and lacking much of the equipment to rebuild it.

The Unions made up the bulk of each Syndicate, but there were also representatives from the third arm of Federationism's economic structure – Co-operatives.[49] With public ownership of companies

---

[48] Ed Dunkley, *Syndicalism for Beginners*, (London: Crimson Literature, 1990) p.31.

[49] An enlightened form of business, where workers in the company automatically gain a proportion of the shares in it, as opposed to shares being sold to outsiders with no interest in the company's success. Workers therefore

(selling shares) banned and co-operatives being the only legal means of running a business, the Union of Britain quickly became 'a nation of co-operation'.[50] Representatives from local co-operatives would sit on Syndicate Committees locally and speak for not only their workers but also to recommend what resources and construction projects were necessary for their businesses' survival and viability. In summary, then, there were three main pillars of British Federationist Syndicalism – the Unions, the Co-operatives and the Syndicates themselves that were made up of representatives from both of the other pillars.

Another area to be explored is the processes by which elections took place within the Union. Elections for both officers of the CTU and the motions put forward at each Congress itself were all done at the annual Congress, that from 1931 onwards took place from the first Monday in September until the third Friday. The Syndicates across the country sent representatives – usually leading to a total of around 1300 attendees, 90% of which were directly elected each Congress by workers' ballot, the rest of whom were entitled to attend because of their position within Syndicate or national committees – all of whom were entitled to vote on motions and officers under a First Past The Post system. All elections, as enshrined in the Constitution, were done under this system, including those within the Syndicates themselves. It is important to note that neither the Constitution nor precedent guaranteed universal suffrage; only those who worked and were part of a Union had the right to vote. This left a high proportion of women – and, in the early years of the Union, men unable to find work – without any democratic representation. On the other hand, there were no regulations regarding the right to vote past the membership of a Union, which generally carried no age restrictions, merely proof of employment. Consequently, the youngest person to vote in the Union of Britain during these early periods (and to this day) was Gareth Burn,

gain a stake in what they are working for as well as some control over the company's decisions.
[50] Tony Crosland, *The Future of Britain*, (Sheffield: Blade Publishing, 1951) p.67.

a 12-year-old boy who voted in the election for Chair of the Ellington Union of Pitmen.

The role of the Congress of Trade Unions and specifically the Federal Council in directing the economy in the years of Federationism was at best minor and at worst cripplingly ineffective. Each Congress, Yearly Aims would be voted on, usually without debate, having been drawn up by the General Secretary, Commissary for the Exchequer and other relevant members of the Federal Council. The problem with the Yearly Aims was not their scope; they regularly called for massive industrialisation, particularly in the steel and coal industries. The problem with them was how unenforceable they were – Federationists feared above all else the accusation of 'Bolshevism' or too much centralist control, and as such the Yearly Aims were just that – aims. There were no penal measures that could, either constitutionally or in practice, be exercised or enforced. This resulted in them being largely ignored by the beginning of the 1930s, and industry progressing at its own rate as Syndicates independently pursued their own aims of either consolidation or small-scale expansion.

The lack of real industrial progress was just one of the many problems that the inherent failings of Federationism brought about. The obsession with debate, fairness and an obscene number of vetos at every level of legislature and administration meant that, in short, nothing ever got done. While it is true that regeneration programmes driven by a sense of working for the common good did heal and rebuild the areas worst hit by the violence of the Revolution and Exodus (notably Dover, Plymouth and Westminster), once this urgency and uniting factor was removed so too was the compromise that made progress possible. The individual Unions and Syndicates simply did not have the motivation or interest to work with one another sufficiently to carry out monumental industrial reform – the only real success stories of the 1920s and early 1930s, such as the rebuilding of the rail network, occurred under the direction of national Unions like the NUR. Personal disagreements, like the infamous feud between Sunderland Union leader Joseph Havelock Wilson and his Newcastle opposite number Joe McCauley, often led to the cancellation or lack of progress on pre-existing agreements regarding factory or road construction. Britain was, it was said, 'littered with half-finished causeways, bridges that cannot support the weight of a small horse and factories that contain no machinery'.[51] It was on this backdrop that the Great Recession would bring down Federationism for good, because of its inherent flaws – it bred stagnation but called it 'consolidation', and in promising freedom to decide how to direct one's own industry on a local level it ultimately relied on a non-existent brotherhood between all workers in the Union to strive for each other's benefit. Such an attitude would not be present until the war and post-war years, and even then only after significant state coercion.

So these were the problems of Federationism – there was no enforced direction of production and consequently a stagnation and gradual implosion of Britain's industry. It had a great many ideals of choice and independence, but ultimately these translated not into a free workers' utopia, but a backwards and barely surviving state. The most lasting impact of Federationism is that it discredited 'Syndicalism' in its purest form for good in Britain. The British as a people had always referred to their Revolution and subsequent state as a Socialist, not Syndicalist undertaking, but the word itself remained in use when it was relevant. The concept of Syndicalism and the radical freedom it offered local communities proved itself unsuited to the mass growth that Britain required in the inter-war years, and eventually, once people tired of what they would eventually call 'the freedom to starve', destroyed its own credibility. It is my opinion that it was this that also frightened off many potential Autonomists from supporting y Glais' cause, explaining to an extent why they have remained a fringe group ever since the mid-1930s. Britain was a Socialist Union. But she had toyed with Syndicalism and the autonomy it granted, and this had been found wanting – dangerously so. Not only had pure Syndicalism, that had achieved so much in France, failed in Britain, it had also taken with it the credibility of the Federationists. The reforms of the Snowden years, covered in the next chapter by Comrade Hobsbawm, were in Eric's own words 'too little, too late'. Nevertheless, the spirit of

---

[51] Eric Blair, *The Road to Wigan Pier*, (London: October Books, 1937) p.32.

the Federationist system – the right for workers to choose their own destinies, discussion between Unions to achieve a greater good and the right to own a stake in your employer through co-operatism – remain ingrained on our Union's political and cultural fabric to this day. The literal survival of Federationism was scuppered by the Great Recession, but some of its ideals shaped even those systems that would destroy it. In this sense, in that no knowledge gained from it was ever wasted, it was, as with all the great systems this country has produced, a thoroughly British experiment.

Too little, too late?

Eric Hobsbawm

'There are times when I honestly believe the next Congress will vote to dissolve itself and invite the King to return if he brings with him jobs and bread.'
Margaret Cole, 13 July 1934

This article first appeared in History Today *in June 1993. Our thanks to that publication for granting us permission to reprint it.*

*

The period between 1931 and 1936 – for want of a better term, 'the Snowden years' – is barely touched upon in our schools, ignored with embarrassment by our leaders and joked about in the press. The failings that came about as a result of the crucified and overstretched Federationist system can not all be laid at Philip Snowden's door, but the one such failing that can be laid squarely at his door is the lack of leadership he displayed. Presented with a golden opportunity for centrist reform, 'the Quiet Man' (as he became nicknamed[52]) simply maintained the status quo and built upon the platform of 'consolidation and compromise' that he had been elected upon. But where John Maclean had, at least in his first years, been driven by a desire to expand industry and keep close relationships with all regions of the Union (with varying success), Snowden seemed to use the newly created Commissaries for Regional Relations as an excuse to not get

---

[52] Sidney Webb noted this in his memoirs, along with the observation that Snowden's style of chairing meetings was that of a 'comatose goose'.

involved himself in the process of keeping everyone on the same level. As such, the Commissaries lacked direction and became little more than local mediators whose job was to offer platitudes from the Federal Council and vague direction when asked (which was almost never, according to J.B. Priestley, whose remit was Northern England). With the exception of his comically lacklustre 'Building Britain' programme, Snowden did little to stem the tide of economic stagnation and joblessness.

There were those who could see trouble on the horizon. John Clynes, old Labourite and confidant of Snowden, warned him that if the economy was allowed to run riot in this way for much longer, the production and supply of consumer goods would begin to suffer, first with clothing shortages and eventually a potential food shortage. Electrical goods such as lamps or wireless sets were also dwindling in production as demand for them grew higher. With this in mind, Snowden used his annual report at the Congress of 1932 (held for the first time in a September) to implore the representatives present to return to their home Syndicates and focus on consumer goods. This measure had little effect. Some, like Mosley in his summing up speech for his failed motion to nationalise the steel, coal and rail industries, blamed the lack of response on Snowden's own failings in the area of forceful speaking. This was only partly unfair, as the Chair was indeed not known for charisma or being able to convince others of the merit of his ideals. He had, after all, been elected after being seen as a 'safe pair of hands' on the strength of his calculative mind and years of economic experience. This experience, however, meant nothing in matters such as the consumer goods shortages because the authority that Federationism dictated to the Federal Council and Congress was so hamstrung by its commitments to liberty (decried by Mosley in 1932 as 'anarchy in Marx's clothing!'[53]) that nothing was enforceable or measurable. Far be it from me to agree with Oswald Mosley, but the result, particularly in those crucial years of 1930-36, was something very close to anarchy rather than Socialism.

---

[53] James G. Brown, *A Short History of Maximism*, (Strathclyde: Perkins Books, 1987) p.94.

As the Congress of 1932 ended, the stage was set for a disaster. Britain, thanks to her isolationist policy and under-reliance on foreign trade bar what it could obtain from Bengal, Sicily and France, was unaffected by the market forces of the world around her and as such would never suffer the consequences of any poorly-managed banking crisis in Mitteleuropa. But her internal economic policy had spiralled out of control and a crash was coming, for all to see. Construction materials were being rapidly over-produced, producing a glut in the market for steel, coal and heavy materials. This was thanks to the 'Yorkshire Triangle' of Sheffield, Leeds and York all producing goods that they could trade to each other with low railway and transportation costs because of their proximity to each other. Despite constant efforts by Commissary for Industrial Relations Harry Pollitt (and his regional counterpart J.B. Priestley) to encourage the local Syndicates to take a broader view and moderate their production to prevent a glut forming, as well as to focus as Snowden had advised on underproduced consumer goods like basic electrics, wireless sets and cars, the Unions paid no heed. Priestley wrote 'it was like talking to a brick wall, and it pained us that good men like Harry and I had fought and bled to build it'.[54] Priestley was not alone in his observations. Tom Roberts told comrades that he had been struggling with the Union leaders in Crewe in an effort to direct their efforts away from industrial level textile production and towards cloth suitable for clothing. Both Roberts and Priestley failed, and it is with this grim picture in mind that we approach the Great Steel Bubble of 1933.

The Bubble was essentially the huge amount of steel being produced and sold between the three most powerful Syndicates in the north of England and arguably the entire country – Sheffield, York and Leeds. In February of 1933, the Leeds Syndicate sent a telegram to Sheffield cancelling all further and existing orders of girders, steel sheets and other construction materials, having completed its 'Riverside Redevelopment' scheme. Sheffield, completely taken aback, tried to open up emergency deals with other Syndicates around the country.

---

[54] J.B. Priestley, *An English Service*, (Leeds: Central Library Publications, 1945) p.40.

However these areas, left out in the cold by years of the 'Yorkshire Triangle', had no construction projects to speak of, and had therefore no reason to purchase the surplus steel. Within days the Sheffield Syndicate held an emergency meeting where it declared it would no longer engage with other Syndicates until its own surplus of steel had been traded for. With no-one wanting to buy steel, and construction already ground to a halt in most Syndicates, basic labour jobs dried up within weeks. For the first time, Unionised factories had to vote to lay off their own workers to ensure their own survival. The Federal Council was largely powerless to act, as the office of the Exchequer could do little more than provide advice on how Syndicates should spent their money. The country's gold reserves had mostly been lost to the Royalist Exodus, so printing more money to insert into the regionally-planned economy was decried by both Snowden and Clynes as 'suicidal madness'.[55]

The collapse of the Steel Bubble was exacerbated by the knock-on effect it had on other steel-producing Syndicates around the country. Sheffield's vast surpluses of steel meant their desperate attempts to be rid of it resulted in local trade deals between Syndicates (despite the best efforts of the Federal Council, most trading between Syndicates was kept at a strictly local level[56]) being undercut by cheaper Sheffield steel. The closures of factories spread, and as the larger industrial employers closed down, so too did local co-operatives geared towards feeding, clothing and caring for workers. The lack of consumer goods production, so feared by Snowden, made matters worse by decreasing spending by families and individuals across the board. The Union's lack

---

[55] Michael Foot, *Old Labour Men and the Revolution, 1925-1936*, (London: October Books, 1969) p.417.

[56] This fundamental flaw of British Syndicalism, outlined far better than I ever could in Bevan's *Our Comrades across the Channel*, was caused by the lack of a '*bourse de travail*' that orthodox Syndicalism called for. Having no central and permanent forum to arrange and compel trading agreements across the country, most agreements reached were distinctly local and not far-reaching or in the interests of the country's economy as a whole. If one thing can be blamed upon the great John Maclean, it is his failure to press hard enough for a Labour Exchange (the presumed Anglicised name for a *bourse de travail*).

of central planning meant it had the problems of a Socialist economy and of a Capitalist one – an entirely insular structure that was unfettered and uncontrollable, while still relying on that great myth of Adam Smith's that is 'market forces'. The flow of money was simply not great enough to sustain jobs and construction during this chaotic period, and was the only logical outcome of the flawed structure of Federationism in its earliest forms. By the beginning of September over 400 factories had closed down, many of them small steelworks established since the Revolution by worker's co-operatives and fuelled by local coal mines that in turn had to lay off workers to stay open, and it was clear that the previously stagnating economy had entered an unstoppable nosedive towards recession.

The Union of Britain's economy officially entered recession on 1 September 1933, having shrunk by more than 2% in the previous quarter – a catastrophe never before seen in the British Isles. Hundreds of thousands were already jobless, with fears of up to a million more becoming unemployed as the winter set in and damaged already fragile industries. The Congress of 1933, therefore, was one of the most highly charged in Union history. Marchers traveled with delegates all the way to London, bearing banners and placards that bemoaned the lack of work in their Syndicates, as well as the apparent 'do-nothing' attitude of the Federal Council. Oswald Mosley, still rebuilding the Maximist movement after the death of Cook in 1931, shocked the country by announcing just before the Congress began that he would not be challenging Snowden for the Chair, and the lack of any other credible candidate (none of the experienced members of the Federal Council wanted to take over the reins at this terrible time) was the only thing that prevented Snowden from losing his post and fading into political obscurity overnight. Instead, a reinvigorated Snowden set out a plan for economic reform that was intended to increase confidence in the economy and so spur on a new wave of independently-backed construction initiatives. Called 'Building Britain', the hastily cobbled together package included plans to further expand the railways (drafted by Clem Attlee, who infamously for the time included a suggestion that they be completely nationalised, prompting accusations of

Maximism), proposals for a series of brand new hydroelectric dams on the Humber, Clyde and Avon,[57] and a vast reconstruction programme for the areas left derelict by the Exodus but untouched since – particularly Covent Garden in London, which was to become a site for a landmark building project that would end the problems of slum housing in nearby areas of London. Noted architects were contacted to produce 'housing with dignity' that was to be affordable in upkeep and presentable to the eye – 'houses fit for British workers', Snowden called them. As history has shown, however, none of these plans came to fruition in the short term, or indeed in Snowden's lifetime.

The Congress was baying for blood, and it would be offered them in the shape of J.R. Clynes, the Commissary for the Exchequer since 1931. A capable and astute man who with more power would probably have seen Britain through the crisis, he agreed to fall on his sword to preserve Snowden's credibility, and the position became open to anyone who could be nominated. Mosley astonished the Congress for a second time by declining to stand for the Exchequer, claiming in a miscalculated speech that arguably set the Maximist movement back by two or three years that 'these men got us into this mess – they ought to bear the burden of pulling us out', gesturing to the largely Federationist Federal Council as he spoke. The statement did little to improve anyone's opinion of Mosley, already being questioned as a man of words and no action, so he made very sure that he spent the following year working to increase aircraft production and design by slowly expanding the power and *de facto* authority of the office of Republican Air Force Commissary. By the fateful Congress of 1934 results were already visible and he enjoyed a return to popularity – but I shall come to that in a moment. After Clynes' resignation in 1933 and Mosley's speech that in fact buoyed support for the Federationists by making them seem like the noble underdogs being put upon by all around, John Wheatley was duly elected to succeed him. Wheatley set about trying to build support for the Building Britain programme (without

---

[57] While the hydroelectric dams, like most of the Building Britain campaign, came to nothing, the plans were adopted almost verbatim by Mosley in 1938, with no mention of their original (by then deceased) author.

success) and providing packages of centrally-raised money to the worst-hit areas of the Great Recession. Wheatley is largely forgotten about in the history books, which is rather a shame. He, like Clynes, was a capable man constricted by the lack of central authority their posts had, but Wheatley himself managed something that all later Commissaries for the Exchequer should envy – convincing an assembled Congress to vote nigh-unanimously for a tax rise.

Granted, it was not a tax rise in the sense that we understand it today, for under Federationism the rate of centralised taxation was voted upon by each individual Syndicate which then paid the amount it had chosen to each year. Wheatley, in his first speech for the Exchequer's office at the end of Congress, spoke passionately of the need to 'revert to Marxism in its truest form' and redistribute wealth centrally. Proposing a flat rate of 20% for all Syndicates to pay each year from the coffers they built through their own local taxes, he was supported by Mosley for his centrist leanings and praised by General Secretary Arthur Horner, whose remit involved much negotiation between Syndicates. The assembled Syndicates and Unions, many of whom had chosen to pay around 20% of their yearly tax intake in the past, rallied together and voted for the motion by 1304 votes to 7. Wheatley was hailed by the Federationists as a 'Marxist champion of the underprivileged', by the Maximists as a 'forward-looking man with an eye for progress', and by the Congregationalists as 'the man to direct us out of this quagmire'. The fortunes of John Wheatley would have changed beyond recognition, however, by 1934.

1934 began with an increase in open dissent against the policies of the Federal Council. Eric Blair, then a young leading light in the Maximists and former militiaman of the Revolution, set off on a journey around the north of England to inspect the conditions of the unemployed during the Recession and chronicled his experiences in a seminal work, *The Road to Wigan Pier*. Explaining the problems of malnutrition, crowding in slum housing and the degradation suffered by miners whose only applicable work experience had been gained down mines when their pit closed,[58] the book sold like the proverbial hot cake under the careful eye of Blair's publisher, Victor Gollancz – who, despite earlier Congregationalist support, had recently found himself (like so many Congregationalists of the day) disillusioned with their support of Federationism and become far more centralist in his beliefs. The book, published and in circulation by May 1934, was a scathing indictment of what Blair saw as the 'pathetic and shirking approach of the fruit juice drinkers and cranks running this country'. Its popularity grew; by the eve of the Congress it had sold 550,000 copies, saying much about the state of the Union and her psyche. The standardised level of taxation had been too little, too late and disagreements had erupted over which areas should gain from the expanded Union coffers. When it came to the Congress, Wheatley (not a well man; he had escaped a fatal brush with illness in 1930 thanks only to the excellence of his local hospital, improved after it had been taken over by a co-operative of doctors and nurses) looked unsteady, weary and not up to the task. As Snowden warily read out the agenda at the beginning of the Congress and asked for any points that attendees wanted to add, a manicured hand rose from the far right of the hall. 'He closed his eyes and bit his lip as he turned to the person whose hand it was, already knowing who it was going to be,' wrote Margaret Cole in her diaries, 'and you could have cut the tension with a knife as he asked him to speak. The deep, refined voice of Oswald Mosley filled the room as he declared "Comrade Chairman, I wish to table a motion of no confidence in the Commissary for the Exchequer".'

Snowden immediately scheduled the motion to be debated and voted upon as late as possible – upon the last day of the period allotted to the election of officers, 12 September – and quickly moved on with the agenda. Better prepared this time for the problems the country had now faced for eighteen months, he tabled his own proposal to merge the offices of Home Infrastructure, Industrial Relations and a number

---

[58] This particular chapter was also released as an essay entitled 'Without a mine', and can be easily found in most anthologies of Blair's writings and in more general collections.

of minor responsibilities carried out by Steering Committees into one department to be labeled as 'the Home Department'. The Congress, now only barely divided between Maximists and Federationists and with Congregationalists, Autonomists and a handful of Unionists[59] holding the balance of power, voted for these proposals by a knife edge, and even then only because some more moderate Maximists supported it in principle (in the days of the old regime's corrupt 'party politics' these men would have been 'whipped' to support the 'party line' – for more on this see my book *The Degradation of Power: Victoria's Whores in 19th century Parliament*). The new role of Commissary for the Home Department would have responsibilities encompassing industry, agriculture and transportation plans. Snowden called it a 'bold step towards real Federal authority' but Nye Bevan, then a young Maximist representative from Wales, belittled it as 'the last hoarse cries of a drowning man with no arms'. The real controversy and lasting damage to Federationism caused by the post's creation was the loss of arguably its leading light after Arthur Horner – Clem Attlee. A Federationist by default ever since his rehabilitation from being an MP, Attlee had gained valuable experience during his time in Bengal helping rebuild their railway network. Here he had ruled essentially by decree, always doing so benevolently and with careful consideration for others' wishes, but nevertheless without red tape or administrative problems. Upon his return to Britain he was bemused to find his comrades at each others' throats whenever the concept of centrally managing anything was even mentioned. His success with the rebuilding of Britain's own railways came largely from his and Jimmy Thomas' close work with the National Union of Railwaymen. As Home Infrastructure Commissary with a great deal of experience, he saw himself as naturally placed to assume the role of Commissary for the Home Department. When the Maximists chose to contest the position by putting up Rajani Palme

---

[59] The somewhat pretentious name adopted by those Union representatives who claimed to not be subscribing to any particular faction but spoke 'for the Union and only for the Union'. Not to be confused with the failed reactionary ideology that dominated the United Kingdom's Conservative Party for much of the 19th century.

Dutt, however, he was called into a closed-session meeting with Snowden that would change his political destiny forever.

The Federationists had found they relied on Congregationalist support to get their man into the post, and potentially (rumours were circulating that Mosley intended to challenge for the Chair on the last day of the Congress) for Snowden's own survival. In a tense meeting between Snowden, Horner and Regional Commissary for South-east England William Benn on the Federationist side and Kenney, Lansbury and famine relief campaigner Helen Crawfurd for the Congregationalists, it was agreed that Crawfurd would gain Federationist support if she stood for the post. Attlee lodged a protest but this was waved down by Horner, who claimed unity against Maximism was a priority 'most absolutely and resolutely held by those of us who have the Union's interests at heart'. Attlee, infuriated, rose to his feet and declared 'then I must loathe the Union, for I'd rather support centralist policies in the clear light of day than shoo-in candidates in a box room!'[60] After storming away from the meeting, he arranged a meeting with Oswald Mosley and agreed to work with him in the latter's capacity as Commissary for the Republican Air Force. Attlee was impressed by Mosley's enthusiasm for central planning and co-ordination of industrial resources and facilities, and the arms industry was one of the few areas that had been tamed to the point that it would do as the relevant bureau of the Federal Council told it. Attlee was also surprised to be greeted by old comrade Ernest Bevin, who had ended his brief retirement to join the Maximist faction as a speaker and organiser. Mosley and Attlee agreed on their alliance once Mosley promised to bring Clem on board for his plans to begin mass production of a prototype aircraft presented by R.J. Mitchell earlier that year.

As well as forcing the hand of the already Maximist-leaning Attlee, the Congregationalist-Federationist deal in September 1934 caught the attention of the Autonomists, who knew their votes might count if an increasingly confident and popular Mosley stood against Snowden.

---

[60] Clem Attlee, *Lessons from Putney: My Autobiography* (London: Cheapside Publishing, 1965) p.101.

Niclas y Glais approached Horner privately and told him plainly that if he was elected unopposed to the post of Commissary for Foreign Affairs, the Autonomist vote could be counted for Snowden. Horner, despite knowing that no Autonomist would ever vote for Mosley unless the Kaiser himself was his only opponent, was too uneasy to call his bluff and nevertheless agreed to the deal. G.D.H. Cole took the news considerably better than Attlee, remarking that he had always had more of a passion for internal affairs. Cole and his wife set about working as a pressure group on Regional Commissaries and Syndicates to improve working and housing conditions, and y Glais was elected in due course as Foreign Affairs Commissary. With both minor factions on side, Snowden looked safe.

Quite why his own faction and those around them wanted to keep Snowden in his job may seem like a mystery now, but it comes down to two things: firstly, he was not Oswald Mosley; and secondly, he had proved himself as an economic administrator before. With the right men and women around him, it was genuinely believed by most of his supporters that he would show some of John Maclean's courage and fire and force his policies through while maintaining a distinctly un-Maximist compassion for worker and Union rights. While most of his measures did turn out to be too little, too late, he did leave one lasting mark on British society – reform of the courts. In 1933, the dilapidated court system that relied so much on the now largely Exiled judiciary was comprehensively investigated and rebuilt by a committee led by Snowden himself. The law remained fundamentally the same, but judges were now to be elected legal officials with at least five years' experience at the bar who would be elected by popular vote (a rarity at this time) for terms of four years at a time, subject to reappraisal by their peers and by the public if a petition of 10% of the population of a region's signatures could be obtained calling for it. Judges also had their role in sentencing decreased, only being able to suggest sentences and options open to the jury (still of twelve people – women were now allowed to take part) rather than impose them. Juries had to vote on the sentence, unanimously for life imprisonment or death. The prison system was also nationalized – the first British institution to be so, and hailed by Maximists as a victory despite this mainly being because of its being run by only one Union that was then simply brought into the national framework. This legal reform is probably the greatest legacy of Chairman Philip Snowden, whose otherwise greatest gift was his ability to manipulate others around him to keep him in the Chairman's seat without doing much to justify his presence there. Nevertheless, it worked and he saw off the challenge to him from Mosley in 1934 by a result of 708-592 with some abstentions.

The final dramatic moment of the Congress, therefore, came not on its last day but in the days before it – the vote of no confidence in John Wheatley. The Congress was once more demanding blood, and Wheatley's chances of survival were slim. Herbert Morrison was quickly drafted in as a potential candidate to replace him by the Federationists, but the damage the Federal Council's reputation would suffer if Wheatley lost would be so tremendous it was debatable whether Morrison would win on the Federationist ticket. As the votes were counted, the colour drained from Arthur Horner's face as he passed the result to Snowden, having checked it in his own capacity as General Secretary. Snowden, with a cracking voice, declared that the motion of no confidence had passed, and John Wheatley would duly be removed from office as Commissary for the Exchequer. Chaos erupted and Snowden remained in his seat, absently reading his notes in what looked to all present to be a daze. Maximists and Federationists in the chamber came to blows, with James Maxton (back, and supporting his former Federationist allies against his archenemy Mosley at any cost) breaking a chair over the back of one snobbish Maximist who called him a 'Caledonian reactionary bastard'. Shouting, papers flying through the air and even some members of the committee rising from their seats turned the room into 'the very picture of anarchy', wrote Eric Blair, until John Wheatley himself rose to his feet and, in a clear, loud voice, asked if he would be permitted to make a statement of resignation. Snowden, in a daze, banged his gavel till all were quiet (this took several minutes) and invited Wheatley to speak.

'Let me begin by saying how sorry I am to have let you all down,' he began, speaking of his genuine regret that his taxation measures were not adequately carried out and how the fault for that lay with him. 'I was not the Commissary for the Exchequer you needed at this trying and troubled time, and for that I am deeply sorry. But let me ask you not to turn upon each other like we have just seen – this is the Union of Britain, and we all live and breathe and work each day in the knowledge that, together, we can achieve great things. Apart, we will wither and die alone. So please, Comrades, I ask you – debate and discuss and criticise all you will, but turn upon one another with violence and we become no better than Robespierre's perverters of our French comrades' first Revolution. Thank you for the support those of you who worked with me gave me, and goodbye.' The attendees sat in stunned silence, and nobody was quite sure what to say. Someone stood up and started clapping. Astonishingly, others joined in and soon a standing ovation was being given to the man who the Congress had just voted to remove for incompetence. Herbert Morrison was duly elected as his successor on a wave of sympathy that Mosley and his Maximists refused to put to the test, and Snowden's glazed eyes and slight smile told everyone in the room everything they needed to know about how lucky he realised he had been. Wheatley retired from Congressional politics and became a Union organiser in Glasgow, working to improve conditions as the Great Recession began to lessen its effects across the 1934-35 working year. Growth returned in May 1935 and the Recession was officially declared over, but there was still much to do. The Coles, the Webbs (Sidney Webb, too, found himself out of a job when Industrial Relations was merged with the Home Department) and men like Wheatley, Bevin and even Mosley worked in their home regions and with their Unions and Syndicates to drag Britain out of Recession by its lapels, improving working and housing conditions and attempting to show that it was not necessary to give the central government a dangerous amount of power to save a Socialist country from recession.

This approach was limited, of course. Britain could not survive on good will and hard work alone, and construction and industry was vital to creating sustainable growth. Snowden's hands-off approach, despite Crawfurd's pioneering work in the area of social justice (200,000 families left poverty in her first six months as Commissary for the Home Department), did little to build these things up and the Congress of 1935 was held in a Britain out of recession but still licking her wounds. Step forward one Oswald Mosley, who stood against Morrison citing his own experience as RAF Commissary and the mass-production plans he had introduced in that role for various aircraft, helping to regenerate areas around the arms factories. On this mandate he was finally elected to the position he had craved for nearly half a decade, and set about putting together various easy to enact and ostensibly Maximist policies and initiatives that would improve his own standing while taking credit for the recovery that was underway. Snowden reminded the departing delegates at the Congress of 1935 (which otherwise saw no other major changes thanks to the new feeling of unity and brotherhood the recovery had brought, although the factions continued to view one another with a wary eye) that he would not be standing for re-election at the next Congress, as if anyone had forgotten.

As 1935 came to an end, parties saw in the New Year across the country. Arthur Horner, standing next to Philip Snowden in Congress House as all around them counted down to the 1936, is said to have remarked 'I have a feeling that everything we've seen so far has just been the beginning, Comrade.' How right he was. The Snowden Years, the Great Recession, the Long Stagnation – whatever you call them – were full of measures that carried with them that fundamentally British timidity that kept our Revolutionary fervour in check for so long. The lack of 'muscle' behind them was what made them too little, too late. The British people and their Union representatives grew tired of 'soft-touch' government and longed for some decisive action to be taken to improve the unemployment, housing and industrial crises. For this reason, the greatest legacy that Philip Snowden left behind will forever be that he set the stage for a man far more extreme than he could ever be.

International Interlude

1926-1935

A World Turned Upside Down

A selection of articles and extracts which provide a cultural and
political cross-section of affairs outside Britain during the time period
covered in the preceding volume.

Letter printed in *The Globe*, October 1926

SIR—

As a Briton exiled from the land of my birth by Bolshevists who
deface the very island of Great Britain by their presence upon it, I
consider it a matter of patriotic duty to put my beliefs and objection on
the public record by communicating them to you in the hope that you
will publish them. Having lived in your fair country for a little under
eight months and, in my time as a statesman and journalist, having
experienced much of it myself, I have no doubt that you will find space
for my thoughts in your respected organ – Canadians, unlike Britons, it
seems, are not frightened by dissent.

Allow me to begin by stating, as I see it, the problem faced by
Britons living in Exile. We (for I most certainly count myself amongst
them) cannot return to our homeland for fear of persecution, torture or
death. A villainous line of working men, brainwashed by depraved

Marxism and that monster Maclean, would tear us limb from limb before we crossed the gangplank. Even this assumes that we would not be blown to pieces in the Atlantic by ships that a year ago bore the names of Kings, but now have, I hear, absurd titles like 'RNS Tyler' or 'Tolpuddle'. We cannot hope to return to our homeland without military action being taken to remove those in charge of the so-called 'Union of Britain'. The Socialists have gained power by making promises that they cannot fulfil, and probably have no intention of trying to fulfil. But as long as they govern the country in a populist and ostensibly sensible manner, the people will continue to support them – such is the power of the venom that now runs in the blood of good British men and women towards the monarchy. Therefore it is clear that such military action will not come from within the British Isles, but must be brought to them by those loyal to the British Empire abroad, myself included.

The problem, as I see it, is that the Canadian government – so happy to welcome seven million Britons into its economy provided they built their own housing – has proceeded to do nothing with regards to liberating the British Isles. My colleagues Mssrs. Baldwin and Lloyd George have found their efforts to establish an official bureau to instigate the liberation completely frustrated and ignored by Canadian government bureaucrats. Your own Prime Minister has only granted one audience to Mr Baldwin in eight months, something I as a Briton believe to be an offensive way to treat the rightful Prime Minister of a sovereign state. It is absolutely imperative for the protection of the Empire, the liberation of the British Isles and, indeed, the defense of your own Canadian state from the scourge of Socialism that we 'Exiles' be taken seriously enough to warrant an office, both physical and metaphorical, of our own.

For this reason I am using this letter to publicly state my intention to establish a permanent office for the British Government-in-Exile. Any official of the Canadian government who has the authority to grant myself, Mr Baldwin and others the right to take up residence in a suitable building should contact me through this newspaper. I hope for speedy results and a successful future. For too long I have seen Britons living in this country with their heads bowed and with no pleasant thought for the future. This must change. The first step toward establishing an official Liberation Committee (alongside my colleagues in the Armed Forces, in particular Air Marshall Brooke-Popham and Admiral Blackhouse) is creating a permanent and recognised British Government-in-Exile. I propose that the current government will reassume the posts they already held before the uprising in Britain, and that elections be an internal matter in which any holder of a British passport may have an input.

To those Canadians reading this who share my desire to restore the Empire and free Britons from tyranny, I thank you for your support. Enlist in your country's Navy if you wish to aid the struggle – I am pleased to say that the integration of Royal Canadian Navy with the larger Royal Navy is one area where your countrymen have been of utmost assistance and highly co-operative. If we control the Atlantic, it will surely not be long before the Royal Standard flies above Buckingham Palace once more. To those Britons reading this, I have only one thing more to say: the time for mourning is over. The time for action is about to begin.

Yours faithfully,

Winston Leonard Spencer Churchill MP

Chancellor of the Exchequer of the United Kingdom of Great Britain and Northern Ireland

Editorial from *Golos*, April 1929

This editorial from the Russian newspaper Golos *(meaning 'Voice') promotes the tenth anniversary of the Conference of Omsk.*

DO YOUR DUTY – CELEBRATE OUR MOTHERLAND'S REPUBLIC TODAY

RUSSIANS,

Today marks ten years since the Conference of Omsk, where brave President Kerensky forged an unbreakable bond between the leaders of the White Counter-revolution. Brave Generals Denikin, Wrangel and Kornilov, along with their fellows, swore allegiance to the then-fragile Republic and united behind Kerensky. Only the treacherous rat Kolchak refused to take part, retreating to his far-eastern army where he pledged his loyalty to the yellow men of Japan over his fellow Russians. This insult is still borne today by Russia, as his rogue state of 'Transamur' sits on our Siberian borders on lands that are rightfully Russian. One day these lands will be reclaimed! One day the 'Empire of the Rising Sun' will be punished for its impudence.

But the loyalty of the other Generals was enough. Within two years, the Bolsheviks had been crushed, their leaders killed and Russia's honour and security restored. Detractors and nay-sayers have since attempted to claim that it was the German military intervention in our Civil War that had the greatest impact on defeating the Bolshevik Reds, but each true Russian knows in his heart that it was our co-operation as brethren of the same state that drove the Red scum back to their strongholds at Tsaritsyn and Moscow, where they died like rats.

Where is Lenin, 'father of the revolution' now? DEAD! His body hung on display in Moscow for three weeks.

Where is Trotsky, the scheming rodent who sent machine gun teams against peasants, now? DEAD! Shot through the neck as he fled true Russian forces and drowned in the Volga.

Where are those who hid behind mighty names, 'the Man of Steel', 'the Hammer' and 'the Giant'? ALL DEAD! Purged from our motherland by the righteous fire of our united White Armies and their bodies left to rot in Tsaritsyn.

Where are those remnants of the Bolsheviks who wanted to destroy our state and enslave us into collectivist tyranny? HIDING! The weasel Bukharin and his motley crew know that true Russians reject them, and if they show their faces they will soon meet their deserved ends. It is only a matter of time, says Security Minister Wrangel, before they shall dangle from lampposts as their Red comrades once did.

But, fellow Russians, ask yourselves also this – where is Russia today, as these men lie in the ground or fester in sewers? RISING! Onwards we go, under brave President Kerensky and our elected Duma! Never again shall tyrants, be they Tsars or Germans or Reds, take away our democratic rights. Never again shall revolutionaries and anarchists seek to murder upon our streets. In the Kaiser's Germany, you may write to your representative in the 'Reichstag', but will he reply? Not unless you are high born to the point that your name has 'von' in it twice! But write to Pavel Milyukov, brave President Kerensky's loyal Prime Minister and servant to all who dwell in Russia, and he will reply to you within three weeks. Such grace, such humility from a man with so much to do – this, fellow Russians, can only be found in a functioning democratic republic such as ours.

So today, *Golos* urges its readers to do their duty and celebrate the Republic. We have freedoms today our fathers only dreamed of. The right to vote, to protest and to dissent are enshrined in our constitution and under the leadership of brave President Kerensky, we shall forever defend these rights from whoever seeks to take them from us. Fly the flag from your home or business today! Throw street parties in memory of Omsk! Shake hands with a soldier who fought for your rights should you pass one in the street! Above all, fellow Russians, CELEBRATE YOUR MOTHERLAND'S REPUBLIC ON THIS, ITS HAPPIEST DAY!

Transcript of *Die Deutsche Wochenschau*, March 1930

This edition of Germany's state-backed newsreel, established in 1929 on the suggestion of a promising ministerial attaché named Joseph Goebbels, deals with various events across the German Empire in 1930.

*

Die Wacht Am Rhein is played. Images of the Kaiser, his son, the Armed Forces and bright views of cities and farms flash across the screen. These fade away to a black card upon which, in white gothic writing, is written 'Die Deutsche Wochenschau'.

News from around the world! All the pictures and quotations that shaped this week in world affairs.

A montage of images of Chancellor Tirpitz appear, along with footage of his casket being transported from his home, draped under the banner of the Reich.

Germany mourns this week as her greatest Chancellor since Bismarck himself passes away. Chancellor Alfred von Tirpitz, who had been in the post since 1924, led Germany through her greatest period of economic growth and imperial glory since the 1870s. In the aftermath of the Weltkrieg, it was he who proposed the consolidation of our African holdings into Freistaat Mittelafrika, and sent war hero Paul von Lettow-Vorbeck to rule the new state. In other overseas matters, it was under his skillful command that Germany intervened in the chaos of post-Weltkrieg China, restoring the rightful Emperor Puyi to his throne and establishing the mighty AltOstasien Gmbh as a company that worked across southern China to build prosperity for Chinese and wealth for Germans.

A noble and respected statesman abroad, Tirpitz was also a skillful and diplomatic leader in internal affairs. As well as keeping the threat of Syndicalism at bay on our borders with France, he steered Germany to a new age of imperial prosperity, while remaining true to our strong imperial traditions. The Kaiser himself mourned him on Sunday, declaring that the Reich has lost its finest living servant. He also announced that he will, 'with a heavy heart', begin the deliberations on who to appoint as Tirpitz's successor.

The emblem of Mittelafrika appears, transposed upon the area of the continent that it controls, followed by images of Lettow-Vorbeck, Goering and Schultz-Ewerth.

In colonial news, flying ace and war hero Hermann Goering arrived in Mittelafrika last Tuesday to begin his role as the new Statthalter of the Freistaat. Paul von Lettow-Vorbeck returned from Africa at the beginning of this month, claiming his work was done. Goering, along with his new ViceStatthalter Erich Schultz-Ewerth, were praised by the Kaiser as they were sworn into their new posts. Goering thanked his majesty for the kind words and pledged to uphold German dignity in her colonies, and expanding where Mittelafrika's interests demanded it. These words caused consternation among members of the Reichstag sitting for the Progressive People's Party, who branded Goering a sabre-rattler unfit for such high office. Ernst Roehm of the Greater German People's Party, however, praised Goering for his 'strong stance against the crawling influence of Syndicalism on the dark continent', a reference to the recent Red insurrections faced by Haile Selassie in Ethiopia.

Images of factory chimneys, road and railway construction and dockyard workers appear in sequence, interspersed where appropriate with pictures of Gustav Krupp and Hjalmar Schacht.

Germany's economic miracle continues this spring, with Gustav Krupp working with fellow senior industrialists from IHK-Mitteleuropa and the Finance Minister Hjalmar Schacht to produce a new document entitled 'Expanding upon Expansion'. The document contains within it ideas to build new and better transport links between Germany's industrial centres, along with an emphasis on developing the long-awaited publicly affordable automobile, the Reichswagen. Mr Krupp confirmed that prototypes are now being drawn up, with the aim of having the car on the road by 1936.

Footage of a football match is shown, with following shots of stadiums, crowds and a trophy in the style of the goddess Germania.

Finally, in sporting news, the final preparations are underway for the first ever Mitteleuropa Cup. The football tournament will be the first formally arranged tournament between the nations of Europe in history, and Germany is deeply honoured to be hosting it. Austria, Ukraine and White Ruthenia are all seen as contenders for the title, but it is the opinion of this news office that the team to back is none other than our Fatherland itself. Whatever the result, the nations of Mitteleuropa will surely enjoy coming together in the best stadiums and bars the continent can offer. Here's to a fine sporting summer!

Extract from *The Great Gatsby*, published 1932

This book by F. Scott Fitzgerald was written as a contemporary critique of American attitudes to society and the wider world. In this extract, the narrator meets with the fiercely nationalist husband of his cousin, and is amused by his outbursts. Fitzgerald intended this, along with those in the book's treatment of Gatsby, as a warning against complacency about 'the American way of life' surviving all transformations, as many of the extremist factions emerging in American politics at this time espoused.

*

"You make me feel uncivilized, Daisy," I confessed on my second glass of corky but rather impressive claret. "Can't you talk about crops or something?" I meant nothing in particular by this remark, but it was taken up in an unexpected way.

"Civilization's going to pieces," broke out Tom violently. "I've gotten to be a terrible pessimist about things. Have you read 'The Rise of the European Empires' by this man Long?"

"Why, no," I answered, rather surprised by his tone.

"Well, it's a fine book, and everybody ought to read it. The idea is we missed a trick by not joining in that Great War. Our businesses got left behind, and we allowed the Germans to dominate the world and – and this is the really depressing part – we allowed them to eventually dominate us."

"Tom's getting very profound," said Daisy, with an expression of unthoughtful sadness. "He reads deep books with long words in them. What was that word we—"

"Well, these books are all scientific," insisted Tom, glancing at her impatiently. "This fellow has worked out the whole thing. If we don't take steps now to keep the world in line, we'll be left behind for a generation and then who knows where we'll end up? Look at our people today – we've got more strikes than ever, fuel shortages in the winter and maniacs like Thomas and Reed telling us we need to emulate that horrible French 'Commune'. Long understands what we have to do about those types."

"We've got to beat them down," whispered Daisy, winking ferociously toward the fervent sun.

"You ought to live in California—" began Miss Baker, but Tom interrupted her by shifting heavily in his chair.

"This idea is that we're Americans. I am, and you are, and—" After an infinitesimal hesitation he included Daisy with a slight nod, and she winked at me again. "—and we've got a right to – to be powerful in the world, because that's who we are. No German or Red has the right to lord it over us, it should be good Americans working together for Americans – see?"

There was something pathetic in his concentration, as if his complacency, more acute than of old, was not enough to him any more. Unwisely, I asked him what this Long fellow proposed to do about this apparently awful situation.

"Now that's the best part—" began Tom, pausing irritably when Daisy noisily tossed her hair back over her shoulder, "—he wants to start these, what are they, programs."

"Programs," echoed Daisy, staring out of the window.

"He wants every man to be able to live like a king," Tom continued, "by letting the state help him out when he needs it – none of this Red nonsense, you understand, that's not what he's about, you see, but – but – oh, it just has to be read to be believed. I understand the problems we've got here now – the rising prices, the property collapse, and this do-nothing we've elected just panders to the state governors. What we need is a stronger union, Nick – you heard it from me first."

When, almost immediately, the telephone rang inside and the butler left the porch Daisy seized upon the momentary interruption and leaned toward me. "I'll tell you a family secret," she whispered enthusiastically. "It's about the butler's nose. Do you want to hear about where we got the butler?"

"That's why I came over to-night."

"Well, he wasn't always a butler; he used to be the overseer for some big company over in New York. Big money, too! Then one day the workers decided they'd had enough of being – what's it called?"

"Downtrodden," suggested Miss Baker.

"Yes, that kind of thing. The workers were – downtrodden, yes – and they banded together into one of those big striking groups and shut the whole plant down for six weeks. Eventually he had to give up his position."

"My," I remarked with a hope that my tone would not betray my lack of interest. Everyone and their grandmother had a story to tell about some villainous Syndicate putting some no doubt equally villainous bosses out of business. Daisy leaned forward again, her voice glowing and singing.

"I love to see you at my table, Nick. You remind me of a – of a rose, an absolute rose. Doesn't he?" She turned to Miss Baker for confirmation: "An absolute rose?"

This was untrue. I am not even faintly like a rose.

Great Men of the Japanese Empire, December 1933

This list, first commissioned in 1930, was published each year to mark out who the Emperor and his government believed had aided Japan and Japanese interests the most. It was considered a great honour to be on the list. Below are some extracts that offer a rough picture of the Japanese sphere of influence during this time.

*

Inukai Tsuyoshi

For years of service to his Emperor and nation, Japan's Prime Minister is once again honoured on this list. A pillar of strength through these dark times for the world, Inukai has time and again demonstrated the might and indefatigability of a just form of democratic government. It was Inukai himself who negotiated with the military to assuage their concerns over Manchuria last year. His diplomatic skill allowed the military to see and respect the value of maintaining the Fengtien Clique's governance in the region, thanks to the careful leadership of Zhang Xueliang. His just hand now guides Japan under the approving eye of his Emperor, who has chosen to honour him this year with his second appearance on the list of Great Men of the Empire.

Zhang Xueliang

The people of the Fengtien Republic know they are ruled by a fair and just hand. Since his father's death and the turmoil of 1928, Zhang has created greater East Asian harmony by steering the Manchurian region that he controls towards greater friendship with Japan. The Emperor is particularly grateful for his work in recent years in reforming his armies on the Chinese frontiers. Zhang represents all that is good about mutual East Asian co-operation with his careful administration, loyalty to both people and Emperor, and just rule. For this reason the Emperor has granted him the honour of being the first Chinese man to appear upon a Great Men of the Empire list. Long may he continue in this way.

Sadao Araki

For service to the military and the Empire as a whole, Sadao Araki is honoured this year by a place on this list. A fierce warrior in our internal struggles against Syndicalism and a Japanese patriot of the highest degree, Japan could not ask for a finer Chief of its Armed Forces. After the historic Inukai-Sadao Agreement of 1932, thanks in part to the stoical nature of Zhang Xueliang, Sadao assured his Emperor that his political ambitions had come to an end. With this move, Sadao laid down a precedent that the Emperor has set in stone – the military shall never again seek control of our country, and democracy shall be upheld to the last. In his capacity, therefore, Sadao also serves as an effective counterweight and safeguard against the potential rise of a new, dangerous cadet class – the last of which are believed to have been executed after the rumoured plans to execute Prime Minister Inukai over the Manchuria Agreement. Sadao's abilities have also been applied to our military as a whole, modernising it and turning it into a formidable force ideal for the maintenance of East Asian peace, whether the threat comes from Sino-German Expansionism, Syndicalism or the Russian Bear. For skills both military and diplomatic, Sadao is honoured by his Emperor on this year's list of Great Men of the Empire.

Aleksandr Kolchak

In pledging allegiance to the Japanese Emperor, this wise Russian Admiral secured the state of Transamur's continued safe existence. A perfect example of the East Asian harmony that exists under the Emperor, Kolchak is not Chinese, Japanese or even Mongolian, yet is welcomed into the Japanese fold after a simple message of submission. Other, racist Empires like the German or former British one would never be so tolerant of command being shared by one whose ethnicity was so alien to theirs. Transamur goes from strength to strength under Kolchak's careful hand, and serves as a powerful and noble naval ally for the Imperial Japanese Navy, providing bases, designs and resources. Kolchak is a fine ally and member of the Empire, and for this reason is honoured this year for the first time with an appearance on the Emperor's list of Great Men of the Empire.

The People of Korea

For the first time, the List Honour has been bestowed upon an entire people. The people of Korea have achieved so much since they achieved the right to be ruled by their fellow East Asians, and Japanese democracy has helped the region develop into a farming, industrial and social paradise. Korea's aristocracy is highly-regarded, her people well-fed, and her industry bustling and growing. All this is thanks to the spirit of co-operation the Japanese-Korean partnership has imbued, and thanks also to the hard work of the Korean people. For this reason the Emperor sees fit to honour them in particular out of all his subjects by adding them as a whole to this year's list of Great Men of the Empire.

Honourable Mention: R.B. Bennett

Although not a member of the Japanese Empire, the Prime Minister of Canada has done great things for Japan in recent months. Demonstrating that the old racism of 'the yellow peril' and refusal to deal with East Asian economies were no way to behave in the twentieth century, Bennett worked with his government and allies to improve trading relations between Japan and her old Entente allies. Though the shame of defeat still hangs heavy on Japan, her allies and Canada (who are in turn host to the defeated exiles of the United Kingdom, driven from their home isles by cruel Syndicalists), Bennett has worked to improve relations with Japan and allows her and Canada to face down the German and Syndicalist threat with strong economies and close friends. With Bennett in charge, Japan knows that Canada shall always be a friend to it. Japan is grateful to have such a loyal friend, and so the Emperor grants R.B. Bennett a special 'Honourable Foreigner' award.

Emperor Hirohito

As is tradition, the Emperor himself is the last name on this year's list of Great Men of the Empire. Without the Emperor, Japan would have lost a large part of her national identity and the solidarity that holds her together in these dark times. After the cruel fate of Emperor

Taisho, so bitterly crippled by meningitis, it fell to his son to rebuild Japan's honour that had been lost at the so-called 'Peace with Honour' with Germany. Hirohito inherited the throne of a country wandering without purpose and lamenting a loss in war. Through wise appointments of ministers, reform of the armed forces and a constant reminder to Japanese people that Japan had gained a great deal from her so-called 'defeat', losing only the German Chinese holdings she had gone to war to gain, and oversaw the claiming of various British Pacific possessions left without a master after the British Revolution in the 1920s. Above all, Hirohito has been a beacon of freedom and democracy in a world caught between absolutist imperialism, unstable republics and murderous Syndicalism. For this reason the Empire's parliament has voted unanimously to once again honour him with the final place on this year's list of Great Men of the Empire.

Minutes from meeting of the Comité de Salut Public, November 1934

This Committee held much of the power in the Commune of France during this time. The extract of minutes below is from a meeting called to discuss the matters arising as the grip of then-Chairman Pivert began to loosen, setting in motion a process that would culminate in his resignation in January 1936.

*

Marceau Pivert, Chairman of the Comité de Salut Public moved the meeting on at this point to discuss the economy. **Pierre Monatte, Delegate to Economic Affairs** was pleased to report that the economy was 'in good shape' on a national level. On a local level, the local governments of the Communes were reported to have largely come into line with national direction thanks to our programme of incentives and fines. Monatte also reported that France looks set to rival Germany for the first time in production of steel by the middle of next year. **Pierre Brossolette, Delegate to Foreign Affairs** remarked at this point that Germany [remark permanently deleted from records]. The Chair echoed this sentiment.

The discussion on the economy concluded that no new reforms were necessary this month, with the present construction rates of railways, power lines and other infrastructure being acceptable to all present. The Chairman moved the meeting on to its fourth point, matters arising under the jurisdiction of the Foreign Affairs Commission. **Pierre Brossolette, Delegate to Foreign Affairs** thanked the Chair and wished for it to be on record that he was aware that this meeting marked his own tenth year in the Foreign Affairs post. For this he thanked those present, the previous Chair Comrade Pouget and wished for it to be put on record that he was intensely grateful to the people of France who had faith in him to represent them abroad in those turbulent days of 1924, even though he was an exceptionally young man. **Charles Rappoport, Delegate to Internal Security** praised Comrade Brossolette, reminding him that it was his own oratorical and literary skills that had endeared him to the French public, and his record of building successful relationships with the nations of the Union of Britain, the Republic of the Sicilies and the Socialist Republic of Centroamerica spoke for itself. Brossolette repeated his thanks for the Committee's support and moved on to matters arising for Foreign Affairs.

The motion to continue funding the German Syndicalist movement the FAUD was once again passed without debate, with Brossolette stating that he wanted the record to show continued sympathy with the oppressed workers of the Kaiser's Germany, with whom France had no quarrel. **May Picqueray, Director of Services de Renseignements Généraux** announced that continued clandestine meetings with the group showed similar overtures from the FAUD itself, and expressed confidence that in the event of war with Germany Syndicalist revolt could be successfully encouraged. The discussion of foreign matters moved on to a debate regarding French aid to Centroamerica. Comrade Brossolette maintained his position that the Union of Britain, with her Atlantic-worthy merchant fleet and strong navy, was doing a fine job of aiding France's Syndicalist brethren in Belize, but Chairman Pivert put forward the case again that internationalism was the key to Syndicalism's continued success and as such, all aid that was possible to spare should be transported to Centroamerica. **Marcel Deát, Commander of the Communal Navy,** supported Comrade Brossolette in that the French civilian and military fleets were in no way suited to such long-distance trade or aid, but made the suggestion that aid could be given to the Union of Britain to be taken among their shipments. Pivert hailed this as a 'perfect compromise' and suggested an immediate shipment of arms and rare materials be drawn up. The final manifest came to 1200 Hotchkiss Mle. 1914 machine guns, 120,000 rounds of ammunition and a license to produce more of the same calibre, and 30 tons of high-quality fertiliser.

Item seven on the agenda was put forward by **Benoit Frachon, Delegate for Bourse Générale du Travail Organisation** as a point of order against Chairman Pivert. The objection regarded the invitation of British pacifist Fenner Brockway to speak at this year's closing of the BGT for the Christmas recess. Frachon said this decision betrayed Pivert and France as isolationist, pacifistic and weak before a rising Germany. **Commander of Communal Ground Forces, General Jacques Doriot** supported Frachon, advising that a more confrontational speaker like Maurice Thorez would be a better choice. Pivert rejected these disagreements, saying that Brockway is a respected internationalist who is a 'pacifist realist'. Far from opposing war with Germany, Pivert stated his belief that Brockway was in fact in favour of the preservation of peace as far as was possible, but accepted that true, lasting peace could not be attained without the removal of the Kaiser's Germany from Europe. Raising a point of order of his own, Pivert chided Comrade Frachon for 'Jacobin leanings', leading to an objection from Doriot. Pivert maintained that Jacobinism is distinctly un-French and un-Syndicalist, and its leaders' plans to replace the BGT and CSP with a single Communist Party and chamber would destroy the good work the Commune had achieved in the last 15 years. Frachon dismissed this as nonsense, pointing out his own belief in the British Syndicalist system involving greater democracy, and attempted to force a vote rescinding Fenner Brockway's invitation, and one was duly called. The record shows that the committee voted against the proposal 7-6.

Letter printed in *The Globe*, 20 December 1935

This letter serves as a useful gauge of successes the British 'government-in-exile' (here referred to always as 'His Majesty's Government' thanks to some personal quirk of the author's) by 1935.

*

SIR—

It has been several months since I last requested that your organ publish an announcement of mine, but I am afraid I must burden your pages with British business once again. I know you and your readers will not mind, for I am acutely aware of the sterling response my letters have received in the past.

Since moving into the newly-refurbished and renamed Britain House offices, His Majesty's Government has gone from strength to strength. Mr Baldwin was in good spirits when I spoke with him yesterday, applauding Lord Beaverbrook's plans to restore the powers of the treasury once Liberation is achieved. My colleague in the foreign office, Mr Lloyd George, is proud that relations throughout the Empire remain strong and that President Hoover in the United States recognised our government's validity in September after his criteria for a democratic poll of eligible British citizens living in Canada was finally completed. Your organ covered the intricacies of which 'seats' (sadly a purely cosmetic term at this time – we shall soon change that) went to which party, but I wish to assure your readers that no serious division exists between my own fellow Conservatives, the National Liberals and the Unionists on the matter of achieving Liberation. Mr Chamberlain at the Home Office tells me that in meetings with his opposite numbers in the other two parties he sensed a deal of consensus in how to run Britain once the United Kingdom is restored, not least on the delicate matter of how to deal with her rampant Trade

Union movement. I daresay my own bombastic views on this matter are unhelpful, so shall not deem them fit for publication here.

While praise is being given, I would be neglecting our brethren overseas if I did not make some mention of the success of the government of Mr Stanley Bruce and Mr William Hughes in the Australasian Confederation. Theirs is a country hurt by Syndicalist and social division, and this was exacerbated by last years' recurring strikes. Mr Hughes has clearly carried the skills he gained as Minister for Trade and Industry into the office of Prime Minister, for his agreement with the Australasian TUC last month hailed a new age of peace, prosperity and cooperation within the Empire's southeasternmost corner. I look forward to working with Mr Hughes over the coming period as His Majesty's Government looks for his support in reclaiming the Empire. Similar overtures have been well received by Lord Linlithgow in Delhi, who assures me that the Jewel of the Empire remains loyal to its rightful government and is ready to tackle the Syndicalist menace of Bengal when the time is right. The Caribbean Federation remains wealthy, and last week agreed to incorporate her navy into the already mighty British and Canadian Royal Navy. With such a force controlling the Atlantic, victory and Liberation are assured.

In closing, I would like to wish all your readers a very merry Christmas and a prosperous New Year. If I may, I would also ask them to pray for the continued good health of our sovereign. His majesty has strained himself far too much in these most recent turbulent years and knowing his people are still suffering under the Syndicalist yoke has taken its toll. I have every confidence that the arrival of spring will see him right as rain once again, but until that time I ask that he be in all our thoughts. I thank you once more for publishing my correspondence, as it has over these last nine years generated a great deal of interest in His Majesty's Government, which now boasts over a thousand of Britain's best bureaucrats, administrators and military minds.

To Victory,
Winston Leonard Spencer Churchill MP

Minister for War, Sea and Liberation
His Majesty's Government

Volume II

1936-1940

The Rhythm of the Age

'There are periods in history when change is necessary, and other periods when it is better to keep everything for the time as it is. The art of life is to be in the rhythm of your age.'

Oswald Mosley

Nineteen Thirty-Six

John Durham

'Comrade Mosley is a capable man. As for what he's capable of, I'd
rather not say.'
Arthur Horner's closing statement at the Congress of the Trade Unions,
3 February 1931

The year 1936 is mentioned in the same breath as 1066, 1848 and
1919 by historians. It was, after all, the year in which the world seemed
to transform in so many ways. Russia went from a quiet, peaceful and
relatively stable Presidential Republic to a violent police state ruled by a
paranoid aristocrat, the United States of America saw civil unrest that
would eventually descend into a Civil War that would end its very
existence, Germany and her puppet states were rocked by a stock
market crash, and in the Socialist states of France and Britain, new
guards took over from the old, in the latter case with huge and far-
reaching consequences.

The year began in Britain with the usual celebrations – the novelty
of fireworks exploding over the Thames was still enough to draw
Londoners from their firesides as 'Big Ben' (the bell inside the tower of
the former Palace of Westminster) rang out the twelve chimes of
midnight. The Federal Council were high on a platform for all to see,
the great red banner of the Union of Britain unfurled below them as
they cheered and raised mugs of cocoa to the crowd (champagne had
been suggested, but unanimously declared to be a reactionary and
highly inappropriate drink to enjoy publicly so soon after such
widespread economic hardship). Helen Crawfurd had ensured that
food was laid on for the Londoners around them, making much of

distributing pamphlets of invitation around the city in the preceding days. The event became, therefore, a display of solidarity and aid as food was distributed from local people who had brought it with them and from big hampers made up by the staff at Congress House. Similar events carried on across the country in most major cities, under the direction of the Congregationalist leaders Annie Kenney and Christabel Pankhurst. Niclas y Glais had in his back pocket 'a telegram from the French foreign minister' (Pierre Brossolette) 'which entreats us all to enjoy the night and ring in a new year of cross-channel co-operation and friendship'. This telegram was generally accepted by y Glais and his Comrades on the Federal Council to be a thinly-veiled attempt to coax the Union into a permanent military alliance with the Republic of the Sicilies and Commune itself.[61]

As mugs of cocoa were passed around and cheers raised, one notable member of the Federal Council was conspicuously absent. Oswald Mosley, the man who would in a few months begin his role as the indefatigable and universally changing force of the Union of Britain, was feverishly at work in his study, with only a sombre-faced Eric Blair for company.[62] Desperate to seize the initiative as the new year began, Mosley intended to take Maximism to its next level – the international stage. Finding common ground with some foreign leaders as well as rising British leaders of industry, Mosley spent New Year's Eve trying to add a final touch to his now deeply refined doctrine – a name.

'There was something unfathomable in the arch of his eyebrows as he pored over the latest figures from Calcutta, Naples or Paris, each with their own linguistic ticks and tells. It had been hours since he had rejected my suggestion of simply using the word 'Maximism', saying a truly Internationalist doctrine could not have fixed origins in any one country. I returned to my copy of *Scrutiny*. At what must have been two or three o'clock in the morning, I heard him slam an open palm into the table and a hiss of triumph escape his lips. With a glint in his

---

[61] Terry Pollitt, *Secret Messages: Reading Between the Lines of Diplomatic Gestures* (Sheffield: Blade Publishing, 1994) p.71.

[62] Eric Blair, *The Long Walk* (London: New Left Book Club, 1954) p.4.

eye almost terrible, he finally raised his head and stared at me. "I've narrowed it down to Totalitarian Socialism, Eric," he said to me in a voice that creaked through a throat untouched by liquid since supper, "what do you think about that as a name?"

I replied that it was somewhat unwieldy and lacked the instant proletarian 'punch' of Marxism or Syndicalism.

"Well," he replied and leaned back in his chair in what was either genuine thought or concealed irritation at my disagreement, eventually adding almost as an afterthought, "what about Totalism?"

I repeated the word. It would do, I said, and returned to Dr Leavis.'[63]

As 1936 began, the most authoritarian brand of Socialism developed since the failure of the Bolshevik Revolution in Russia came to be. Mosley, never one to balk at completing several tasks at once, took it upon himself to begin as great an industrial reform as he could while maintaining the favour of his more liberal comrades on the Federal Council while at the same time organising the international conference that would finalise what Totalism stood for. The Birmingham Conference was held on 11 January 1936 and was attended by Georges Valois of the French Sorelian faction, Benito Mussolini of the Sicilian National-Syndicalists, and Lavrenti Beria of the Socialist Republic of Georgia. Only the last of these three men was in power in their country, and – given that Mosley himself had not yet claimed the prize of Chair of the CTU – was oddly the most powerful man present. Mosley recorded in his diaries that 'I do not trust Beria. His eyes are always flitting from person to person around the room – the idea of Socialist solidarity seems most out of character with him. His interest in Totalism is, of course, useful and I appreciate it so far as it remains so. But I cannot be sure of good relations with Georgia while he remains in charge.' This presumptuous last sentence, in which Mosley speaks of his own opinions dictating the country's foreign policy, are symptomatic of the triumphalist attitude expressed by most

---

[63] Dr F.R. Leavis, literary critic and prominent forward-thinker among leftist intellectuals in the Union during this time, was the editor and chief contributor to the influential *Scrutiny* literary journal.

Maximists during the months leading up to the Congress of 1936. As they hustled and bustled their way around the corridors of Birmingham City Hall as the Totalist Charter was being prepared, Clem Attlee and Nye Bevan were often said to jokingly greet one another as 'Comrade Commissary' in anticipation of the posts they hoped to take at the next Congress. Eric Blair wrote that he was 'looking forward to finally getting on with the real business of changing people's lives, after so many years of merely writing about them'. The Conference was, for the Maximists, a complete success. Totalism was hammered out in strict and unequivocal terms – a belief in the importance of the total involvement of the state in the running of the economy, industrial base and infrastructure. This was at its core, and along with it came the various concepts of rule by a centralised organization of Trade Unions (having come from Syndicalist roots, Totalism did not call for an adoption of some kind of political Party structure, alienating the French Jacobin faction who wished to build a new 'Communist Party') with minimal interference of 'local government' (a term Mosley considered an oxymoron). Totalism might just have easily have been called 'Centralism', if that term did not have connotations that indicated a very different place on the left-right spectrum to the position that Totalism itself held. Once Totalism had been ratified and agreed on by the representatives present, it was announced to the world on the airwaves of the BBC and simultaneously condemned and applauded all over the world. In Russia, Mikhail Bukharin began distributing a pamphlet stating his full support for the doctrine, saying it was the logical internationalist development of the great work of Vladimir Lenin (the spiritual leader of the Bolshevik Rebellion). In the United States of America, William Z. Forster upset his Comrades in the more de-centralised Combined Syndicates of America by coming out in favour of Totalist thought and ideas, as well as earning himself a brief spell in prison for causing a breach of the peace when he made his announcement. Finally, in the Kaiser's Germany the announcement was welcomed by Ernst Thalmann, a strong-willed agitator and long-time proponent of leftist revolution in Germany. Totalism had been a complete success, and the Maximists appeared to have taken their first step towards a truly internationalist foreign policy beyond Mosley's general support for 'interventionism'.

The foreign policy of the Union in those opening months of 1936 was relatively subdued. The assassination of President Kerensky in Russia was responded to with a message of condolences by y Glais, eager as he was to build relationships with non-Syndicalist nations. The move came to nothing; during the chaos that ensued when the Security Minister, Pyotr Wrangel, began to seize the apparatus of state, the memorandum was presumably lost or discarded as Syndicalist trash by an aristocratic plutocrat moving into the Russian Foreign Office. The developments in Russia were eyed with caution by Philip Snowden in particular, who had long believed that Russia was no threat to the free Socialist peoples of the world while she was constrained by 'parliamentary democracy' and the jostling factions of the military, aristocracy and democrats. Now, in the shape of Wrangel, Russia had a strong, uncompromising leader with years of experience in crushing dissent. Mosley argued at a Council meeting on 6 January for an immediate show of force and support for Mikhail Bukharin, then broadcasting from a seized radio station in the Moscow suburbs. Bukharin would go on to elude capture, but Mosley's show of support was voted down almost unanimously. The Union was, it should be remembered, a distinctly isolationist nation at this time.

The last moments of Federationist foreign policy were personified by Arthur Horner's attendance of the Congress of the Third International, held in Paris in May. Britain, by attending, was maintaining an ultimately non-interventionist stance in the short term while building long-term relations with Syndicalist allies in Europe, and less close to home in Central and Northern America. Horner, making much of his own skillful manoeuvrings in telegrams to the CTU and BBC, made vague statements of support at the various caucuses of the Congress, assuring Jack Reed of the CSA that British aid would assist his Second American Revolution when the time came, 'providing relations with Canada will not be unduly damaged – we have no wish to enter the waters of the Royalist lion just yet'. A similar get-out clause was promised to the men of the CNT-FAI when they argued for foreign aid should they rise against the oppressive Kingdom of Spain, which had begun suppressing the trade union movement there. Horner agreed that Britain would aid 'how she could' and expressing, controversially, an interest in docking rights in Gibraltar should the CNT-FAI take over the country. This was coolly received, to say the least. Other matters raised at the Congress included a condemnation of 'white terror' (the persecution of socialists worldwide by imperialist Russian, German and American governments) and various attempts by the governments of the Republic of the Sicilies, the Union of Britain and the Commune of France to establish more favourable trade agreements for themselves. Bengal brought exciting news to the table, its delegate – the impeccably-spoken Mohandas Gandhi – declaring that economic progress within the country was at an all-time high, thanks in part to his own social-reformist measures. The moves were applauded by Horner but privately derided by Mosley at home as 'the musings of a comically liberal babu'.[64]

The Britain that Horner returned to was one that was in, as Sidney Webb put it, 'moderately good shape'. The worst of the impact of the Great Recession was over, and unemployment levels had steadied at around 650,000. Oswald Mosley was taking much of the credit, both in his capacity as Commissary for the Exchequer and in referring to the steps he took in his previous role as head of the Republican Air Force to encourage greater aircraft production.[65] As Snowden presided over the weekly meetings of Federal Council in the months between May and September, there was a sense of helplessness, described by William Wedgwood Benn as 'the feeling that everything was slipping from our

---

[64] Eric Hobsbawm, *Mosley: From Baronet to Comrade to Tyrant* (Birmingham: Onward Publishing, 1984) p.51.

[65] As well as being a popular economic move to generate jobs around traditional armament-focused towns, the RAF was uniquely positioned within the armed services as a force that was accepted to be highly lacking by all but the harshest of pacifists. Mosley used skilful rhetoric to play up the importance of building a strong force of fighter aircraft to defend Britain's skies, saying that while they were of some use in an offensive war, their main purpose (and the one to which they were most suited) was the defense of the British Isles 'from those who would bring us war even if we strive to avoid it'.

fingers'. Mosley was dominating the discussion time and time again, despite being the only Maximist on the Council. Snowden had attempted to make political gain in February by chiding him for his actions 'outside his brief' in calling the Totalist Congress, but this was waved aside by Mosley, who declared (quite correctly) that he had acted in his capacity as a free man of the Union, not as Commissary of the Exchequer. *The Chartist* ran headlines praising the initiatives of the current government, calling it a 'Federal Council of all the talents', but even the state's official mouthpiece (whose editor had a receive-only phone connected to a direct telephone line from Arthur Horner's office) could not mask the fact that most of the economic measures being taken now were coming straight from Oswald Mosley, and were Maximism in all but name. Coupled with this was the propaganda campaign being put forward by Mosley and his Maximist allies. Blair published a new essay every month urging reform, William Joyce secured a regular fifteen-minute 'post-script' on the BBC Home Service and Nye Bevan was making tours of the Welsh heartland, undermining the Autonomists' key area of support with fiery rhetoric that only Nye, as a (by political standards) young son of the valleys could bring forth. Ernest Bevin was in charge of wooing trade union and Syndicate leaders around the country, making particular headway in the southwest, a Federationist stronghold since Spargo's defeat by Maclean in 1931. A man of strong personal appeal and impeccable union credentials, his own experience of the world stage from serving as the Union's first Comissary for Foreign Affairs gave him gravitas and diplomatic skill that he brought to bear on the most stubborn trade union leaders who feared the consequences of Totalism being brought into action by the Maximists. Snowden and Horner (his obvious successor) tried in vain to keep up with this onslaught, warning on the wireless and in the streets of 'the tyranny of centralisation', and Horner himself personally visited several union leaders in an attempt to convince them that they were in effect voting to marginalise themselves. Mosley countered with sympathetic pamphlets that called the Federationists 'fearmongers', and pointed out that the centralized authority called for by Totalism had been born out of the CTU and its equivalents abroad. 'Far from voting to remove your power,' Mosley said in a famous speech to the National Union of Railwaymen, 'you are increasing it at the national level! All that is expected in return is some relinquishment of regional authority, in the interests of oiling the wheels of the apparatus of state.' With the Congregationalists depicted in cartoons and pamphlets as at best meek do-nothings and, at worst, nagging women with hen-pecked husbands, the Federationists looked to be out of time and friends. The Autonomists had lost the endorsements of the most powerful Welsh unions, and only Willie Gallacher and his Scottish clique maintained some support there for the movement. As the Congress drew nearer, it became clear that the vast majority of representatives from across the Union intended to travel there to vote Maximist. Sidney Webb, however, with more foresight than he knew, observed in a column for *The Chartist* on 19 August that 'an awful lot of people seem to want to vote for the Maximists, but it seems that an awful lot of them don't actually know what the Maximists plan to do.'

The 10th Annual Congress of Trade Unions opened at Congress House on 1 September 1936. Maximists had been circulating pamphlets entitled 'FINALLY', detailing within them their plans should they (as was expected) see a huge boost in support and take control of the Union's government. As representatives, elected or appointed in August, filed off the trains at Britannia (formerly Victoria), Euston and Liberty (formerly King's Cross) stations, it was clear that such a boost would be taking place. Margaret Cole, herself elected for the tenth year in a row as a representative from Oxford thanks to her administrative role within the city's Syndicate, noted the following on her own journey:

'I sat opposite a young woman from Chichester who told me that this was her first Congress, and that she had been elected to represent the girls on the sewing machines in the factories south of Kingston. I asked her therefore if she was supporting the Congregationalists, but she looked at me in something close to horror and declared that she most certainly was not. Looking me fervently in the eye, told me the only group in the country who had the mettle necessary to pull us out of these troubled times was the Maximists and that charming Mr Mosley. I held my tongue and quietly read through my notes. She was not the first Mosleyite I had met on the journey, and it was becoming increasingly clear that she would not be the last.'[66]

Even as the delegates were on their way, Horner's diaries record emergency meetings being held with the Congregationalists in the early hours of the morning on 1 September. Horner was a seasoned veteran of such backroom deals, and declared he would offer 'whatever it took' to convince Annie Kenney to mobilise her faction in his favour. His advances were rebuffed, however, when Kenney (who was a close friend of Snowden) objected to the current Chair's absence, remarking dryly that he was perhaps too dignified to attend a meeting where people squabbled over his corpse. Horner lost his temper and made what is believed to have been a sexist remark but of which all records are lost, and Kenney stormed from the meeting, announcing at the first opportunity she got that she intended to stand for the Chair's position, creating a three-way race for the first time since the Great Recession. Niclas y Glais, hearing the news, seized the initiative and, after assuring Willie Gallacher 'he would have his turn', announced his own intention to stand. The amount of support both candidates received in nominations surprised both the Maximists and Federationists. In particular, Mosley himself was taken aback; by the time the Congress was underway in its earliest most formal stages at noon on the first day, began emergency meetings with his fellow leading Maximists and warned them that the fight would be harder than expected. A walkover had been anticipated, but with the anti-Federationist vote now split, the Maximists might not get all their officers elected, nor all their policies supported.

The first item on the agenda under policy debate was the economy. The Federationists, spoken for by Arthur Horner, praised the existing design of the economy as flexible, liberating and providing for all. In an attempt to swing support from the Maximists, however, he did say it was time to expand it, suggesting elaborate new industrial construction

---

[66] Margaret Cole, *Living for Britain: My Diaries* (London: Penguin Publishing Cpv., 1945) p.111.

plans in Birmingham, Sheffield, Glasgow and Cardiff. This allowed Mosley, speaking for the Maximists, to counter perfectly with a very potent question of how Horner intended to bring these plans to fruition when his own faction's commitment to 'freedom' (Mosley 'spat the word', according to Cole) meant they could not impose any construction orders on any Syndicates. Helen Crawfurd for the Congregationalists praised the plan but stressed that top-down orders from the central government was not the way forward, while Gallacher argued for more inter-regional co-operation in Scotland and Wales to build 'self-sufficient industrial bases for our Home Nations'. Mosley countered once more, concluding the debate just as time ran out with a scathing attack on all three of his opponents, saying that their plans were all well and good but without Totalist economics being applied to Britain, none of them could come to fruition. At this he detailed the Maximist plans for the economy, involving vast swathes of industrial expansion and the centralisation of all construction legislation, giving that power solely to the central government, which he hinted would be renamed from the Federal Council to the Central Bureau, and have its powers vastly expanded. At this, some of the more 'fairweather Maximists' balked. A mineworkers' leader from Newcastle heckled Mosley, saying 'you mean to take our freedoms away!' Mosley replied that the only freedom he wished to take away was the freedom to harm oneself through irresponsible economic activity, and the most efficient way to do that was to ensure that everything was checked and double-checked centrally before it was put into practice. When another heckler, a leader of a Syndicate in Kent, questioned the role of 'our union men' in all of this, Mosley reassured him that the role of the trade unions would be preserved and, in fact, strengthened – Totalism was not Communism, relying on some clique-run political party, he said. The CTU would maintain its 'vital place' in British governance and would be consulted far more regularly than the 'paltry tip of the hat' that the Federationist system offered it each September, he continued. At this juncture, Philip Snowden, presumably irritated that what was supposed to be a debate had become a question and answer session to the Chairman-in-waiting, banged his gavel and concluded the economics debate. The Maximist motion narrowly passed, to gritted teeth in various corners of the room.

The second of the four most highly-charged debates at the Congress of 1936 was regarding military matters. Horner praised the work of Tom Wintringham as overall commander and overseer of Britain's military, which by this point consisted largely of local popular militias and one central army of three divisions. The Federationist motion wished to expand both these institutions, proposing an additional four divisions for the army by the end of 1937 and a quadrupling in size of local militias. The pacifist Congregationalists abstained from the debate, with only George Lansbury rising to say that, as ever, the Congregationalist motion was a proposal to destroy all weapons of war currently in the Union of Britain. Niclas y Glais spoke for the Autonomists and said that the Home Nations should have stronger militaries to defend themselves independent of London – he proposed a standing army in Cardiff and Edinburgh to complement the one in Birmingham. But once again it was the Maximists who took the debate by storm, with their illustrious backer Basil Liddell Hart giving an incoherent but impassioned speech about the importance of centralising military authority as quickly as possible, so the construction of a modern, tank-driven army could begin. His and Mosley's oral depictions of brave socialist soldiers riding into battle atop armoured beasts that spewed righteous fire and belched the black smoke of Revolution caught the imagination of the Congress, and once again the Maximist motion passed, this time by a considerable margin, despite controversy over the abolition of popular militias (something Mosley called 'incorporation into the wider armed forces').

The third debate centred on foreign affairs, and what stance the Union should take towards other countries in the world. The Federationist Sidney Webb gave a short speech arguing in favour of the status quo – that Canada was the Union's mortal enemy and France and Sicily had proved themselves good friends to Britons – but this was unexciting and upstaged by Mosley's fiery speech in favour of 'turning words into actions' through a build up of military strength and a more confrontational style. Ernest Bevin stood up next and supported

Mosley, saying he would not flinch from pressing the rights of the workers of all the world if he ever had to negotiate with reactionaries in Berlin, Moscow or Ottawa. This, coupled with some unimpressive and controversial performances from Annie Kenney and Niclas y Glais (who respectively argued for a totally isolationist foreign policy and a reconciliatory attitude to the Royalists), ensured Maximist victory once more. Philip Snowden let his head slip into his hands as a quivering Arthur Horner announced the result of the vote, the General Secretary's own face white with fear.

The Federationists would find their fortunes had changed by the middle of the final key debate of the Congress, regarding internal policy. Mosley spoke first on this occasion, and called for a reduction in power of the Syndicates over regional matters, saying their first and main duty should be to 'speak for their peoples' rights' while the Central Bureau would, under a Maximist system, deal with issues of construction, price-fixing and taxation along Totalist lines. When pressed on how the business of government would be done, he announced plans for 'National Directives' that would be issued as and when they were required, and would be constitutionally binding by their nature. Someone shouted 'so you'll rule by decree!' from the back of the room. At this, the chamber erupted into shouting, whooping and heckling, some of it positive and some of it negative. Many trade union leaders who had attended with an intention to vote for the Maximists because they were sick of Federationist weakness suddenly realised how strong-handed Mosley intended to be in reducing the power of local authorities. Horner seized his opportunity and tore into Mosley, claiming his proposed 'modifications' to the Union's constitution were 'only a step short of tearing it up'. Kenney remained silent throughout the debate, unsure of where to stand, while y Glais leapt to his feet and, knowing he would be better off as an Autonomist under Federationists than he would be as the champion of a lost cause under the Maximists, joined the attack. Proposing separate CTUs for Scotland and Wales, he claimed that one did not have to be born a Baronet to be radical – the first such attack on Mosley's high-brow background. Mosley turned red with rage, gaining ground with some delegates but losing it with others as the spittle flew from his lips. He attacked once more the weakness of Federationism, shamelessly praised his own Maximist measures as Commissary for the Exchequer and RAF Commissary, and above all insisted that no personal slight based on where he happened to be born would deter him from his 'unending crusade to rid this republic of stagnation, backwards-looking economics and lies'. The vote was incredibly close, requiring three recounts, but eventually passed in the Maximists' favour by a mere 21 ballots. Mosley was visibly shaken, however, and nothing was certain about the vote the following day for the officers of the government of the Union of Britain.

The atmosphere was intense as each candidate made their statements and speeches, proposing this and rejecting that. It was clear the Maximists were to make massive gains, but the resurgence in Federationist support as their Totalist agenda became truly clear left a big question on everyone's minds – would Mosley be able to lead a 'Central Bureau' (as he wished to call it now) of Maximists, or of compromise? The elections looked to be going his way, as Maximists Clem Attlee, Nye Bevan and Ernest Bevin gained the important roles of the Exchequer, Home Department and Foreign Affairs Commissary respectively. The moment that would bring total silence to the delegates as they held their breaths to see what happened next, however, came when the results of the election to the office of General Secretary, the Union's second most powerful position and, as it were, administrator-in-chief, were read out by the current General Secretary, Arthur Horner. James Maxton recalled the event in tantalising detail.

'His eyes widened as he took the paper from an aide. He cleared his throat to speak, and the murmuring subsided. "I hereby declare the votes for each candidate are as follows," he began. "Lewis Jones," (the Autonomist, a Welsh agitator) "121 votes." There was no applause. All were frozen in their seats or where they stood.

"Christabel Pankhurst," (the Congregationalist) "209 votes." "William Joyce," (the Maximist, a propagandist and all-round thug) "454 votes."

There were gasps. Quick mental arithmetic meant Joyce had surely not gained enough to win outright.

"Tom Mann," (the Federationist, a popular man who was seen as their best chance to hold the position) "80 votes."

Gasps again, and one shriek. It seemed impossible that Mann, a hero of the Revolution, could lose so ignominiously. The Federationists were surely damned. But then Horner's mouth broke into a tiny smile.

"No Preferred Candidate – Keep Current Officer," he declared with a throaty confidence, "490 votes."

There were cheers and roars simultaneously. Somehow, Arthur had won the confidence of just enough people to keep him in the job, even though he wasn't standing for it. It was clear to him even then that he wasn't going to become Chair, but everyone (especially, I imagine, the people who had voted that way) knew that he would be a perfect counterweight to Mosley's excesses if, as expected and as he turned out to eventually do, the bloody Baronet won.'[67]

Maxton was right. Mosley did go on to win, beating Horner by over a third of votes cast, with y Glais and Kenney failing to scrape even five percent between them. Hopes that Mosley would see it as a hollow victory were dashed when he took the podium from Philip Snowden for the first time, cutting the old man's farewell speech short by starting up the applause before he had concluded his statements. Re-stating his rhetoric from earlier in the Congress, he was optimistic about what could now be achieved with a Maximist government in charge, and cold towards his General Secretary. Rather than, as was expected, stating he looked forward to hearing what Horner had to bring to the table, he made a veiled jab that indicated he hoped Horner's experience in 'the old regime' would not taint his 'progressiveness' when it came to the 'imperative task of moving our Union onwards to a brighter future'. Horner replied with an icy stare, foretelling much of the relationship between the two men over the following years. But the taste of an unlikely coalition at the top aside, the reality was clear – Britons had voted for Maximism, and Maximism

[67] James Maxton, *Memoirs of an Undesirable* (Paris: Bastille Books, 1947) p.341.

they would have. Apart from Horner (and Wintringham, who hung on thanks to his powerbase in the military) the only other non-Maximists in the new 'Central Bureau' were Annie Kenney, somewhat patronisingly invited to become Commissary for Female Workers after the re-elected Jesse Eden refused to serve under Mosley, who had no prominent female supporters of his own, and Willie Gallacher, who was elected to serve as head of the Intelligence Bureau thanks to his own experience in union espionage and diplomacy, rather than backing from his own Autonomist supporters. Some changes were brought in in the military positions, and the first ever Central Bureau of the Union of Britain, therefore, notable for being the first such national body since 1931 not to contain 'Regional Commissaries' (Mosley thought them irrelevant now the central government would operate on everyone's behalf in all matters), was made up thusly:

Chairman of the Congress of Trade Unions Oswald Mosley
General Secretary of the Congress of Trade Unions Arthur Horner
Commissary for the Exchequer Clem Attlee
Commissary for Foreign Affairs Ernest Bevin
Commissary for the Home Department Nye Bevan
Commissary for the Intelligence Bureau William Gallacher
Commissary for Female Workers Annie Kenney
Chairman of the Home Defence Committee Tom Wintringham
Chief of Staff (Army) Walter Kirke
Chief of Staff (Navy) Ernle Chatfield
Chief of Staff (Air Force) Hugh Dowding

As September 1936 drew to a close, Britain entered a new age with a new form of government. France had done the same at the start of the year, with Georges Valois' Sorelians taking control of the Bourse du Travail and Committee for Public Safety. Russia was by this time relatively under control, a total police state now in place under Wrangel's despotic rule, but the same could not be said for the United States of America. With presidential elections approaching in November, the country in poverty and two radical factions emerging from the left and the right, Chairman Mosley's first foreign affairs priority was to have a series of reports written about the state of affairs across the Atlantic. His plans, should things go his way, would shape the American-European relationship for a generation. For Britons, the impact he would make on their lives would last a lot longer.

Reform and reaction

Terry Pollitt

'Tradition is that most English of concepts: a system of values and processes that change beyond all recognition and yet stay essentially the same.'
Eric Blair

The changes that took place in the early years of Mosley's Chairmanship were nothing short of cataclysmic. And by 'changes', the reader should understand that I mean changes in nigh-on every single part of life. The rights of the worker, of his Union representative, of the Syndicate and of the soldier all changed dramatically. The standard of production and expected levels of success increased fivefold. The Union of Britain, at the heart of the matter, went, over the course of three years, from a devolved, isolationist economy with an above-average industrial base that was under the direct control of the workers who operated it through some degree of democracy, to a centralised, state-socialist, Totalist and internationalist economy with a magnificent industrial base over which the worker had nominal ownership but little real authority. A worker's state built on socialist principles we remained. But if any had doubted it, the Syndicalist experiment of the Union's earliest years was over. This chapter will endeavour to examine these changes, firstly in civilian life and latterly in military affairs.

As Georges Valois sent a telegram congratulating Mosley on his election, he was himself performing very similar changes in France, having come to power with his Sorelian allies in January of 1936. As the country's labour exchange was dissolved and replaced with a central bureau similar to that which Mosley intended to devise, he warned Mosley in a private letter of pushing the Unions too hard. 'Totalism was born out of Trade Unionism and the rights of the working man,' he wrote in October 1936, 'just because we have applied centralised authority to those rights and, in economic terms, expanded them, does not mean it is our duty or our right to demolish the instruments by which men can achieve fair standards and wages for their labour.' This note, known as the Valois Memorandum, was kept in the top drawer of Mosley's desk,[68] and shall here be argued to represent the core idea that drove Mosley's implementation of Totalism in the Union of Britain. Just as Communism (a doctrine popular before the First Great War, notably espoused by Marx himself and the leaders of the Bolshevik Rebellion) had its roots in parliamentary democracy and so called for a 'Communist Party', the roots of Totalism lay in Syndicalism, and therefore rejected fickle Party structures for a stronger and more unified Congress of Trade Unions. Jimmy Thomas, now languishing in retirement but still by 1936 a highly respected Union man, speculated that Mosley's insistence on maintaining the CTU's role as a legislative body was because 'he knew damned well he didn't have a choice'.[69] This was undeniably true. Mosley, even though he had no Trade Union background himself and was a delegate appointed by his local Birmingham Syndicate (until becoming Chairman, when for obvious reasons he no longer required nomination to attend the Congress), was a fundamental believer in their value and, whatever his own autocratic tendencies, believed it vital that they protect the worker from exploitation and provide him with a forum through which to voice his interests. Where Mosley's understanding and respect for the Unions differed from the status quo set by Snowden, Maclean and Horner was that he (like many in those frustrated pre-war years) felt that giving every man a say in what to build where and how it should be built was a road to ruin.

What Mosley meant to do, then, was to present the CTU with a set of amendments to the constitution that would permit what he

---

[68] Eric Blair, *In The Highest Quarters In The Land*, (London: New Left Book Club, 1955) p.259.

[69] Ian Hislop, *Royalists, Rioters and Rabble-rousers: A History of Dissent*, (Sheffield: Blade Publishing, 1990) p.94.

called 'the unrestricted implementation of true Totalism'. They were, among other things, a reassessment of the authority of local Syndicates, which now had to hand over all authority regarding construction projects to the central government. The Congress of Trade Unions itself would meet regularly each September, as before, and would still have to vote on some matters and elections. William Joyce, smarting from his defeated attempt to become General Secretary, wrote a widely distributed pamphlet that argued against the 'dangers' of creating a corrupt representative parliament by calling on the CTU too much. In a masterstroke of what was ultimately propagandising, Mosley convinced the Congress of 1937 that some matters were best decided by the central government as and when a decision was required, rather than construction orders being ratified once a year by the Congress. This was an expansion of the National Directives concept that Mosley had touted during the internal affairs debates of 1936, and dictated (pun intended) that the Central Bureau could call for any construction orders that it saw fit, in line with its Three Year plans and additionally 'in response to whatever changing conditions might apply'. This incredibly vague final clause entitled Mosley and his allies to rule, for all intents and purposes, by decree.

As Britain wrestled with her collective conscience over trading regional and occupational liberty and self-determination for what James Maxton called 'a few scraps of tainted bread', opposition was forming to the Maximist measures taken by the government. It came not only from men like Maxton and traditional foes of the Maximists such as Niclas y Glais, but also from one man within the government itself – Arthur Horner. Horner, in his capacity as General Secretary, served as the Central Bureau's link to the CTU. The Central Bureau met once a week in Congress House (though one of Mosley's first policies was to order the construction of a new building to house all administrative departments and to be called Britain House[70]), and

---

[70] Mosley originally intended to partially demolish Downing Street and construct a series of buildings there, but was talked out of it by Eric Blair who, rather cryptically at the time, told him he 'didn't want to look like he was moving back into the farmhouse'.

heated exchanges often took place between Attlee, Bevan and Mosley on one side and Horner on the other. Horner repeatedly advised against measures he believed the Congress simply would not tolerate, and on one occasion (when Mosley tabled his idea at the Bureau meeting of the second week in March 1937 that Congress ought only to be called once every three years, in line with the new three-year economic structure of the Union's plans) flatly warned him that he could expect a General Strike if he pushed the Congress too far. 'We'll have men going on strike for political reasons, damaging the industries they own, Comrade,' he declared, 'and none of us want that, do we?', allegedly lingering for a second too long between 'that' and 'do we?', eyeing up Mosley as he said it. His message was sound – Mosley could not yet treat the Union's constitution and her Syndicates like his plaything. By 1938, the Syndicates had had their power all but eliminated in matters of industrial construction or production quotas. Taxation remained completely centralised and the Syndicates no longer had any say in matters of infrastructure after the Congress of 1937, where a great deal of power was passed to the Central Bureau in exchange for some representatives from the CTU attending the weekly meetings. These five elected officials, some of them already holding minor administrative roles in the Home Department, came to represent the government's appeasement of the more traditional Trade Unionists, who disliked the increased power of the Bureau at the cost of the CTU's relevance. The posts in fact served as a Machiavellian means to manipulate those who held them into seeing the benefits of Totalism – it was here that my own grandfather, Harry Pollitt, moved from being a Federationist with an interest in Trade Union autonomy to a Maximist with a belief in moderate Totalism. Whether this was opportunism on his part or a genuine change of heart is for other, less emotionally involved historians to debate. It is clear, though, that Harry was not alone in his conversion. Jimmy Thomas, not two years after his sly utterance regarding Mosley still being beholden to the Unions, joined the Central Bureau as Special Observer on behalf of Transport Workers. The election of these officials split popular opinion[71] and the Congress. Some, including the hardline Maximist pressure group known as the Comrades of Arthur Cook, were strongly in favour of them. Others criticised the representatives as being traitors who were visiting (by the time of its construction in 1938) 'Britain House for little more than beer and sandwiches'.

Pithy jibes aside, there was real opposition to the Maximist takeover of the Union. It became most pronounced when the more 'Bolshevik' elements of Totalism were enacted, starting in the winter of 1937. Having enacted a massive construction schedule from Attlee and Stafford Cripps' Three Year Plan that included the building of ten new hydroelectric dams to put the last vestiges of the unemployed workforce into employment, Mosley's eyes came to rest on the bloated and inefficient agricultural policy of the Union of Britain. Private landownership, already illegal since 1926, had its definition broadened to include ownership by Syndicate. Mosley gave an impassioned radio address on New Year's Day 1938, saying that the ownership of the 'common land' by Syndicates was an 'obstructionist and potentially damaging relic of the failures of the last decade that degrades the very spirit of the Diggers and Levellers'. His reference to the common land and to 17th century agitators that took it over and farmed it in common interest (for more information on this, see my book *Winstanley: The Revolution's Prophet*) both enraged and inspired elements of the British population. The remnants of the middle class – now a largely intellectual subset as the economic middle classes either fled in the Exodus or had their property stripped from them – were overcome with 'Revolutionary nostalgia' for a tragic, bygone period of British History and came out in support of Mosley's collectivist plans. The working classes, however, were less clearly in favour. Syndicate representatives believed (correctly) that landownership was their last means of remaining relevant and that Mosley intended to strip it from them as the final step to marginalising them beyond recognition. They

---

[71] Although opinion polling was not conducted at this time (partly due to the lack of universal suffrage making it largely irrelevant), archived complaints to Syndicate and Union representatives can give us a rough picture of the public's psyche during this period.

also saw themselves as the true successors of Winstanley and the Diggers, and in some more outrageous pamphlets painted Mosley not as agitator, but as Lord Protector or 'King by another name'. In the wake of this uproar, Mosley was forced to backpedal furiously, calling a meeting with Arthur Horner and seemingly admitting defeat. Horner proposed eliminating Syndicalist control through introducing local co-operatives that would mean collective ownership of the land by each man who farmed it, but from a legal perspective meant the state and Central Bureau was the *de facto* administrator. 'I took Arthur's suggestion on board immediately,' remarked Mosley to Blair, 'it's the best way of taking control of our assets without giving the impression of tyranny.'[72]

It was not known how James Maxton became aware of this exchange until many years later, but today it is generally understood that Eric Blair was in fact the one who 'leaked' it to him. Seizing it on it with a hitherto-unseen rage, the Caledonian firebrand took to his typewriter, hammering out one of the most inflammatory political pamphlets in British history. 'The Impression of Tyranny', as it was called, highlighted what Maxton called 'the ugly face of Totalitarian Socialism'. Citing production figures and anecdotal evidence of the falling standards of living of many in inner-city industrial centres, Maxton decried 'the workers' state where the worker owns his factory but goes home to a house a government two hundred miles away decided must be demolished to make way for another, larger factory'. Maxton even gained the opportunity to address the nation by radio on a rainy Sunday evening in April. By June 1938, the pamphlet was in wide circulation and Mosley responded with the methods that he would become infamous for. Writing a curt note to the General Secretary of the British Broadcasting Co-operative, he declared it 'no longer in the national interest' for James Maxton to be permitted time upon the airways, or any mention of him. Nye Bevan was summoned to Mosley's office and instructed that it was very much in the national interest for the printing presses that had produced the pamphlet to be

---

[72] Eric Blair, *In The Highest Quarters In The Land*, (London: New Left Book Club, 1955) p.301.

found and confiscated. Bevan, his head shaking as he left Britain House, nonetheless complied. Maxton found himself gagged and powerless, eventually being barred from attending the Congress of 1938 for 'counter-productive activity'.

The response to Maxton's expulsion from Union politics was a degree of public outcry, particularly in Glasgow. The Bureau's response was the re-opening of an old Victorian psychiatric hospital as Broadmoor Political Re-education Centre, where 18 Scottish dissidents were sent in the first year of its operation. By the end of 1939, it would have over 200 inmates, and plans for further centres would be underway. From Maxton's perspective, he was lucky enough to not be arrested himself, but felt this was only an even greater insult. The upshot of it all is that he was driven underground, maintaining contacts with old Comrades in Clydeside and working to build up his powerbase with carefully distributed leaflets printed on home presses. Maxton noted that even when he so much as said a few words to workers assembled in a pub, he was sure of 'at least two or three men in distinct black coats following me from the establishment to whatever residence I happened to have at the time. On the one occasion I turned to address them, they vanished behind a locked up street-vendor's stall. Five minutes later, they were behind me again. I am being tailed for disagreeing with the Chairman. Is this what Connolly, Lenin and Maclean died for?'[73] With Maxton kept quiet, the 1930s drew to their close with a relatively stable political situation in the Union, with Mosley and his Maximists deliberately quashing any figure who looked like they might attain the same level of spiritual leadership of oppositionists that Maxton inspired through his own dissent.

Thus did civilian life change beyond all recognition in the late 1930s. But the very spirit, construction and organisation of the Union's armed forces underwent similar changes. One of the core tenets of the Maximist platform (and one they had received a clear mandate to pursue) was the massive expansion of the British Army, Republican Navy and Republican Air Force. Annie Kenney was dismayed at this but convinced to stay in her post as Commissary for Female Workers

---

[73] James Maxton, *Memoirs of an Undesirable*, (Paris: Bastille Books, 1947) p.31.

as, when more and more women began to enter factories to construct armaments, the need for a dedicated representative to defend them from discrimination became clear. The Navy, still relatively large and modern thanks to the number of mutinies in 1925 that had caused much of the British fleet to stay in the Home Isles, was nonetheless in need of expansion to keep up with the German and Canadian naval programmes. Ernle Chatfield announced in December 1937 that plans had been successfully drawn up for a new class of Battleship, the Union Class, and that six of this model would begin construction in early 1938. More modern destroyers, cruisers and light aircraft carriers were also developed thanks to the work of the recently-nationalised British Naval Development Agency, with an intention that a newly rejuvenated fleet could take to the seas by 1940.

British Capital Ship Construction, 1937-1940

Battleships, Union Class
RNS *Union*
RNS *Worker*
RNS *Winstanley*
RNS *Clydeside*
RNS *Maclean*
RNS *Hardie*
Light Carriers, Chainbreaker Class
RNS *Chainbreaker*
RNS *Freedom*
RNS *Liberty*
RNS *Maximist*
Cruisers, Internationale Class
RNS *Marx*
RNS *Sorel*
RNS *Thalmann*
RNS *Gramsci*
RNS *Engels*
RNS *Khrushchev*

The Air Force, already undergoing some Maximist developments thanks to Mosley's having worked there for much of the early 1930s, was similarly expanded. Money and expertise were poured into the Research and Development Department (R&D) and new designs tested on a regular basis. By 1938, the prototype that R.J. Mitchell had first put forward in 1932 had been tweaked, refined and eventually adopted as the Spitfire, with construction rights issued to the United Southampton Naval and Aviation Works (Mitchell's employers and, until the Revolution, a company known as Supermarine). Mitchell, sadly, died in mid-1937 and never lived to see production line Spitfires enter the new 'Air Columns' of the Republican Air Force. The Southampton Spitfire was accompanied in its role as fighter by the newest Interceptor design under construction by the United Bristol Engineering Cooperative. The Bristol Hurricane, while somewhat more primitive than the Spitfire, was easy enough to produce and was an important political tool in winning over unsure Maximist support in the west of England, traditionally a hive of autonomists (with a small 'a'), with plants producing parts for them spreading across Gloucestershire and even into Wales. The re-organisation of the RAF, overseen by Hugh Dowding, saw what had been little more than a loosely-joined group of flying circuses operating under local Syndicate control (Gloster Gladiators had notoriously been observed dusting crops in Somerset) turn into a tightly-regimented national air force. Wings of aircraft were organised into Air Columns, four of which made up an Air Army. Each Air Army from around the country came under the relevant command for its region, be it Home Command for the southern interior, Scottish Command for the Scottish, and the appropriate Coastal Command (which co-operated to some degree with the Fleet Air Arm).

The Army, long and quite justifiably known as 'Wintringham's plaything', was the toughest nut to crack. It is here that one requires some knowledge of the political operations and theories that were invoked in the mid-to-late 1930s when it came to the Army. Wintringham had been a moderate Federationist politically, but an authoritarian populist in his own personal methods of operation. It was this that granted Mosley some common ground which he could exploit in his dealings with 'the People's Field Marshall'. Wintringham had for years been unhappy with the low level of politicisation within the officer corps of the Army. Brooke, Kirke and Vereker had been permitted to train a largely apolitical army on the model pursued by Bernard Montgomery. In exchange, they pledged loyalty to the people of Britain, regardless of the government of the day. This position was much the same as that which had been held by the Army before the Revolution, but with 'the people' replacing 'the crown'. Mosley presented Wintringham with a deal that would shift this attitude to the left. In exchange for the abandonment of Wintringham's pet project of 'popular militias' making up most of the Army, Wintringham would have free reign to create a Political Education Unit that would make it its business to ensure leftist thought drove at least the common soldier to do his duty. Other duties of the PEU (its operatives nicknamed Peuvies) included expanding the reading lists required for officers going through training school, and the creation of a system by which enlisted men could elect promising peers to be put forward for officer candidacy. Officers were also to be subject to peer and subordinate review by secret ballot at the end of each year, though this provision was to be suspended in times of war.[74]

As Mosley held up his end of the bargain, Wintringham held up his. Beginning in late 1937, Wintringham used the popular calls to aid the Anarcho-Syndicalist rising in Spain (for more information see 'Britain and the Catholic Wars' by John Durham later in this volume) to dispose of some of the more troublesome militia commanders. Sailing off to fight and die in the Spanish heat, they did not suspect

---

[74] This last point was subject to a deal of contention between Mosley and Wintringham. Wintringham demanded the elections regarding confidence in officers be maintained during war, but Mosley insisted that they be suspended 'in the name of unity in the face of the enemy'. The debate spilled into civilian life, with Eric Blair going so far as to give a radio address extolling the virtues of a company of men led by a man they have placed electoral faith in but at the same time warning of the dangers posed by 'a villainous, reactionary Hun advancing on defenceless women of Europe because their defenders are up in arms over votes of no confidence and debates as to who ought to carry the ammunition'. After a month of heady debate in public and private circles, Wintringham acquiesced.

that those of them that returned would find their militias disbanded and reconstituted as more traditional columns within the new divisions of the British Army. Between 1937 and 1939, using the tensions of Europe to his advantage, Mosley worked with Wintringham to stage a massive recruitment drive (though did not introduce conscription) to build 'a workers' army'. The democratic element of this new, centralised force proved popular, and the popular figures at its helm soon showed themselves to be Kirke, Vereker, Montgomery and Wavell. These largely younger faces marked a clean break from the 'stuffy' Field Marshalls of yesteryear, and were popular with the enlisted men. It was this popularity and level of freedom offered to the common soldier that softened the blow that the remnants of the Autonomists beat their breasts over – the popular militias were gone, and in their place were non-region-specific Columns that recruited from around the country. Mosley said it was to avoid the catastrophe caused by the 'Pals Battalions' of the Great War, but y Glais (himself under increasing surveillance and largely resigned to being a radical poet for the rest of his days) wrote in the Welsh language poem 'Song of the Llangrannog men' that 'they joined to fight for workers, Welsh and pure/but find themselves stationed upon the Humber for an autocratic Baronet'.[75]

But the 'New Army' project was not simply the expansion of the British infantry columns.[76] Basil Liddell Hart had spoken in Mosley's favour at the Congress of 1936 and was promptly rewarded with the post of Special Military Attaché for Mechanisation. Mosley shared his dream of an entirely mechanised British Army, and saw fit to start the process with the construction of a largely motorised infantry force to operate alongside a series of fast tank formations. Although Hart reportedly begged Mosley for authority over the Republican Air Force to encourage the design and construction of more bombers, of the tactical and dive variety, Mosley warned him he could only push the

---

[75] These lines are typical of y Glais' shift to more virulent Welsh nationalism in his later, more marginalised years. For more information, see my book *Whatever became of the Autonomists?*

[76] In the Army, the term came to replace 'Regiment'.

'self-defence' line so far when it came to rearmament, and pointed out that Britain's island status meant the construction of strategic bombers, like the Southampton B.12/36 prototype, was more suited to the ranged war she would one day fight. Hart therefore contented himself with working with engineering and construction Unions to oversee the development of the first Two-Year Plan. Distinct from the Three-Year Plans, these shorter structures operated on a purely military basis and called for various new weapons, vehicles and armaments to begin construction and training. By 1939, the intention was to have high-calibre, quick-firing artillery units equipped with fast tractors to provide mobile artillery support where required, with some money being diverted into the development of native mobile artillery vehicles, like what would become the GW2-era A12 Firebrand. Tanks were also to play a central role in the New Army, with the first Two-Year Plan dictating a need to build enough for four 'tank divisions' that could operate at the head of an assault. With British steel production at an all-time high, the only setback to this plan was the oil required. Through careful diplomacy, Ernest Bevin arranged a tri-partite pact with the Socialist Republic of Georgia and the distinctly reactionary (but poor) state of Azerbaijan, which at this time controlled the oil fields of Baku. The Republican Merchant Navy was equipped with a fleet of oil tankers under the provisions of the first Three-Year Plan, and so Hart's fear of tanks sitting idle in depots while wars were raged to win the oil that could fuel them were put to rest. The tanks that would equip the British Army boiled down to two competing types of design; Hart's preferred 'Cruiser' design, which sacrificed armour for high speeds and a high-velocity gun, and the more Great War-based 'Lumberer' designs. Backed by some within the Army and in particular by the more militant Unions around Sheffield (where the Lumberer prototypes were produced), these tanks favoured low speed, thick armour and low-velocity guns that could lob devastating high-explosive rounds into enemy formations or structures. Hart liked the designs but found them incompatible with his plans for 'a quick war'[77] and

---

[77] Hart 'knew' the inevitable war against Germany could not afford to drag on, because of her resources overseas – ever the army-focused thinker, he did not

therefore was forced to reject them. Only industrial and political intrigue prevented the Lumberer from being completely rejected as a design, and consequently Hart was forced to put together his first 'Ironsides' (named after the Civil War-era Cavalry units, not the contemporary Royalist Field Marshall) tank division as a mix of the two types.

The tank divisions were a propaganda and theoretical success. The early Comrade and Leveller models would have been largely replaced by the time the Union entered the Second Great War, but this was not important at the time – Mosley had promised full employment, greater industry and a stronger Britain. In these tanks, be they hulking behemoths or lithe jaguars, he provided all three. The Unions were impressed, the Army happy and workers around the country involved in steel, fuel and explosive production, to say nothing of the impressive mechanical skills imbued in British engineers during this time.

The 'caterpillar track revolution' had been a success, as had the politicisation of the Army, but it was also during this period that one of the more famous developments of the mid-20th century history of our Armed Forces came to be. On 5 January 1938, on a cold beach just west of Plymouth docks, a bedraggled but steely-eyed man sank to his knees and ran his fingers through the sand. He had not been in his native land for 19 years, and his face was hardened and darkened by the Arabian sun. His name was T.E. Lawrence, and his arrival would send shockwaves through the political and military establishment. Lawrence had served in the British Army against the Ottoman Empire during the Great War, and aided the Arab Revolt to a large degree. His skill at harassing the long, winding supply lines in the deserts of Mesopotamia and interest in Arab custom had earned him the nickname 'Lawrence of Arabia' among both Briton and Arab. During the British retreat from the Ottoman campaign in late 1919, he stumbled across the plans that had been drawn up regarding what to do with the remnants of the Ottoman Empire had it been defeated. Outraged by the jingoistic and patronising plans of the British and French to turn upon the independent Arab tribes and impose new

---

bring into the equation the might of a potential Internationale blockade.

'mandates' upon them after they had beaten their Ottoman masters, Lawrence deserted and lived with his Arab comrades for the rest of the war. Eventually finding refuge in the emerging and semi-autonomous Arab state of Hejaz, he served as a military adviser for much of the 1920s and 1930s. Tragedy struck in 1937, however, when Ottoman agents, armed and accompanied by German intelligence officers, attacked the palace of the Sheikh and murdered the crown prince and many of Lawrence's friends. Lawrence himself escaped death only thanks to his service revolver. Escaping on a motorcycle (and narrowly avoiding a fatal accident in the process), he travelled for months across the desert until buying his way onto a boat bound for the ports of the Italian Federation, where he slipped across the border into the Commune of France and requested passage to Plymouth. His first action, he would later write in his memoirs, was to feel the British sand between his fingers and inhale the sea air. His second, as no-one needed memoirs to know, was to telegram London immediately and offer his services.

Wintringham, Mosley and the rest of the Bureau were entirely unsure of how to respond. Lawrence had offered to lead a new team of agitators and special operatives with the aim of wreaking havoc in Germany itself when the war came, but made no mention of his own political allegiances. Arthur Horner expressed concern that he had no real socialist credentials and was a loose cannon at best, but Mosley said his skills at leading a protracted revolt could be extremely useful in the industrialised border regions of Germany which, if the correct political officers travelled with him, could be 'easily induced to rebel' if support from local German trade unions could be obtained. After meeting with Lawrence, Wintringham became convinced of his commitment to liberation of the oppressed. Even when pressed, he expressed no love for socialism, but a deep hatred for Germany and her allies, as well as any imperial power that would deprive others of their liberty. When asked if he believed the oppressed workers of Germany and central Europe shared the cause for revolt that the Arabs in the Ottoman Empire held, Lawrence told Wintringham that, when boiled down to the simplest of human conditions rather than reading into the proud history of both groups, yes, they did. Wintringham left the meeting pleased and told Mosley, 'He's no socialist, I grant you, but he's a damned useful iconoclast.'

The final piece of the puzzle to construct a revolutionary (in every sense of the word) army had been found in the shape of Lawrence. His Revolutionary Exportation Directive (RED) was nicknamed 'the Agitators' by those who knew of it, and word spread within the forces that young men looking for real adventure, particularly those with revolutionary fire in their bellies and a working knowledge of German, should ask to be considered for it. It was at a conference for joint intelligence staff from the navy and army that T.E. Lawrence, now in full British Army regalia for the first time since 1919, bumped into a young naval attaché by the name of Ian Fleming. The two men found themselves working together on the same table and within a short while Fleming had been asked to become Lawrence's adjutant, a role he quickly accepted. The RED took shape, and by the end of 1939 comprised of 600 well-trained and educated men, 'as mighty with rhetoric as they are with a machine gun'.[78]

We must come to a conclusion, then. The opening years of Maximist governance in the Union saw reform, reaction and upheaval in all quarters of society – industrial democracy decreased while raw industrial capacity expanded. The Armed Forces managed to increase democracy while expanding in size threefold, and modernising significantly to boot. Individual liberty was curtailed more now than under any Federationist measure, with printing presses broken and dissidents driven underground or imprisoned for 're-education'. But, as has been the burning question for a thousand historians since the Mosley period came to an end, were those repressions and the worse ones that would follow necessary to allow Britain to survive the war that Mosley, more than anyone else, knew was coming? When taking the scale of the Second Great War into account, one must surely reply in the affirmative, however controversial it may seem today. But within the context of the period of 1936 to 1939 being viewed as it would

---

[78] Alistair Maclean, *Lawrence of Germania* (London: Penguin Publishing Cpv., 1960) p.213.

have been by those who lived, worked and died during it, the matter becomes less black and white, and enters that most hated of realms of historical debate – the morally grey.

The Second American Civil War

Noam Chomsky

'Never before in our Republic's history have the threats been so strong from all sides. I call for calm, and I call for peace.'
President Charles Curtis, 20 January 1937

'We hold this truth to be self-evident: that all people are created equal. It's as simple as that.'
General Secretary Jack Reed, Combined Syndicates of America, 22 January 1937

'The United States of America is a corrupt, bloated and plutocratic mechanism designed by the bureaucrats of city hall to keep the common man down by turning the rich man against him. Why shouldn't the industrialist have his say in government? Why can't he make his case directly to his employees and let them decide if they want to work for him any more? Why should the factory owner have to prostrate himself to government wishes to gain subsidy or funding? Wouldn't all this be solved, my fellow Americans, if government and business were one and the same thing?'
Governor Huey Long, proclaiming the American Union State, 25 January 1937

'Comrade Chairman, would you care to join me in the War Room?'
Ernest Bevin, Commissary for Foreign Affairs, 29 January 1937

We are delighted to include this piece by one of America's greatest living thinkers. It chronicles not only our Union's involvement in the Second American Civil War, but also the finer details that are perhaps less widely known to students of history and to the general populace.

*

I have been asked by John to do something that really should be considered impossible. To summarise the Second Civil War is to summarise an event that changed the course of human, not just American, History. The forces that emerged would play a role in reshaping the old world into the new, and would tear apart a continent united for almost two centuries. Volunteers came from around the world to fight for three great and competing ideologies – Democratic Capitalism, Organised Syndicalism, and Corporate Populism.

The Failure of Progressivism and the Revolving Door Presidency

It is, I suppose, necessary to provide an introduction to the feeble, crumbling state that was the United States of America by the time of 1936. Its troubles were rooted in the years before the Great War, during the so-called 'Progressive Era'. The failings of this movement, characterised by Jingoism, misplaced optimism and the righteousness of mass politics, were never clearer than during the aftermath of the Great War. The reactionary government of the early 1920s reluctantly instituted women's suffrage after two years of violent and civil struggle on the streets. The action was too little, too late for many women who had found the self-evident righteousness of industrial democracy far more appealing and joined their comrades in the union movement in forming the One Big Union and, eventually, the Industrial Workers of the World (both forerunners of the Combined Syndicates of America). The Great War, so nearly entered by the United States in 1917, had ended in the outcome Americans wished to avoid, and then some. A German-dominated Europe was far from friendly to the country that had given substantial loans to her enemies during the war. To make matters worse, these loans themselves became untenable after the revolutions in France and Britain caused the countries to, in effect, cease to exist (Marshall Foch, leading the provisional government of 'Legitimate France' to Algiers, sent a telegram to Washington shortly before leaving Marseilles which read 'MY FINANCE MINISTER TELLS ME YOU ARE PRESSING US TO KEEP UP OUR REPAYMENTS STOP OUR NATIONAL SHAME IS GREAT ENOUGH TO TOLERATE DEFAULTING ON LOANS TO A FRIEND WHO DESERTED US').

This insolvency heightened by the British default in 1925, President Lowden was forced to issue a humiliating 'call for action' as the economy officially entered recession. Confidence flatlined and Lowden's speech was derided as a 'cry for help' from a poor, unstable and unfriendly Russia and a distant and uneasy Japan (the only large economies left in the world who had not fallen under total German dominance). Germany herself chose to kick the United States while she was down when Chancellor Tirpitz imposed punishing tariffs on trans-Atlantic trade, something quickly emulated by Germany's satellites and overseas territories.

The recession of the mid-1920s led inevitably to the Great Depression of 1926. Union membership skyrocketed as 'fat cats' began closing down factories, and Populism gathered strength as ideologues like a young Huey Long toured the dilapidated and un-industrialized farms of the south and Midwest. The farmers were more than happy to accept Long's take on America's problems being a struggle between 'us' and 'them' – the working man and the elites who control him with unfair deals and high prices. As the depression continued, Lowden was assassinated by a lone gunman while leaving a function in Minnesota. Few mourned the ineffective President as the ageing and equally incompetent Vice President Sproul was sworn in to succeed him. When the latter died in 1927, chaos reigned in the Republican Party and on the streets as Long stepped up his rhetoric, claiming that the 'deal' – where the working man would let the elites run his life if they did it competently and in his interests – had been broken. That had changed, cried Long from every rooftop and Father Charles Coughlin from every radio set, and it was time for the chaotic and slapdash

parties at the top of the electoral system – the Republicans especially –
to be swept away by a new generation of Populists who wanted to
'work for you'. Workers in the South flocked like lemmings to this
madness, while industrial workers continued to band together in more
and more powerful union organisations. President Kellogg,[79] an
amiable and humble man, was all that prevented a complete
Republican wipeout in Congress and from the national stage when he
lost the election decisively to Democrat Cordell Hull.

The Hull presidency was just as shambolic as the beginnings of the
'Revolving Door Presidency' under the Republicans before him. Efforts
to stimulate the still-depressed economy (the Great Depression would
outlast the United States itself) by printing money resulted in bouts of
hyperinflation and the German tariffs meant the only economies the
US could be competitive in when it came to trade were those in Asia.
The Qing Empire, although installed with German support, was not a
slave to Berlin and so provided some fertile ground for agreement, with
the Wang-Roper Agreement[80] stimulating fertilizer exports and
production, as well as providing new ground for ambitious railroad
companies. However, the trickling-back of money from these Asian
markets was slow, and the whole agreement fell apart in 1931 when
AltOstAsien Gmbh, the German state-directed business under
Alexander Falkenhausen that was in *de facto* control of southern China,
signed an agreement of its own with the Qing government that all but
replaced the benefits the Chinese had gained from the Wang-Roper
Agreement.

The economy continued to stagnate, and joblessness increased by
millions each year. Shanty towns were set up in most parks in major
industrial cities, known as 'Lowdenvilles' and later 'Hulltowns'. Hull
himself, and the Democratic Congress, were perceived to be ineffective
and unable to represent either the working man or the businesses that
could provide him with work. Alexander Berkman's radical anarcho-

---

[79] The Secretary of State became next in line to Sproul when the latter took
office without a VP of his own in 1927.
[80] Named for Wang Jingwei and Daniel C. Roper, the Qing finance minister
and US Secretary of Commerce at the time.

Syndicalist rhetoric, as well as the Utopian writings of Jack Reed, found favour with those left at the bottom of society. Berkman, Reed and William Z. Foster worked to build strong links between all major trade unions in the United States, eventually forming the Combined Syndicates of America in 1932. Huey Long, meanwhile, had been elected governor of Louisiana in the late 1920s and, gaining the affectionate nickname of 'The Kingfish', had set about pushing the executive power of the role to the absolute limit, providing businessmen with massive state loans in exchange for 'a closer welding of government and business'.[81] His repeated confrontations with the Democratic establishment resulted in his expulsion from the Party in 1930, but he shrugged this off and went straight to the Republican Party, which as a friend of business was only too happy to have him. The increasingly corporatist moves made by the Long governorship raised eyebrows in Washington, but Long's personal popularity meant Hull's hands were tied as Long seemed to glide effortlessly towards the Republican nomination for President.

The Republican establishment, however, were terrified of Long and loathed the very idea of him becoming the nominee, much less the President. They threw their entire weight behind a man who, to many, was the acceptable face of business-focused government: Herbert Hoover. A former Secretary of Commerce and praised for his efforts under the Kellogg administration, Hoover had escaped much of the blame for the Depression that Hull had gained, and beat Long to the nomination in 1932. Outraged, Long left the Republican Party and denounced both parties that had now shunned him, saying they had 'no place in them for a true visionary who can fix this country', and established the American Union Party on a platform of isolationism, protectionism and the corporate state. Hull wearily agreed to run for a second term, knowing he would be demolished by Hoover come November. He was right.

---

[81] In reality this meant that government officials were represented on the boards of all public companies who agreed to loans, while in exchange a 'Business Senate' housed leaders from each business that was part of Long's programme, known as 'Share Our Wealth'.

Hoover's time in office was marked by strikes, natural disasters and more economic failure. The Dust Bowl catastrophe, slowly emerging since 1930, became worse in the first year of his term and he proved totally incapable of dealing with the problems it caused, from joblessness to unusable farmland. In 1933, the radical Argentine republic of La Plata announced it would cease trading with the United States after German relations with the country reached new heights. By 1934, with the collapse of Brazil into Syndicalism, the United States was without any major trading partners in South America and the economy was in tatters. To make matters worse, the Federal Reserve was by all accounts nearing bankruptcy. Hoover found himself paralysed both internationally and domestically. When, in 1935, the American Union Party and Combined Syndicates of America both announced they would be fielding candidates in the 1936 Presidential Election, panic gripped the Democratic and Republican Parties. Hoover had begun grooming Charles Curtis, an intelligent, enlightened but ultimately weak figure who Hoover hoped would unite the country in sympathy, while the Democrats (and, as some said at the time, 'democracy itself') had one last ace to play – former Governor of New York Franklin D. Roosevelt.

Roosevelt, or 'FDR' as he was known, was a distant nephew of former President Teddy Roosevelt. After declining the Democratic nomination in 1932 (all, including President Hull, could see it was a poisoned chalice), he travelled across the country and rose to national prominence when he established the 'Tennessee Valley Volunteer Service', an organization dedicated to rebuilding the land devastated by the Dust Bowl. He announced his candidacy for the Democratic nomination in March 1935, but while on a whistle-stop tour of Louisiana in September, tragedy struck as loyal Longite militiaman Carl Weiss, fearing that Roosevelt would ruin his beloved leader's attempt to gain the Presidency, gunned down the former Governor. As Roosevelt lay dying, he is reported to have remarked 'This can't be right.'

The hopes of the Democratic Party died with FDR. John Nance Garner, a Southern 'business Democrat' was nominated in his stead in

1936, in the vain hope that he would steal some more moderate voters from Long's business supporters. The CSA, meanwhile, nominated Jack Reed as its candidate. Alexander Berkman had been ill for much of 1935 and died in 1936. Reed had seized upon this and, using powerful rhetoric based on his time in Russia during the Bolshevik Rebellion, implored the Union men, Socialists, Syndicalists and Anarchists of the CSA to strive together to build a more moderate alternative than the polarized Anarcho-Syndicalist and 'State Socialist'[82] factions currently dominating the movement. On a Radical Socialist-Syndicalist platform, Reed secured the nomination, arguing in favour of the democratic process that saw him beat out Paul Mattick and William Z. Forster (the latter of whom was not a strong supporter of democracy within the movement) and choosing Norman Thomas as his running mate.

As the election loomed, Hoover and Curtis campaigned heavily on a platform of anti-extremism, and urged 'the democrats in the Democrats' to vote for 'the democracy-supporting candidate who can win'. Garner strongly objected but had the matter taken out of his hands when the so-called 'Berkman Letter', allegedly written by the late Alexander Berkman on his deathbed, was 'intercepted' on its way to Democratic VP nominee Harry A. Wallace. Though acknowledged as a fraud today, the letter indicated that Wallace, a known member of the left wing of the Democrats, was in fact in league with the CSA and had promised to 'deliver the Presidency' to them. With Garner's bid for the White House all but destroyed thanks to his personal support for Wallace (the old man quite legitimately believed that the letter was a hoax, and would years later be proven right), the Presidential election of 1936 went from a four-horse race to a three-horse one within days.

As the Great Heat Wave continued, the Dust Bowl became a testing ground for the increasingly paramilitary CSA and American Union Party. As 3000 people died in some of the harshest heat ever to hit the North American continent, skirmishes and brawls broke out between left and right as militiamen began protecting farmers from the opposing side. Longites would torch what little land survived on farms

---

[82] This element of the CSA would later adopt the moniker 'American Totalist'.

they perceived as 'submitting to the Syndicalist yoke', while CSA men, it must be admitted, were just as free about the destruction of property owned by pro-Long farmers. On this backdrop, President Hoover became increasingly concerned about intimidation at the polls. After riots in central DC in September, the President summoned General Douglas MacArthur to the White House and requested that he make arrangements for the army to be deployed at polling stations around the country in November. Hoover himself made arrangements with state governors for the deployment of the National Guard, and the plutocrats of City Hall around the country were only too happy to 'protect each citizen's right to an unmolested democratic process'. What this translated to was a joint Democrat-Republican conspiracy alongside the military to keep voters identified as 'leftist' from the polls. The Kennedy Memorandum, composed by junior interior attaché Joseph P. Kennedy (who would later defect to the AUS), wrote that 'Long getting a few congressmen and Senators elected is an acceptable sacrifice if it keeps the extremists of the left out of Capitol Hill and, heaven forbid, Pennsylvania Avenue'.[83]

Men and women across the country were followed into the booth by soldiers, who were often carrying rifles. Elsewhere, more subtle tactics such as the curfews imposed on slum districts in Chicago prevented many working men from getting to the polls in time. As the sun set on Tuesday, there were already riots over what many were calling a rigged election. As Wednesday dawned, and 'President-elect' Charles Curtis issued a patronizing and self-righteous radio address urging calm and unity, it was only a matter of time until the levy broke.

Escalation, Outbreak and the Opening Plays

---

[83] Steven Colbert, *A Most Unholy Stink: Corruption and Plutocracy in the last days of the United States* (New York: United Printers, 2001) p.89.

After Curtis' radio address (and Hoover's subsequent speech in support of the President-elect) failed to stem the increasing unrest in cities across America, the President-elect agreed to meet with Reed and Long to 'discuss the implementation of governmental and electoral reforms'. What the press called 'The Leaders' Conference' began in DC on November 20, and continued until December 3 with limited success. Riots calmed down and it looked like the threats by Reed of a General Strike and by Long of 'drastic action' would not be carried out. Disaster struck on December 3, however, when a Longite Minuteman struck and killed a placard-bearing CSA protestor, beating him senseless with a club while the police stood and watched. On hearing the news, Reed rose to his feet and immediately left the conference, refusing to meet with any representatives of the American Union Party. Curtis tried in vain to maintain order, even proposing that Long be represented at the meeting by one of his deputies, but Reed was adamant and returned to Chicago on the next train.

Curtis was visited by General MacArthur on Christmas Eve 1936. The General proposed an immediate state of emergency be declared after January 20 (the date of Presidential inaugurations after a recent change in the law) which would allow MacArthur and the Army to round up and execute the leaders of the Syndicalist movement, and imprison or blackmail leading American Union figures. Curtis rejected the move unconditionally, threatening to strip MacArthur of his commission if he mentioned it again. News of the proposition leaked, however (reportedly because of MacArthur's highly temperamental exit from the President-elect's residence attracting much attention from a nearby Unionised newspaper seller), and Reed went public with the news on December 26. A joint session of the IWW, One Big Union and the North American Socialist Congress (the three main constituent parts of the CSA) approved a motion for an indefinite General Strike to begin on January 1. The final stage of the escalation was about to begin.

When Long heard of the General Strike, he told supporters that 'the Reds have given us exactly what we wanted'. 'Minutemen' were immediately called together and instructed to 'assist the federal authorities in breaking the strikes by whatever force Chapter Leaders[84] feel necessary'. What followed in the first weeks of January (called 'the winter of democracy' by some dry wit in the outgoing Hoover administration) was, in the eyes of revisionist historians, a state of undeclared war between federal government, Longites, and leftists. Whatever intellectuals may like to describe it as, it was bloody, it was destructive, and it was horrific. In Birmingham, Alabama, a small group of steelworkers who struck in solidarity with their fellows were herded into a furnace by Longite thugs – who carried with them US issue Tommy guns and Springfields – and burned alive. In Baton Rouge, Louisiana, Long exercised his emergency powers as Governor (he had been re-elected to an unprecedented third term in November) to round up all heads of CSA-affiliated trade unions (which, by this point, was all of them) and imprison them. Eighteen men were shot 'trying to escape' during this chaotic breach of liberty.

Inauguration day came. President Curtis called for 'calm and peace'. Nobody listened. Having received an affirmation from President Curtis that no negotiations would be undertaken while workers were on 'political strike', and with his eyes red from weeping over the deaths of sixty-four strikers shot to death at mining picket lines in Colorado, Jack Reed went on every CSA-controlled radio frequency in the country on the evening of January 22 and declared the 'workers' state'. Much debate has been had over the truly revolutionary impact of the declaration, with some arguing that it was in fact simply a move from *de facto* to *de jure* rebellion against the state. Almost the entire state of Illinois, all of Ohio and many bordering states were under the control of CSA militias and administrators, with the Governors boarded up in their mansions, cowering behind National Guard troops. The Combined Syndicates of America were formed within a week out of the states of Pennsylvania, Ohio, Indiana and Illinois. Michigan and Wisconsin saw popular uprisings against their Governors in the following week and had joined the CSA by the 27th. Any Federal army

---

[84] Local elements of the Minutemen were named Chapters. This was just one of the various pieces of Church nomenclature that the American Unionists adopted in these early days.

units within the new 'state' were given 24 hours' clemency to either report to a CSA recruitment station or cross the borders into Canada or the 'USA proper'. Reed made no secret of his intentions, however – he declared a 'war of liberation', which was met by President Curtis with a withering declaration of a 'police action' against the CSA. Refusing to accept the CSA's legitimacy as a state (Vice President Frank Knox called it 'a bunch of Marxists, illiterates and gangsters agreeing they don't yet hate one another enough to stab each other in the back'), the Curtis government called up all reserves and began amassing troops on the de facto 'border' between the CSA and USA. The US Army at the time could only muster six full-strength divisions, and so an immediate 'fight for freedom' campaign of conscription was launched.

Sensing that it was now or never, Long seized his chance and declared Lousiana an independent 'Union State'. In his 'speech of secession', he stressed three times that this was not to be a repeat of the 'heroic failure' of the Confederate States of America. 'The Union State,' he said, 'is not the weak, flimsy organism that the Confederacy was. All territories that join with us in the coming days will share our values – strong, corporatist government, the right of the businessman to have his say, and a fair deal for the working man!' The rhetoric found favour with the Governors and state legislatures of Florida, Alabama and Georgia, and Longite militias in South Carolina, Tennessee and Mississippi made short work of the opposition to joining the 'American Union State' in those states. Arkansas became the final state to formally become part of the AUS during peacetime by signing the Little Rock Agreement on January 31. Finally, on February 1 1937, Long declared war on 'all enemies of the Union State', meaning the CSA and USA.

Curtis' response to the AUS was the same as his response to the CSA – ruling out a pact against the Syndicalists, he immediately mobilized all nearby divisions and sent them into the territory of the American Union State with the intention of crushing it immediately. The move backfired hugely when the a huge section of the invading army defected *en masse* to Long's forces, including Colonel Patton.

Patton would be quickly promoted by Long to the rank of Major General and play a large part in AUS actions during the war. Similar disasters befell Federal forces in the north when they tried to drive on Chicago – soldiers, many of them from working class backgrounds, were easily won over by the local militiamen and rhetoricians. After mutiny in two divisions, 'Soldiers' councils' voted to join forces with the CSA, which was already raising its own formations from untrained militia. The highest profile defector was George C. Marshall, who had been approached before the war by Jack Reed through a series of letters, and had slowly become a moderate Socialist in his beliefs. Sick of the corruption and plutocracy of the United States, Marshall became the first General of the Popular Front in February 1937.

As the situation worsened, the CSA launched its first 'General Offensive' of the war, under the direction of the Army Council of Robert Merriman, Oliver Law and George Marshall, aimed at driving into New England and securing its coastline. The reactionary Canadian government, fearing the worst, unilaterally occupied all of New England before the General Offensive could arrive. Reed, furious, had to be talked out of declaring war on Canada by Norman Thomas, who argued that pragmatism dictated they must not be at war with two capitalist giants. The offensive was halted on February 20 and new objectives issued: a drive on New York, Washington and Richmond, to deny the USA access to the coast. The offensive was a huge success. The demoralized, underequipped and sympathetic US troops fell or defected to the primitive human wave tactics of the Syndicalist forces, but heavy resistance was encountered north of Washington DC. Calling a halt to the advance for two days, Marshall regrouped his forces and ordered the shelling of the fortified positions in the DC suburbs – a controversial move because US military governors had forbidden evacuation in the hope that this would grant them a kind of 'human shield'. Nevertheless, though civilian casualties were incurred, CSA forces broke through and took Washington at the beginning of March. They were inadvertently aided by the AUS assault on the south of Maryland, and when the latter took Dover, the USA lost all her East Coast ports.

The elements of the Navy present in those ports had a choice between trying to get through the Panama Canal and siding with one of the rebelling factions. Most chose the latter. Many ships suffered mutinies and consequently defected to the CS Navy – the most high profile gain for the Syndicates was the USS *Colorado*, which was promptly renamed the CSNS *Joe Hill*. The Joe Hill squared off with her former sister ship, the USS *Maryland* (renamed in Union State hands as the UNS *Consolidation*) at the Battle of New York Bay. The Joe Hill came off better, but the encounter was largely inconclusive according to scholarship (naval history is not one of my strengths). By mid-April, the US Army was retreating into the mid-West (the new capital of the USA was declared to be Denver) and AUS and CSA troops skirmishing along the informal frontlines they had developed when they squeezed the USA away from the coast. It was on this backdrop that President Curtis suffered another, massive heart attack and died. General MacArthur moved quickly to take over the Federal Government and became military dictator in all but name, with VP Frank Knox pushed into the sidelines and made Secretary of the Navy. As MacArthur suspended elections, he triggered the event that probably cost the USA its last chance of surviving the war – the Western Secession.

Frank Merriam, Governor of California, pledged to 'preserve the Constitution of the United States' by creating the Pacific States of America. Democratic and opposed to war with any of the other three factions of the Civil War, the PSA was joined by Oregon, Washington, Nevada and Idaho within a month of California's secession. National guard and defecting Federal Army units set up guard on the borders of the country but took no offensive action. And so it was that by July 1937, the once mighty United States of America had been reduced to a rump state in the Midwest, with Texas as its strongest region.

Stalemate, Mass Mobilization and the Deal with the Devil

As skirmishes continued along the CSA-AUS border (though no offensives were launched past the rough border that stretched east and west of where Syndicalist and Longite troops had met and engaged in southern Kentucky) and the USA began to dig in, the enormity of the fight for the survival of the United States sank in. MacArthur appealed to each and every able-bodied man in the remaining states of the union (Montana, Wyoming, Colorado, New Mexico, Texas, Oklahoma, Kansas, Nebraska, North and South Dakota, Arizona, Utah and Iowa) to join the local elements of the National Guard and fight for the Union. The Texas/Louisiana front was one of the deadliest of the war, with troops from both sides dying in their hundreds by the hour as the USA and AUS attempted abortive offensives into each other's territory. In the North, a front line running roughly along the state lines between Illinois and Wisconsin and the remaining US states had degenerated into Great War-era trench warfare, with much of the decisive action in the war taking place in the air as the factories of Chicago and Detroit churned out more and more aircraft for the Syndicates.

As fall turned to winter in America, the quick collapse of the United States that Long and Reed had hoped for became less and less of a reality. The USA was re-arming and rebuilding its armies and successfully digging in. The Syndicalists, therefore, had to compete. Regular army units were starting to enter the field under woefully inexperienced political officers, but the CSA had an ace up its sleeve – foreign volunteers. Oswald Mosley of the Union of Britain, still relatively new to his job as Chairman, promised Jack Reed support in the shape of the Republican Navy escorting troop ships loaded with volunteers to the ports the CSA controlled. The AUS did not engage these convoys, not wishing to incur the wrath of an established naval power. By November 1937, when the stalemate set in, Mosley and his Foreign Commissary, Ernest Bevin, consulted with the Army and agreed to send some of the newer elements of the British Army to North America. This was apparently in contrast to the British attitude to the Catholic Wars in Spain – the older, more anti-Totalist elements of the Army were sent without support to the Spanish plains while the newer, more professional and industrialized divisions were sent to North America to test out armor strategy alongside heavy air support from the Republican Air Force. Whatever the British politics behind the deployments, Reed and the CSA were extremely grateful as the 'John Beckett Formation' and 'Mosley Column' (among others) took up positions in the trenches next to their American brethren. Across the frontline in the west, and with some French volunteer units taking up positions in the south against the AUS, the world's first truly Internationalist army stared down its capitalist and corporatist foes.

Similarly reinforced were the AUS armies on the Texas front. Sicilian Mafia men, angry at their lack of freedom to break the law under Socialism, fled in their droves to Long's corporatist state, goaded by the broadcasts of Father Charles Coughlin who spoke of the 'Christian duty' of any good Catholic to support the 'anti-Syndicalist crusade'. With both armies bolstered by foreign volunteers and internal recruitment (thanks to their doctrines being popular with working men both sides of the border), it became clear that the outbreak of open warfare, rather than the declared 'war' between the two states that had amounted to little more than some skirmishes and the odd naval encounter, was inevitable. As 1938 began, plans for Spring Offensives were drawn up by all three states while Frank Knox and what remained of the civilian government of the USA tried in vain to negotiate the Pacific States' peaceful return to the Union. After these attempts failed – but did not provoke Merriam into declaring war on the USA, as Long had hoped – MacArthur focused all his efforts on co-ordinating the war effort against the CSA and the AUS. As the winter began to thaw across the Midwest, all three sides seized their opportunity. In late February, the AUS began an offensive north into CSA-controlled northern Maryland, while the CSA began an attack on March 1 into North Carolina and Tennessee. Both attacks stalled after two days, and counterattacks ensued. As the planned 'war-winning offensives' turned into hopeless meat-grinders for both sides, the USA launched its all-out last-ditch attempt to save itself: Operation Gettysburg.

Moving quickly into Wisconsin and Illinois, the USA used armor reserves against the well-entrenched CSA and Internationale positions. The Syndicalists lacked anti-tank weaponry, so it came down to air support, artillery and the use of explosive charges when the M2s rolled into battle. MacArthur's plan looked to be a huge success until the British 1st Ironsides Division – a freshly-arrived armor unit – hit the left flank of the Federal supply lines on March 8, just as the US troops could see Chicago on the horizon. The Syndicalist forces rallied and MacArthur's attack stalled. Meanwhile in the South, similar events had been underway. The USA had attempted, as part of Operation Five Forks, to throw the corporatist armies out of Louisiana and, if possible, drive deep into Georgia. They had less success than in the North, however, as Long's forces had obtained greater numbers of former regular army troops for their cause. Nevertheless, an initial breakthrough did occur, and shells even landed on Baton Rouge at the end of March before the USA's overextended supply lines crippled their advance and cleared the way for a Minutemen comeback.

The 'twin battles' of Norfolk and Richmond are perhaps the most significant of the Civil War. In two cities at the same time, AUS and CSA forces clashed in a bloody, inconclusive stalemate; both eventually withdrew claiming victory. Happening between March 6 1938 and April 2 1938, the battles cost 80,000 lives between them. The strain was simply too much for Jack Reed, and for Long, too, ever the pragmatist – he could not continue to mount casualties at such a rate if he was in a two-front war for his survival. And so it was that Long summoned Joseph P. Kennedy, rising star in the US diplomatic service and former Congressman from Rhode Island who had defected to the AUS in a motorcar with blacked out windows in January 1937. Kennedy had the position of *de facto* Foreign Minister in the provisional AUS government, and had proved his worth negotiating interim trade deals with Cuba and the Dominican Republic. Now he had a slightly more daunting task – to meet with Ernest Hemingway, Secretary with responsibility for Foreign Relations of the Combined Syndicates of America.

The Kennedy-Hemingway Pact, agreed to in principle by both sides on April 30 1938, was thrashed out and eventually signed over the following two months. The text of the Pact was simple enough, requiring only two points after weeks of negotiation.

Kennedy-Hemingway Pact of 1938

The Combined Syndicates of America and American Union State are hereby no longer at war.

The Combined Syndicates of America and American Union State will hereby recognize the borders established from the findings of the Mattick-Lindbergh Commission.

The Mattick-Lindbergh Commission sat concurrently with the Kennedy-Hemingway negotiations, with teams of negotiators and administrators on both sides sometimes being able to get along amiably, other times not quite as amiably as could be hoped. Norman Thomas, infuriated by the very concept of this 'deal with the devil', threw his papers to the floor and roared at the 'corporatist pigs' on the other side of the table as the Commission remained deadlocked after seven hours of negotiation over the exact borders in the former state of Tennessee. Prescott Bush, then a Business Minister for the AUS, fumed over Paul Mattick's suggestion that workers in the AUS should be granted an amnesty and grace period to cross the border into the CSA 'where they might be better treated'. But the Commission eventually agreed unanimously on the borders – both sides effectively got to keep the territory they had won from the USA, and they recognized that any further territory that they might have wanted was so deep inside the opposing state's borders that it would have been tremendously difficult to make Syndicalism work with Tennessee businessmen in their way, or Corporatism popular with Unionized dockworkers in Delaware.

The End of the USA

With the signing of the Kennedy-Hemingway Pact, the death knell of the USA sounded. The July-August campaigns from both the South and North drove deep into US territory and all but ended the war by September. The CSA reached the border with the Pacific States of

America on August 20, while the AUS bogged down in eastern Texas. With the CSA now stretching from Virginia to Utah, the USA retreated back into Texas, its most loyal and, by this stage, industrialized and militarized state. While the CSA launched its 'Rio Grande Offensive' under the meteorically successful Generals Merriman and Law (they reached the border between New Mexico and Mexico on September 21), the USA entrenched itself alongside Texas' huge state militia and National Guard. By September 30, the 'United States of America' had become no more than the Lone Star State. Even Alaska (seized by Canada) and Hawaii (declared independence and looking to Japan for protection) were no longer territories of the Union. Guam, Puerto Rico and Colon had been snapped up by nearby powers, and so it was that Governor Allred became *de facto* civilian head of the government of the United States of America, with General MacArthur at his side. As the AUS and CSA attempted to break the impressive 'Alamo Line' that had been dug all around the state and race one another to the sea, matters were taken out of their hands when a coup was undertaken on the morning of November 1. Armed men broke into the Governor's mansion, arrested MacArthur and his entourage and shot Governor Allred to death. W. Lee O'Daniel seized control of the reins of power, saying the time of the USA had passed and the constitution was now 'null and void'. Proclaiming the Republic of Texas on November 2, that date became famous as the day in 1938 that the United States of America, in *de facto* and *de jure* terms, ceased to exist.

The Texan question hung in the air for the Syndicalists and Longites. Should they invade? While a tired Reed was weighing up the ideological and practical ramifications of such action, the matter was taken out of their hands when Governor (now President) O'Daniel revealed his admiration for the work of Huey Long and the American Union State. Citing the economic and agrarian problems being faced by Texas at the time, he invited citizens to a plebiscite on joining the American Union State, to be held in the last week of November. The Yes campaign was the only one legally permitted to walk the streets and contact voters, so it was unsurprising that it returned 98.7% of the vote. On January 1 1939, the short-lived Republic of Texas gave up her independence and merged with the American Union State, with Huey Long giving a radio address in which he expressed his gratitude and applauded the 'forward thinking' of the people of Texas. Long promised a 'New Deal' for the people of the Union State, free from 'kleptocrats, bureaucrats and plutocrats'. The Constitution of the American Union State was signed into law by Long on February 1, officially abolishing the state structure of the United States in favour of 'the Union State' – one overarching body that ruled all territory from Miami to Houston. Long, in his new capacity as Governor-General of the American Union State, returned to the airwaves to congratulate the people on the success of their 'second Revolution'. As the new AUS national anthem, the Battle Hymn of the Republic, swelled, citizens around the South readied themselves for a new brand of tyranny.

The CSA had had a relatively good outcome from the Civil War. It controlled much of the industrial Midwest, a chunk of the Northeast (though it had yet to reclaim New England) and a handsome military. As the Revolutionary Congress of 1939 got underway, Jack Reed was unsurprisingly returned by all delegates to the new constitutionally-created post of President of the Supreme Council of Workers, with Paul Mattick at his side as General Secretary of the Congress of Industrial Workers of the World. Reed, too, took to the airwaves and announced a degree of demobilization for the armed forces – the Civil War was over, he said, and the CSA was a peaceful nation with no further interest in expansion at this time. Negotiations would take place with Canada on the return of New England, but now was not the time to restart conflict over land – that most bourgeoisie of behaviors. The Pacific States of America was no enemy of the workers of the Combined Syndicates of America, Reed continued, adding that he looked forward to working with President Merriam to secure trade agreements between their two nations. This softly-softly approach angered hardliners like General Law and William Z. Foster (the new Secretary with responsibility for Production), who wanted to continue the war or at the very least state an intent to reclaim the Pacific and New England territories by force. One thing the CSA's leadership was united on was a lack of interest in invading the AUS. 'Long can have his corporatist mess', said Reed, citing the popular support for Long as showing 'ground infertile for the seed of Socialism'. The Congress concluded with all members rising and raising their left arms as they sang the new national anthem of the Combined Syndicates of America, *God Save The Free*.

The foreign volunteers returned home as victorious heroes. Mosley met the boats bringing back the battle-hardened British units and applauded them until his hands were red. In France, Valois shed a tear as the Air Legions embraced their wives, comrades and fellow workers as they disembarked from the homebound convoys. But beneath the sentimentality, valuable lessons had been learned. Britain had gained a great deal of experience in combined arms operations, particularly in using armor alongside aircraft, and the French had been able to share valuable technological advances with their American comrades when it came to miniaturizing radio sets for their tanks. The Kaiser and von Papen knew from 1939 onwards that when the next war came, they would have to be ready to fight tactics a world apart from those used in the last one.

And so the dust of the Second American Civil War settled. Out of the ashes of one failed state came three stronger ones – democracy, corporatism and Syndicalism found their place on the North American continent. The three states would experience very different fates as the 20th century continued, but for now they were happy to begin the arduous task of rebuilding a country shattered by war. As the soldiers returned home from the front in the Combined Syndicates of America, they sang 'Joe Hill', 'God Save the Free' and 'The Internationale' as they dug their shovels into the earth. If you will forgive me using a cliché, they had won the war. The time had come to win the peace.

Britain and the Catholic Wars

John Durham

'The isolationists would have us cover our eyes while a crocodile
eats all our friends, in the hope that it will not see us.'
Oswald Mosley, 1937

The Catholic Wars – or, as they are separately known, the Spanish
Civil War and Second War of Italian Unification – are notable in
British history for marking both a beginning and an end. They were
the first wars that the Union of Britain had become indirectly involved
in since 1925 and, alongside the Second American Civil War,
represented one of the most significant gambits regarding the Armed
Forces Reorganisation Plan executed during the period of Maximist
consolidation. Domestically, the Catholic Wars saw tempers run high
in Britain House and on the streets, while internationally they reshaped
the British relationship with much of Europe. Militarily, British troops
in formations considered 'problematic' by the Mosley government were
sent to Spain, while more favoured units were sent to the mountainous
front in Italy with full training and support.[85] Diplomatically, the
Catholic Wars therefore represented an end to British Isolationism and
beginning of the direct action that came to symbolise the foreign policy
of the Mosley years. As former Foreign Commissary G.D.H. Cole
wrote at the time, 'we are coming out of our shell, but I fear Comrade

---

[85] Tank units, as outlined in the previous chapter, were mainly sent to America.

Mosley does not realise that in doing so we are leaving behind our strongest shield'.[86]

'The Catholic Wars' being a catch-all term, the two conflicts and one area of diplomatic crisis that they represent ought to be examined separately at first. The first shots of the wars would be fired in March 1937, when the Carlist royalists of Spain declared the claim of Javier Carlos to be 'righteous, noble and true', and demonstrated quite how strongly they felt about the matter by ordering their followers to form militias and open fire on offices of local government. The Kingdom of Spain reacted with a deal of tardiness (Mosley remarked to Ernest Bevin that 'it seems that Spanish Practices apply even to warfare'), but after the toppling of the ineffective José María Gil-Robles y Quiñones and the appointment of General José Sanjurjo to the office of Prime Minister, an immediate crackdown and deployment of what remained of the Army (approximately a third of it, in dribs and drabs, had moved to side with the Carlists) against the Carlist strongholds in the north of the country ensued. As curfews were imposed across the country and workers' rights suspended in the interests of keeping Spain's industry at full pelt, sporadic strikes broke out. These were met, as in America, with harsh and disproportionate force. Sanjurjo eventually banned strikes entirely in May 1937, leading to a massive uprising on the part of the CNT-FAI (Federación Anarquista Ibérica). The uprising was quelled in many parts of the country, but became popular and largely successful in Catalonia. The French, seeing an opportunity to expand the Internationale, sent advisors and diplomats to assess the ideological purity of the movement. One report was filed which came to dictate French attitudes to the civil war:

'It is undeniable that leftist fervour exists in all those I have met. There is a genuine desire to build a workers' state from the ruins of the old as the two forces of reaction destroy one another in a petty squabble over crowns. But I cannot help but feel a sense of isolation from those I speak with – they are Anarchists, unquestionably, and the values of Totalitarian Socialism will be hard to convey to them.

---

[86] Mark Phrythian, *Notes on Foreign Policy, Volume I (1925-1940)* (Oxford: Ruskin University Press, 1995) p.491.

Nevertheless, I feel this is an opportunity to bring one more great nation of Europe into the leftist sphere. More paramount even than this, however, is my sense that it is our moral duty to liberate those less fortunate than ourselves, should the opportunity arise. Here we have such an opportunity – only the most reactionary among us would be able to refuse it.'

– Report filed by Diplomatic Special Envoy To The Spanish People On The Behalf Of The Workers Of The Commune Of France, Albert Camus[87]

Camus' final clause had the effect of an 'Emperor's New Clothes'-like statement. Though Camus was then a mere diplomatic runner for his masters in the *Palais du Travailleurs*, his report moved Chairman Valois so much that he circulated it to all departments in the government, and indeed to Mosley himself by way of telegram. It was here that French debate over military aid for the CNT-FAI ended, and that the British one began. As crates of rifles, shells and artillery guns flooded over the Pyrenees, Mosley convened an emergency meeting of the Central Bureau and read aloud the Camus Memorandum. Eric Blair (attending the meeting in his capacity as Private Secretary To The Chairman) immediately applauded it (some accounts say he did so literally) and tabled a motion to follow the French lead. Mosley himself, however, was more cautious. As the architect of Totalitarian Socialism he had more at stake if another country 'fell' to the 'backward-looking' force of Anarchism. 'We had near-anarchy for 11 years on this fair isle,' he told the Bureau, 'can we, with all compassion, sentence another land to that inefficiency, violence and discord?' Clem Attlee made the point that the country's coffers were in no state to wage a war in Spain as well as America, with Tom Wintringham adding that the military was in no state to do so either. Eric Blair, desperate for the Bureau not to turn its back on this opportunity, volunteered to personally travel with a shipment of French arms and report back on whether British interests would be served by aiding the Anarchists. Arthur Horner, himself deeply opposed to all overseas military action, seconded Blair's proposal in what he would refer to in

---

[87] Pierre Hiribarren, *Les français siècle* trans. Jean Chrétien (Paris: Rousseau, 1999) p.190.

his diary as 'a fit of romanticism I had not experienced since John [Maclean] died'. Mosley relented, and Blair was duly dispatched to France by dirigible. What he sent back would become a defining epistle in the history of the Union's foreign policy.

'COMRADES—

Let me begin by saying that there is no doubt in my mind that these fellows are Anarchists to their core. What we understand as Socialism is to them as alien as the concept of popery to us. Where we propose an aiding state, they see voluntary contract between brothers in leftism as the only way forward. But there the differences between our people end. When I look at the grimy, besmirched and, occasionally, bloodied faces of the men and women (for they allow women to take on practically any role) about me, I see the same optimism shining behind them that I saw on the faces of those I brawled, wrote and sang alongside in 1925. The Bureau no doubt requires more than high-minded romanticism to be convinced of the virtues of our engaging with this conflict, so I shall remind them of the highly useful position of Spain within Europe's geography.

While we are not members of the Internationale alliance, it is quite obvious that it is only a matter of time before Comrade Mosley contacts Comrade Valois to finalise our accession. Even were this not the case, expanding the influence of the leftist sphere (as Comrade Camus so poetically called it – this is a good phrase, and one I think to my shame I shall have to steal) would be entirely in our interests. When referring to a landmass of similar size to France and controlling the straits of Gibraltar, is it better to have an Anarchist country – if such a thing can exist, but I shall leave such hypothesising to the cranks and fruit-juice drinkers – that naturally leans towards us in the event of war, or a Kingdom that will naturally side with reactionaries, be they Papist or Prussian, when the war does come? I shall leave this question with the Bureau. For my part, if Britain will not send arms and men to Spain, I will remain here. Perhaps through my small contribution – I know how to fire a rifle, dig a latrine and cook for a dozen men – the shame of a nation that did not act to prevent tyranny can be assuaged. If Britain will listen to the people of Spain in their hour of need, I am more than happy to return to London and take charge of the operation myself.

In Unity,

Eric'[88]

The letter was sent to all members of the Bureau, via their home addresses. This coup of personal interaction allowed them all to read it without censorship or the guiding hand of Mosley's presence. Mosley himself was, however, also moved by it, and was impressed by Blair's simple but undeniable logic regarding the usefulness of a friendly, if non-aligned Spain. Blair was recalled from Spain with an assurance that Britain would indeed be committing some level of aid to the struggle there, and a Central Bureau 'war cabinet' meeting called for 10 August.

But the playing field had shifted since May. The Crisis of the Italian Peninsula of 1937 is one of the more complicated cases of geopolitical strife in recent times, rivalling even the Schleswig-Holstein question for sheer complexity. In April of 1937, Benito Mussolini's National-Syndicalists had gained a majority in the elections for the Congress of the Greater Sicilian Union. A Totalitarian Socialist of the first degree – he had been the first man invited to the Totalist Congress in January 1936, and the first to respond – he was also known for advocating a swift war of reunification against the 'Papist North' of Italy. Referring to the Italian Federation at this time as 'Papist' is somewhat unfair and inaccurate – the nominal head of state was the Pope, but real power lay in the hands of the local dukes, who were only Papist to the degree that they attended Mass and feared their god. However, the Republic of the Sicilies was not the only part of the Italian peninsula to undergo political change in 1937 – a mere month

---

[88] Blair's assertions regarding the nature of Spanish leftism were broadly true, if something of an overstatement. Non-Anarchist leftism did exist in Spain, but had been largely marginalised by the almost universally Anarchist Trade Union movement. For more information regarding the chaotic splits of the Spanish left, largely precipitated by the death of Juan Negrín, Indalecio Prieto and others during the 'Red Scare' of 1933 and 1934, see Zapatero's seminal *The Spanish Left*, published in 2004.

after Mussolini's election, Pius XI died. This spurred the Austrians into action. Mindful of their weakening grip on European affairs in light of the icy Ausgleich negotiations that had been undertaken in February (the Austrians had pushed for further centralisation of the monarchy, but were forced to back down by Hungary, which had been enjoying its new degree of autonomy since 1927 a little too much to hand it back again), they pressed the Italian government to recognise the claim of Duke Giuseppe di Toscana, an Austrian who would bring the north of the peninsula well and truly under the Hapsburg boot. The Vatican, in conspiracy with the Italian Dukes that controlled the regions outside of Rome, acted quickly to fill the void so as to avoid this Austrian imposition. Cardinal Innitzer, a hardliner who nevertheless commanded enough authority to be elected without delay, was installed as Pope Julius IV within two days of the first Austrian telegram demanding the claim of Duke Giuseppe be considered.

In seeing off one diplomatic foe, the Italian Federation had created two more – the Republic of the Sicilies, which now felt it had a duty to act against the Federation before its newly aggressive leadership acted against the Republic, and Julius himself. The new Pope was a hardliner in almost every sense, and had mad dreams of a Catholic Bloc, first proposed to him by the now-warring pretender to the throne of Spain, Xavier Carlos. He, like Mussolini, had visions of a united Italian peninsula once again. As he set about expanding the power of the papacy and making overtures to Catholic nations worldwide (setting up an economic bloc between the Italian Federation, Carlist Spain, Ireland and the French 'state-in-exile' in Algeria) and Mussolini gave increasingly fiery speeches in which his rhetoric edged closer by the day to open discussion of war, Chancellor von Papen of Germany, President Wrangel of Russia and Chairman Valois buried their heads in their hands.

Into this swirling diplomatic catastrophe stepped Oswald Mosley. As he called the meeting of the Central Bureau on August 10 to order, he asked if he would be permitted to begin with a small piece of unscheduled business. When murmurs of acceptance granted him his moment, he began. 'Comrades, it is my duty to inform you that this morning I made a telephone call to Comrade Mussolini of Sicily. I assured him that whatever the outcome of the rising tensions on his peninsula may be, Britain will stand by his side. Totalitarian Socialist solidarity must come above all national interest.'

There was a lengthy pause, during which Eric Blair's jaw had to be picked up from the floor (Horner genuinely included this in the minutes of the meeting, a rare written sign of his scathing spoken wit). When an official burst into the meeting with the news that Sicilian troops had crossed the border into the Italian Federation, Mosley was 'grinning like a Cheshire cat' and Blair looked to be furious. Horner was simply dismayed, and Wintringham beside himself with rage. Mosley took control of the meeting once again and outlined the plan he had developed, in connection with the Special Advisor to the Chairman on Matters of Reforming the Army, Basil Liddell-Hart. Wintringham was further outraged to hear that the New Units (the specialised infantry divisions raised at Mosley's request thanks to a volunteer-soliciting campaign by the Maximists) would be sent to the Sicilian front forthwith, with no provision in the war plans for any deployment of the Popular Militias that still existed around the Union. Mosley revealed that he had hoped that Blair would have a role for the Popular Militias in his folio entitled 'Intervention in Spain'. It was of no coincidence that Blair had exactly that. In the days leading up to the War Cabinet meeting – which, we must remember, had been called to discuss the war in *Spain* – Mosley met with Blair and suggested the deployment of the Popular Militia as volunteers in the country might be the least internationally controversial way of aiding Britain's Iberian brethren. Blair was unaware, however, of Mosley's conspiracy with Mussolini and thus was under the impression that the more substantive Army units – the New Units – were in no fit state to be deployed to Spain. As Mosley calmly explained how the Sicilian Navy would co-operate with the Republican Navy to ship British soldiers to the peninsula, Blair sat in stony silence, his eyes narrowed as he stared down his mentor. He had been had, and he knew it. He would not forget it for the rest of his career.

Wintringham was still up in arms over this apparently unilateral decision to declare war on the Italian Federation while British 'advisors' were rolling tanks along the Mississippi and British 'volunteers' were about to strengthen the line outside Barcelona. He expressed his strongest objections to Mosley's encroachment on his own brief as Chairman of the Home Defence Committee (essentially the defence minister and Chief of Staff) and, at the end of a twenty-minute rant, threatened a very public resignation. Mosley played to Wintringham's weakness – his own sense of self-importance – and convinced him that while some secrecy had been necessary it had, of course, been regrettable and would be avoided in the future. 'But,' he continued, 'the reality of the matter is that we will be at war with the Pope as of midnight tonight, so we really need our best man to oversee our Army while we prepare to defend ourselves.' Ernest Bevin chimed in that it was unlikely the Germans – themselves undergoing a minor anti-Catholic surge in the wake of the 1937 Reichstag elections (the Zentrum Party had disputed results across the country and caused minor disturbances in the streets) would act with anything more than a condemnation unless the Austrians had their own sovereignty violated. Clem Attlee, usually silent throughout Bureau meetings, suggested that Wintringham would be best placed organising the introduction of a new, nationwide round of conscription – officially there had been none since 1921, but 'volunteer-drives' had been held in certain populous areas since 1936 – for a larger Army was surely going to be vital to defend Britain should the war escalate or, heaven forbid, another war with Germany or the Royalists were to break out at some later time. After a final consoling word from Arthur Horner, Wintringham consented to remain in his post. Mosley announced that John Beckett, veteran of the Great War and rising star in the New Units, would take charge of operations in Italy from a strategic and logistic standpoint, with the usual command positions going naturally to those members of the Officer Corps that had passed Wintringham's Tests Against Reactionary Thought. The meeting adjourned as a total success for Mosley – Hobsbawm considers it 'the moment Britain became a dictatorship' because of the complete demolition of opposition that Mosley managed to achieve on a matter of such great importance.[89]

The almost immediate deployment of the New Units – they began loading onto ships on 20 August – and the greater popular fervour on the side of the Spanish volunteers, whose trains rattled through provincial towns and villages to waving flags and cheering crowds, meant that Mosley was in a uniquely strong position at the Congress of 1937. The Pope gave him a greater propaganda coup than he could have ever created for himself when, two days before the Congress, he declared the war against the Sicilians a 'holy Crusade' and said it formed part of a wider 'battle for Christendom' that the Carlists of Spain were also fighting.[90]

The Pope had effectively united the two conflicts into one – the Catholic Wars.

The first Congress to be called under Maximist rule had a decidedly more theatrical flair to it – Liddell-Hart and Beckett gave a joint presentation on how, in less than a year, the groundwork for a 'new New Model Army' had been laid down and the first recruits into these more professional units would soon be seeing action in Italy. No elections of officers were held, to some dismay from some Syndicate leaders, and the motions in support of the interventions in Italy and Spain were subtly but very definitely a courtesy that the Congress could bestow on the operations, not an opportunity to prevent them from taking place. The Congregationalists were naturally furious, with George Lansbury attacking Mosley for ending Britain's period of 'splendid isolationism, peace and prosperity'. Mosley responded with typical venom, talking of the impossibility of walking away from fellow

---

[89] Eric Hobsbawm, *Mosley: From Baronet to Comrade to Tyrant* (Birmingham: Onward Publishing, 1984) p.109.
[90] This move is genuinely accepted as being an attempt by the Pope to secure military aid from the Carlists. Unfortunately for the Papacy, the Carlists were in no position to aid them, apart from the fighter wing of aircraft that were sent under the name 'Angels of War'. The outdated Spanish planes did little against the more modern Sicilian and British designs.

Socialists in their hour of need, and stressing the need 'to make the Armed Forces, and the country, ready for any eventuality'.

The other issue brought to the fore by the Catholic Wars at the Congress was the ongoing debate about the place of religion in Union society. Every faction seemed to have their own view of God, the Church and, most controversially, Catholicism. The Archbishop of Westminster Arthur Hinsley had been quick to distance British Catholics from the Pope's remarks, stressing that the Catholics of Britain meant no harm to the Union or its armed forces, while calling for those Catholic soldiers who asked to be discharged during the present wars to be treated with sympathy. While there were some motions – notably from William Joyce – to ban the Catholic Church and detain all its officials, the general mood of the Congress was more sympathetic.[91] The debate turned, therefore, to the wider question of religion's place within the Union, something that had been deftly sidestepped since 1925 whenever it came up. Mosley, however, now in control and heading the Maximist faction that, in accordance with Totalitarian Socialism's tenets, rejected all religion in the name of Marx and preferred to promote patriotism and glorification of the working man, decided to permit an open debate to see what came of it. The current Maximist line was that conscientious objectors were to be mercilessly persecuted, as they were putting their fictional 'god' before the defence of the Union. Many of the Maximist leaders were, however, born into Anglican backgrounds (and it was not uncommon for them to still consider themselves lapsed Christians), so no further action was either taken or proposed – merely hinted at with fiery language.

The Autonomists thought the status quo was perfectly acceptable. A tired Niclas y Glais gave a rambling, hard-to-hear speech about the virtues of the current state of affairs, claiming religion was somewhere

---

[91] This was not typical of the country as a whole, however. Sporadic violence against Catholics broke out, with whole communities turfed out of some towns and villages before Popular Militia stepped in to restore order. It is estimated that this episode, one of the most forgotten in British history, cost over two thousand lives.

the state had no business interfering in. The Congregationalists had a more radical plan – thanks to their own highly religious background, they pressed for complete religious freedom and the abolition of the Church of England and Church of Scotland, to be replaced by the Popular Church of Britain. Britain's state religion (it had had none since 1925) would become Congregational Christianity, with the election of ministers and bishops a norm. Unsurprisingly, Mosley despised this idea – 'it tears down a respected English institution and replaces it with a democracy!' he bellowed to the Congress, spitting the final word. The Federationists (or what was left of them) were split down the middle – the 'Marxist Radicals' who echoed the Maximist calls (in theory) to ban all religion, and the largely Scottish section of their faction who were, like John Maclean, drawn to Socialism through the Kirk. They put forward the idea of the Church being worked with more closely by the state as an extra layer of bureaucracy and civil service. In the end it was the status quo which won the day, with a few provisions for freedom of religion being renewed. Bishops, for example, had taken on many new recruits since many of their number fled during the Exodus, but those that remained under Federationism were protected, largely thanks to Maclean and Maxton's insistence that Popular Militias had 'the protection of places of worship, and of the homes of members of their respective clergy, where necessary' inserted into their constitutional brief. Mosley relented at the Congress of 1937 to renew these lapsed protections, as well as proper recognition of the Quakers as a religious group (he remained steadfast against their conscientious objection, however, but vowed that the justice system would treat every case of Cowardice individually and without bias). The Congress was concluded without any other debates of real substance, continuing the trend of the Bureau (and, increasingly, Mosley) ruling by decree.

The first British troops arrived in Spain in late September 1937. The Solidarity Brigades, as they became known, took on names and identities quite distinct from the British Army they had left behind in the Union. Units took names ranging from the romantic – 'John Maclean Battalion', 'Spirit of '25 Platoon', and the famous 'Tolpuddle

Brigade' to name a few – to the industrial – at the Third Battle of Abrera in 1938, the 'Sheffield Steelworkers and Shop Stewards' came to the rescue of the 'Newcastle Dockers', supported by the guns of the '2nd Tin Miners' Battery'. While the sacrifice and bravery of the British volunteers cannot be called into question, their military effectiveness can. The Anarchists of the CNT-FAI were unable to hold a coherent front line for much of 1937, and it was only when the French officer training programme began to produce frontline-worthy officers that attacks in any meaningful sense began to succeed. The British, Spanish and French troops along the thin front outside Barcelona knew they were surrounded on all sides, but also that brave holdouts in the south of the country were in the same position. On the reactionary side of the war, the Carlists were making serious gains against the increasingly Sanjurjo-led Kingdom. Alfonso XIII was weak and there were rumours he had suffered a debilitating stroke, but Sanjurjo took a greater and greater control of the country, imposing stronger curfews and, at the end of 1938, a blanket draft of all men over 18 and under 45 to report for duty. This signalled the beginning of the end for the Kingdom, as the Carlists had already completely encircled Madrid and left the Kingdom holding little more than a few holdouts on and near Gibraltar. British volunteers at the Barcelona front wrote excited letters home about the coming attack against the distracted Carlists, but dithering, infighting and inefficiency meant in never came. On 30 January 1939, mere hours after the formal surrender of Sanjurjo to the Carlist forces (the King was indeed dead), an army of Carlists launched a full-frontal assault on the Barcelona Line, assisted from the south by a defecting Kingdom army led by General Francisco Franco. The Anarchists broke *en masse* and engaged in a messy fighting retreat to the city itself, which was then bombed for three days solid in a previously-unseen show of airpower from the Carlists. Eric Blair pleaded with Mosley to redeploy one of the interceptor wings in Italy to Barcelona while there was still time, but Mosley refused, saying (probably accurately) that it would be an empty gesture that would simply delay the inevitable at the cost of British lives. As the bombers pulled back, Franco and Xavier marched into the ruins of the city to claim their hollow victory. The Spanish Anarchists of the CNT-FAI had fought hard, extending the front at one point to threaten Tarragona, but it was ultimately futile. As the front had collapsed, Valois in France had panicked and, fearing an immediate Carlist invasion of the Commune, ordered all French troops to retreat to the sea and refuse to engage. All regular army and air force units withdrew immediately, marking what is still known today as 'the great betrayal' in Spain, but many French volunteers stayed with their comrades and, together with the Spaniards they came to liberate and the Britons with whom they had common cause, manned the ruined barricades as long as they could.

Eric Blair would later write this poem about the conflict, which, when published on his death, which despite its debatable quality (Blair's strengths lay in prose, and his few dalliances with poetry were heavily modernist and shapeless) became a hugely popular piece, often read or quoted in memorial to those who fell:

Homage to Barcelona

When I was in Barcelona I met a boy.

His name escapes me

But he was fourteen years old.

I asked him why he was carrying that rifle

He told me it was so he could be free.

I told him I had fired a rifle, and it had not made me free

He laughed and said that was because I was already free.

As I left Barcelona

I saw this boy again.

He told me he had joined the militia

And would be taking up a position to the West of the city.

When I saw off our volunteers as they set off for Spain

I told them of this boy

Of his pride

Of his optimism

Of his bravery.

The Britons who went to join him

Were proud

Were optimistic
Were brave.
To be sat behind a desk
While others you have sent
Die
Alongside those you have known and admired
Is worse than hell itself.
But my self-pity is nothing
Compared to what Spain now feels
She cries out in anguish, even now
Her people under the monarchist yoke
While we pat men on the back
And give them rifles
So that we may go on being free.
A soldier, a man from Newcastle
Returned from Spain and told me
He'd fought with a boy who said he'd met me
And that this boy was the bravest man he'd ever known
To this boy, it was not politics
Or wealth
Or land
Or bread.
But all that mattered in all the world
Was that he could fight
So that he could be free.
The boy, like Barcelona
Fought to be free, and failed
He was everything that was good about the people of that city
And a rifle's bullet found his heart while he refused to retreat.
So said the man from Newcastle
When we sat in my office I was behind my desk.
One day I will go back to Barcelona
And I will find where that boy fell.
I will kneel down and kiss the land
Feel it on my lips

For I will know
And I will make sure the world knows
That that place
That place he fought
That place he died
That place he believed
Is free, and has always been.

Xavier was crowned King of Spain in February 1939, and immediately ordered a 'period of renewal' for the country which his followers began to enact. Spain became a closed, isolationist and reconstructive country, torn apart by lengthy war and mourning the loss of so many. Valois and Mussolini panicked for a time that they would be attacked by a vengeful, righteous Catholic Spain, but these fears were assuaged when the true extent of the damage done to Spain's pool of manpower, industry and armed forces became clear. The Internationale had lost this war, but at least it faced no further danger from its opponent for now.

The war in Italy, by contrast, was a far greater success. Britain's New Units went from strength to strength as their disciplined command structures held up in the face of the enemy. Within one month, Sicilian forces had maintained their positions across the border with the Federation and had begun their advance on Rome. The British were responsible for guarding the eastern flank of this advance, which culminated in the Battle of Monte Porzio Catone. British Lieutenant-General Bernard Montgomery led a force of regular infantry, mountaineers, marine troops and mobile artillery teams against the Italian Federation's First Army, commanded by Field Marshall Graziani. It was the first full-scale battle the Union had engaged in alone in the history of the country, and occurred on 23 May 1938. As the sun burned in the sky, Montgomery's troops took up defensive positions in the mountains around the town itself and proved immovable, utilising what would become Montgomery's preferred tactic of 'attacking through defence'. A young Terence Milligan served as a Corporal at this battle, and wrote: 'through the smoke of the guns we could see figures lumbering towards us. "Papists!" came the cry from our Sergeant, a man by the name of Jack Jones whose name I thought I ought to remember, and I ordered my gun team to feed a belt into the Vickers. As we awaited the command to fire, someone began singing 'The Red Flag'. Within moments, the entire line had erupted into song. Poor Catholic buggers. They must have been terrified – advancing towards a ridge of heavily armed atheists in good voice!'[92]

Milligan's experience was not unique. 'The Singing at Monte Porzio' became a legend throughout the Army, and was quick to spread to civilian life in Britain itself. A popular play about the events would later become a feature film in 1941, starring John Mills and Noël Coward. Like the film, the battle was a great success. The Federation's army routed, but not before over seven thousand prisoners had been encircled. The way was clear to Rome, which duly fell to Mussolini's Army Of Liberation in June of 1938. The Vatican encircled but not entered, Mussolini, Montgomery and Mosley (via telephone) debated over what action to take next. Entering the Vatican and arresting the Pope was out of the question, for nothing was more certain to provoke an uprising of all Catholics in the Syndicalist world. The course of action eventually decided on was to offer the Vatican the chance to surrender peacefully, at the cost of deposing Julius in favour of a man Mussolini approved of personally, Achille Liénart. A liberal French Cardinal, his total lack of political ambition and modernising attitude towards the Church made him the most acceptable candidate to the victorious Syndicalist powers. After a week of chaos inside the Vatican, Julius IV was pronounced dead, having 'hurled himself from a balcony during a fit of some great strength', and Liénart was declared Pope John XXIII. The new Pope called on all Catholic soldiers to stand down and allow the Sicilians to take control of the north of the country 'in the interest of lasting peace and religious freedom', having received a guarantee of the latter from Mussolini, himself a lapsed Catholic.

The Dukes that made up the rest of the Federation, however, were not so easily talked round. Their armies continued to clash with the

---

[92] Terence Milligan, *The Pope: My Part In His Downfall* (London: October Books, 1971) p.49.

Sicilian-British force as it made its way to Milan, but were rarely more than a poorly-supplied nuisance. The Italian Federation officially ceased to exist when the flag of the Republic of the Sicilies was raised above the town hall of Milan, and Mussolini proclaimed the Socialist Republic of Italy from a balcony in Rome. As France reclaimed the city of Nice (the Italian Federation had gained it as booty after the Great War), the Austrians were flabbergasted and terrified of what might happen next, and so demanded that Mussolini give an assurance that the SRI laid no claim to Austrian-held Trento. It was after von Papen announced that Germany had an interest in preserving the status-quo in the Adriatic that Mosley displayed a degree of hubris that would bring about his only negative experience from the Catholic Wars – he contacted the Austrian Chancellor and proposed a conference at Munich to discuss the Trento matter, with himself, Mussolini, Valois and the relevant Austro-German parties in attendance. The Munich Memorandum was, for want of a better term, laughed out of the room. The Austrians refused to even dignify Mosley with a formal telegram, treating him like a meddling commoner[93] and causing widespread humiliation for the man who had commanded the world's airwaves in the wake of the Totalist Charter. This led to a particularly embarrassing cartoon by David Low, published in *The Globe* in Low's home of Ottawa (he had fled there in 1925). Portraying Mosley as the 'first among commoners' trying to give the appearance of being a 'proper world leader', the cartoon depicts him as being snootily turned away, along with his grubby workers, from the Austrian Chancellor's home, labelled as 'Heartbreak House' after the anguish Mosley must have felt. Mosley was furious at the cartoon, and ordered any copy of it found in Britain destroyed and the possessor imprisoned for a minimum of ten years. In the wake of the failure of the Munich Memorandum, Mussolini's refusal to negotiate over Trento and the

---

[93] This was coherent with the policy of 'Non-Legitimation' that was pursued by some of the central European reactionary powers during the 1930s, that avoided all recognition of Syndicalist or Socialist heads of state as anything more than common citizens with no right to negotiate on behalf of their exiled legitimate governments, wherever this was possible.

Austrian reluctance to respond would grow into one of the major causes of the Second Great War.

As the Catholic Wars went on, Britain domestically underwent a degree of change. Attlee's first Five-Year Plan was well underway, with more and more arms and goods factories being built on previously undeveloped land. The Central Bureau tried to ease the strain the wars were placing on the economy by lowering prices somewhat, but this resulted in a brief spike in hoarding and confusion internationally over the value of the Republican Pound (£) so was halted immediately. The main issue effecting Britain, however, was her relationship with Ireland.

Ireland and Britain had shared a détente since 1926, when Bevin (then Foreign Commissary, now back in the job) had travelled to the country and personally arranged the handover of the six counties of Ulster that had briefly made up 'Northern Ireland'. When she joined the Catholic Bloc, Ireland risked shattering that détente. President Collins had been deeply unsure about the decision, but his hand was forced by a collapse in the nationalised Southern Ireland Peat Mining Company that provided a huge section of employment in the south of the country. With unemployment skyrocketing and exports low, the country was crying out for aid, and British tariffs had increased towards nations of 'impure ideological background'. Collins took a decision and joined the Catholic Bloc, receiving a loan from the Italian Federation almost immediately and seeing a small amount of economic recovery. His joy was short-lived, however, when the wars began to turn against the Italian Federation and the Carlists urged Ireland to send help to Italy. Mosley, furious, expelled Jim Larkin (the Irish Special Representative in London) from the country and sent a viciously-worded telegram to Dublin warning of 'the consequences' if Ireland were to ally with the Catholics. Collins was relieved that he now had an excuse to back away from the Catholics, and spoke in such terms to the Dáil on the matter. Shortly after the crisis faded, however, an emergency meeting of Cabinet was called by the Prime Minister, Eoin O'Duffy. It had become clear that with relations with Britain had cooled dangerously, and with the Carlists a spent force rebuilding their own country and the Pope no longer Ireland's friend in anything more than words and prayers, Ireland would need to find new friends. For this reason was Foreign Minister Éamon de Valera dispatched to Canada.

The impact of the Catholic Wars on Britain cannot be overstated. It shifted the balance between civilian life and military life, it placed even more governmental control on various parts of the armed forces, it significantly changed the balance of British diplomatic relations, and drove Ireland out of the comfortable détente that Britain had enjoyed with her quite happily for more than a decade. The New Units returned from Italy a battle-hardened and exemplary force. The Popular Militias, and with them Wintringham's spirit, had been all-but annihilated under the Spanish sun. Wintringham resigned himself to oversee the drafting of more and more men into the New Units (soon after they became simply known as 'the Army') and spending his spare time writing out lengthy tracts to be read by Political Officers before troops went into battle. Mosley and Blair's relationship was permanently altered by the wars – Blair realised he had been cheated by his mentor and was from that point on a far more determined political operator, as well as, it was said, a distinctly sadder man. The British economy surged onward, fuelled by semi-wartime fervour and further Nationalisation under the cover of 'the war economy'. The British people went with it with bated breath, wondering what the 1940s would hold for their fair isle.

Breaking Point

Eric Hobsbawm

'I hate you, Arthur. I hate what you want to do. I hate the way you
want to do it. In the top drawer of my desk there's a brown folder with
details on how to have you killed.'
'I know, Comrade. That's why there's a revolver in the top drawer
of mine.'

*Oswald Mosley and Arthur Horner, in a disputed passage of Eric Blair's
classified memoirs, December 1939*

The conclusion of the interwar period was the setting of some of the
harshest and bitterest political rivalries in British history, as well as
serving as the scene of the final radical changes to Britain's peacetime
economy. To paraphrase Marx, the locomotive of history here made its
last stops before steaming ahead to the clash of ideologies that would
define the rest of the century. Despite this, it has been remarkably
difficult to analyse this period particularly successfully, thanks in no
small part to the significant weighting of evidence in favour of the
political intrigues that nearly tore our Union apart, rather than much
being done in terms of exploration of the lives of individual working
people during this time. Thankfully the work of near-constant
Commissary for something G.D.H. Cole (himself a major player in the
upheavals of the late 1930s) and his wife Margaret provides us with
some oft-overlooked evidence regarding the daily lives of workers and
their families. Their *Report Into The Condition Of The Union*, published
quietly in 1941, features interviews, statistical tables and the like, and
serves as an extremely useful tool to provide a wider picture of life in

the Union during the chaotic pre-war decade. This article will make much use of their work.

Nevertheless, to ignore the intrigue that has been written, speculated and talked about at a greater length than perhaps any great political rivalry before or since would be folly. The rivalry between Oswald Mosley and Arthur Horner, two men who never thought they would work with each other as Chair and General Secretary in a thousand lifetimes, was so bitter, so heartfelt and, at its core, so genuinely ideological that it is remarkable that the country survived the chaos it created between them. This too must be addressed in connection with the major reforms of the late 1930s and early part of 1940, in particular the Second Agricultural Revolution that nearly reignited a level of discontent last seen on British streets during the Great Recession.

First, however, we shall examine the work of the Coles, in particular three case studies that provide, in my opinion, a suitably brief but nevertheless detailed account of life in our Union during this time. The first of these is a coalminer at Ellington State Colliery named, for the sake of anonymity, Comrade P. Comrade P worked an 11-hour shift – a slight reduction from pre-revolutionary days thanks to the early stages of the Relocation Directive that came in in 1937. One of the building blocks to the Second Agricultural Revolution of 1939 was the gradual moving of 'non-essential mercantilist classes' from town centres into bases of rural agriculture or coalmining and the 'proposed re-employment' of those transported individuals in the pits. This was partly a continuation of the Federationist doctrine of 'redistribution of the idle', but that process had been entirely voluntary (at least on paper). The ULNER (United London and North-Eastern Railway, commonly pronounced phonetically), PSR (Popular Southern Railway), FMR (Federated Midland Railway, the spiritual successor the LMS) and AWR (Amalgamated Western Railway) all received Directives from the Central Bureau in April 1937 to begin to set aside locomotives and rolling stock for 'an amount of passenger cargo' to be transported from urban areas into countryside settlements, both old and new.

In the case of 'the new', one of the more enduring impacts of Maximism on the British landscape is the construction of Newtowns in the late 1930s, usually built to incorporate mass-collectivised farmland, mines or new power-stations. A brainchild of A.J. Cook, their devisor's death placed their future in doubt (Mosley was apathetic towards them) until George Bernard Shaw volunteered (from retirement, no less) to head a committee exploring their implementation.

Although construction was disrupted by the war, three landmark Newtowns, namely Hardie in Lancashire, Winstanley in Kent and Pankhurst in Northumberland were completed by the end of 1939 and have continued to grow since, Pankhurst in fact gaining city status in 1981. The towns themselves are a long-standing monument to the brutalist architecture of Totalitarian Socialism and the foibles of the intellectual elite that sat at the heart of Maximism. Much like the urban blocks of flats that they accompanied, the houses and factories of the Newtowns were tall, angular, and grey. It was in one of these buildings – specifically, Block B of Ellington Miners' Accommodation Station, begun in 1934 by the local Syndicate to provide the slum-dwelling miners of Ellington with clean, safe housing with running water and electricity and formally nationalised as part of the 'Imposing Elements Of Newtowns On Existing Settlements' integration plan in 1938 – that Comrade P lived with his wife and two sons. Although not old enough to have worked the pits before the Revolution, he worked closely with men who had, and in his interviews with the Coles had nothing but praise for the state of his work at the time. He was grateful indeed for his 11-hour shift and the Relocation Directives that had made this possible. He remarked that one of his closest friends was a former accountant from Newcastle who had been unemployed for much of the 1920s and early 1930s until an RD offered him the chance to move to Ellington. Comrade P also shared with G.D.H. Cole a story where, after an unpleasant and fatal accident with a piece of drilling apparatus, he had discovered the dead drill operator, a towering pillar of a man he had solemnly nodded to each time he passed him and tried to avoid catching his eye, had been born the second son of an Earl and had previously worked in a desk job for White Star Line until the events of 1925 saw him rapidly in need of new employment. The Coles cite this admittedly anecdotal piece of evidence as proof that 'socialist class mobility', touted by Maclean in his more education-focused years, could cut both ways.

Comrade P's working week was therefore fifty-five hours long, something still considered unacceptable by then-Commissary for the Exchequer Attlee, but he earned a substantially improved wage compared to his 1925 counterparts, even adjusting for inflation and the radical changes in the backing of Pound Sterling post-Revolution. His home in Block B was free and maintained by his trade union, and his wage, thereby liberated from the constraints of rent (although utilities payments were made on a flat, non-metred quarterly basis) granted him the purchasing power to support his family more than adequately. P's situation was an unusually good one, however. While the reforms he benefited from were being gradually enacted across the country, progress was slow and, in some areas, erratic. Mosley's decrees took time to filter down through the quagmire of bureaucracy that the Federationist system had left in its wake. Nevertheless, in Comrade P's example a modern student of history can get a relatively reliable picture of the best possible life for a coalminer in the late 1930s.

The second example that we shall glean from the Coles' work is that of Mr G. Naylor of Croydon. Comrade Naylor did not request to be anonymised like Comrade P. A man in his fifties, Naylor had led one of those remarkable yet entirely unremarkable lives that were so ubiquitous in the early years of our Union. A member of the lower-middle class from birth, he attended a grammar school and became a factory foreman at D.P. Garrard and Co. Steel in west Croydon after returning from the Western Front in 1919, and remained at Garrard until 1925. During the Revolution, he was arrested and put on trial by the Popular Militia, charged with Exploitation and Industrial Neglect. These charges were grossly unfair, it seems, with the real blame lying with the departed Mr Garrard and his accountants (no record of their arrival in Canada exists, so it is speculated by the Coles that they were some of the thousands that drowned in the initial chaos of the Exodus). Luckily for Mr Naylor, his former employees took the stand

and spoke in his favour. Eleven men came together to exonerate him, including the shop steward he had worked with to attempt to improve conditions. After a two-year period of political re-education in the grounds of Portsmouth's Fort Nelson, he was declared Rehabilitated in 1928 and returned to his former post at the newly-Syndicated "Amalgamated Metals Plant (Croydon)", a large complex built up around the buildings of the former Garrard and Co. works. The plant would be nationalised in 1937 but keep the name. His job at the time of his interview was similar to his previous one but with additional layers of bureaucracy – he had to oversee production on the factory floor, comply with quotas set by the Three-Year Plan and served as Secretary in the weekly meetings of the Workers' Council (held in the upper room of Croydon's Green Dragon public house). In a reversal of the pre-Revolutionary situation, he reported directly to Shop Stewards regarding improvements to workers' welfare and, while all matters of pay were dictated by the very top level of government, the issuing of 'assistance bursaries' to workers struggling for any reason, for example an injured or sick family member. The relationship with the Shop Stewards and the inherent link with local rather than national trade unions is one part of the Syndication process that was left in place during Nationalisation. It is a system left unchanged to the point that its incarnation today is never referred to as a remnant of the Syndicalist system; indeed, it became and has remained synonymous with 'British model Socialism'. When asked to comment (clandestinely) on his life since Maximism, he told the Coles he had 'less clout but more dosh.' These five words succinctly summarise the impact of Maximism on British society far better than any poet ever could.

The final example to be consulted in this article is that of a young Portsmouth mother named Mrs A. Raising two boys aged four and seven, she was also pregnant at the time of the interview and wearing state-issued maternity clothing. She described it as reasonably comfortable and obviously hand-made, bearing the hallmarks of a state-backed co-operative in nearby Waterlooville. Her husband was a navy man whose wage was sent directly to her while he was on a routine voyage on the RNS *Agitator*. Food prices were undergoing a government-precipitated slump at the time of the Coles' interview, but times were still hard for Mrs A. Raising two children while preparing for a third was difficult enough, although the help from her friends and neighbours had been invaluable. This, according to the Coles, was symptomatic of the 'wider condition of Britain's towns and villages'. Volunteerism and friends helping one another had always been a cornerstone of working class British life, and under socialism it had flourished despite attempts to regulate and incorporate it into a more rigid structure. Arthur Horner had a rare success in dissuading Mosley from something when he convinced him that 'a neighbour carrying a basin of hot water to an overcome friend is something we should celebrate, not legislate'. Mrs A nevertheless had to work part-time to continue to provide for her boys, even five months into her pregnancy. The naval wage only went so far (it had been calculated, infamously, as being fit to provide for '1.4 children') and consequently Mrs A worked Wednesdays and Thursdays at the local Administrative Bureau, typing up drafts of the latest Three-Year Plan quotas. While working at the Bureau she would leave her boys with the local church crèche, another example of a non-state institution that had been largely left alone by the Maximists because it had been judged, in a hair's-breadth vote preceded by nine hours' debate at the Congress of 1937, to be 'capable or more good than harm'. Mrs A herself had no real political opinions, though was prepared to tell the Coles her local Congress representative (George Flydale, elected for the 1938 CTU by the unions of Hilsea North) had begun lobbying on her behalf for an adjustment in the price of coal, or at least an extension of the Naval Subsidies, with Nye Bevan's Home Department.

Mrs A's two boys attended Portsmouth North District School; a new-build, massive building that held three thousand students and had 'quite unfriendly architecture'. The school was, like all new schools built in the late 1930s, a towering structure that represented everything wrong with Mosley's dispassionate building programmes of the 1930s. On Thursday evenings the boys were members of the 2nd Portsmouth Column of the British Vanguards, an early iteration of the youth organisation founded to replace Baden-Powell's now-illegal (and disturbingly Royalist) Scouts. Mrs A beamed with pride when she told the Coles of her elder son's promotion to the position of Flag-bearer General within the column, and his authority over the group of five other boys that made up Potemkin Troop (his brother, as per regulations, was a member of a separate subdivision within the 2nd Portsmouth, Bastille Troop). The 2nd Portsmouth had recently sung *The Red Flag* to a packed church hall the preceding Sunday, something Mrs A assured the Coles it was a shame they had missed. Mrs A's life was typical of any young mother or housewife in the Union during this time – not particularly different to the time before the Revolution, but not worse by any stretch of the imagination.

Between them, these three case studies provide a useful cross-section of Union life across the different spheres of society. Manual labourers, the (officially) unemployed and the administrative classes all had their part to play in the building of a new Britain for a new era, or so the propaganda said. All these changes had, with some exceptions, come about within 'the great British tradition of gradualism' as the reactionaries in the Union and elsewhere called it. Since the Revolution and those drastic changes of 1925-1928, no radical top-down reform had been imposed over any length of time shorter than a year. Mosley would seek to change that when, on 11 August 1939, he sat down in front of a microphone and said these words:

'Good evening, Comrades. I would like to thank you for listening to this broadcast. In it, I shall be outlining what I and our comrades in the Central Bureau believe to be the final building block on the road to Totalitarian Socialism. It concerns the single most important good that this country produces, something that is the lifeblood for our Union. I am, of course, talking about the very food we eat.

Since the Revolution, British agriculture has taken great leaps forward in matters of modernisation, mechanisation and mutualisation. The co-operatives established towards the end of the last decade have served this country well, but have not been without faults. Those of you who work in Britain's fields or have friends and relatives that do will know that when we of the Maximist faction took power in 1936, we immediately undertook a process of limited Collectivisation. This meant that, in some areas where co-operatively run farms were not achieving their full potential, they were taken under the direct control of the local socialist authorities and the folly of private property was brought to an end. These collectives have proved so successful that it is now time to move to the next stage of our agricultural development. On the third of September of this year – that is, three weeks from now – the Central Bureau will formally nationalise all land used for agriculture in the Union of Britain. All existing co-operatives are to be broken up and rebuilt as stronger, better and more efficient farms. They will in several instances be combined with other nearby farms and will be given the latest machinery and expertise when it comes to extending their reach across our countryside. Comrade Attlee has presented me with figures that predict a growth in the size of Britain's farming industry by over 15% in the coming three years. This will mean a more self-sufficient Union, a more powerful trade presence abroad, and better quality of life for us all.

This brings me to the final new directive that the Bureau is poised to carry out. It would be folly to suggest that the existing agricultural labour force is capable of working on these new expanded farms in their entirety. For this reason, and with maximum efficiency as its utmost goal, the National Agricultural Labour Force is to be created. The NALF will contact those invited to join via letter and inform them of their posting in one of the many new 'superfarms' around the Union. Facilities for families to move with chosen labourers will of course be provided, and the impact on the communities they leave behind will be minimal – skilled factory labourers, builders and other manual workers will not be chosen, but administrators, teachers in areas where no more are required, and other members of the less active, more intellectual classes will be prioritised. This, I am sure we can all agree, is the fairest way to avoid any great social or economic upheaval in our Union. I am delighted to announce that these optimisations, transportations and reallocations will be overseen by Edwin Gooch. Comrade Gooch is a formidable administrator and has worked in socialised agriculture for the entirety of his life, and I have every faith that he will not allow this vital step in the development of true

Socialism to fail. He will take the new post of Commissary for Agriculture tomorrow, and will update us all on the progress being made through wireless broadcasts like this one.

I will conclude this broadcast with a call for unity and cooperation. The next few months will be hard, and many of us will struggle to deal with the changes that this will bring about. But make no mistake – Britain and her economy are ready for this. The infrastructure, the utilities and the resources are present. All that is required of us all is to work together and make this second Agricultural Revolution the great success that we know it can be. Goodnight, and onwards, Britain.'

The immediate response to this broadcast among the general populace is difficult to gauge. There were no riots, and it is said that the night of the eleventh passed eerily quietly, as if the people of Britain retired early to their beds, apprehensive about what the morning would bring. The immediate response of the political classes, however, is a far easier phenomenon to chronicle. Arthur Horner was beside himself with rage, partly because he had been completely left out of the lead-up to this decision but mainly because it was against everything he stood for. Top-down 'snap of the fingers' nationalisation combined with a massive, repressive movement of the population in the name of 'efficiency' was every Federationist's nightmare, and as their spiritual leader and as General Secretary of the Congress of Trade Unions, it was a bitter, bitter pill to swallow. So he decided not to swallow it. After a shouting match with Mosley in the Chairman's office, he contacted old comrades and allies and tried to outmanoeuvre Mosley. To his horror, he found that all positions on the Bureau – the only institution in the Union that had any semblance of democracy by this time, it is important to remember, as the Congress was packed out with a massive Maximist majority and only voted once a year when in its official three-week session – were firmly in the Mosley camp and had all played a part in the planning for the Second Agricultural Revolution. Resistance to the plans as they began to be implemented, however, would not stop at Horner.

George Douglas Howard Cole had, by 1939, led quite a remarkable life. An intellectual and principled 'libertarian socialist', he had served as a junior writer during the constitutional debates of 1925 and had believed himself to be living in paradise under the Syndicalism of the Federationists until 1936. He had served in various commissary roles, including that of Foreign Affairs. When Mosley took charge, he had become quickly disillusioned and retreated to the sidelines of politics, working to subtly undermine the Maximist authorities with quietly dissenting works like the above-mentioned reports on the condition of Britain. When he heard about the Second Agricultural Revolution, however, he was forced into action. Something else had to be done, he thought. Summoning all his courage, he established the Guild Socialist League, an organisation dedicated to 'the promotion of co-operatives and decentralised socialism'. The League was not immediately banned but was blacklisted for any reference in the media, but this did not prevent word travelling like wildfire across towns and cities. Collectivisation was resisted wherever it was emerging, with workers petitioning representatives of the Central Bureau for the right to mutualise their plants or factories. Matters came to a head when representatives of the League staged a two-hundred-man sit-in on farmland earmarked for nationalisation in January 1940. The crowds dispersed after a machine gun position was set up on a nearby hillside and fired warning shots over their heads, but the move frightened Mosley, who summoned Cole and told him to shut down the League or face imprisonment. Refusing to back down, Cole used his time in Britain House to meet with Arthur Horner and propose a united front against Mosley and the seemingly unstoppable tide of liberty-reducing Totalism. Horner agreed and began to form a broad coalition of anti-Mosley support using his resources as General Secretary. Dissident James Maxton, long ago forced underground, made contact and offered his support to any potential anti-Mosley coup. Disgruntled Federationists and Autonomists in the shape of J.B. Priestley, Niclas y Glais, Lewis Jones and Harry Pollitt agreed to meet with Horner with the intention of cornering Mosley with a list of demands.

All was not well with the Second Agricultural Revolution. Those unfortunate intellectuals sent to work the fields had not only their own problems to contend with but also the displeasure of the locals too.

The 'Goochers' – as they became known, after Commissary Gooch – were reviled for perceived ladymanishness, incompetence and laziness. Most of this was unfair, but that did not prevent severe levels of unrest in rural communities during the January to March period of 1940. The situation became more desperate in May, and began to indicate a wider discontent over nationalisation even outside agriculture, when fighting broke out during the construction of a new nationalised slagheap in Kent. Three hundred people were injured and one police officer was killed. Mosley, furious, summoned Horner and was surprised to find him flanked by all his new allies bar the still-shady Maxton. Horner and Cole accused Mosley of acting without any mandate from the workers or people of Britain, to which Mosley scoffed. Totalitarian Socialism was about the enlightened acting in the interests of the workers, not the other way around, he said. Top-down reform could not be rigorously and sufficiently imposed if reforms had to be approved by those at the bottom. Horner, Cole and their comrades left the meeting in disgust, determined that an attempt to bring down Mosley through the ballot box at the next Congress was their only option. Mosley, guessing this, at first moved to have them all arrested, but Blair, mindful that the recent Liberty Cross station riots over the forced Transportation of over five hundred teachers, tailors and nursing staff to the fields of Gloucestershire had come dangerously close to open revolt, advised against any further moves publicly calculated to suppress dissent. Instead, Mosley shored up his own support by building up a cabal of his own – Attlee and Bevan, Bevin, Gallacher, John Beckett (a loyal Mosleyite and experienced soldier, he would later succeed the distinctly un-Mosleyite Wintringham as head of the Army) and of course Eric Blair surrounded Mosley at nearly all times and met, plotted and telephoned those delegates to the Congress they had the slightest doubts over. Mosley knew suspending the Congress of 1940 would, in Blair's words, 'leave everyone with a bad taste in their mouths that only our blood could wash out' and so it was to go ahead as planned.

By the end of August, one year on, the Second Agricultural Revolution was in full swing and Congress loomed. Agricultural production had superficially increased, but massive incompetence accompanied by huge levels of unrest on some of the seven new 'superfarms' had put the process significantly behind schedule. The Mosley and Horner cabals came to the Congress with two distinct agendas – the latter wished to remove Horner, the former wished to depose Mosley. All other matters took second place. Mosley had only glanced over and eventually signed the crucial documents relating to the deployment of higher-density naval patrols in the seas around Iceland, and in the months following Horner had barely batted an eyelid as he stamped the requests for more political 'advisors' to be sent to Reykjavik to assist the fledgling government in completely throwing off the imperialist shackles of the former Danish colonial occupiers by adopting socialism. It is of note that on the agenda for the Congress of 1940, compiled by Horner himself, 'The Situation in Iceland' is number forty-two, and scheduled to be discussed in the middle of the second week. The entire affair – the naval deployments, the sending of political advisors and the success thereof, the displays of force against the also-interested Canadians – had been carried out by the 'backroom boys' of the Union; the undersecretaries, the junior commissaries, the deputy treasurers. The closest thing the Union had at this time to a civil service had co-ordinated a major international incident while their leaders squabbled and plotted each other's removal and while their countrymen fought off attempts to be forcibly relocated or worse. It is a wonder things did not turn out even worse than they did.

As the Congress of 1940 began, one could hear the sound of knives being sharpened. In his opening address, Mosley dropped regular hints about a need to purge 'obstructionist elements within the apparatus of government'. Horner spent much of his time in fringe meetings, trying to convince influential members to join his side of the split that had been a long time coming. While support for the successes of Maximism was still strong, many union leaders agreed that the Second Agricultural Revolution was a step too far and they would not have minded a return to the level of power they had exercised under Federationism. Those aware of the split – a large majority of the Congress and the country remained blissfully unaware – knew that something would have to give. Either the last vestiges of orthodoxy would crumble and die in Horner, Cole and Pollitt, or Mosley would find himself toppled by a country longing for a simpler, less authoritarian time.

It was on the penultimate-but-one day of the Congress – the twenty-sixth of September, to be exact – that Horner rose from his seat to make his move. Eric Blair would later write that 'he gripped the podium with a white-knuckled grasp, visibly shaking and biting his bottom lip as he straightened up, as if conscious that he looked as dishevelled as he probably felt.' Mosley sat stony-faced as 'his' General Secretary set the stage for a scathing attack on the excesses of Maximism and the Chairman in particular. But, as we all know, as Horner reached the card of his speech that explicitly spelled out his intentions and goals, the world changed forever. Not with a bang, nor with a shout, but with the sound of a pair of running feet, the banging of double doors, and the weary, tired croak of a man who had been up all night. As Ernest Bevin's secretary spoke, the whole Congress listened, and as he finished speaking Horner and Mosley locked eyes, an unfathomable expression shared between them.

'Our men have been blockaded on Iceland,' said Harold Wilson. 'It's the Canadians.'

A Very British Emergency

John Durham

'A ragtag pack of bandits, novelists, halfwits and drudges. If these are the best men our once-Sceptred isle can provide, we shall be in London by 1942'

Winston Churchill, Minister for War, Sea and Liberation, 'His Majesty's Government', 1 October 1940

Britain was stunned. During the time it took for Undersecretary Wilson to stagger towards a seat at the end of a pew in the Congress Hall, the room erupted into a chorus of panicked shouts, angry cries and screams of terror. It was obvious to everyone that war was the Canadian intention, and as far as they knew the Union was completely unprepared for such a conflict.

Mosley rose from his seat, visibly supporting himself on the arm of the Chairman's chair. With a sudden, loud banging of the gavel, he called the Congress to order. 'Comrades,' he began, apparently quite oblivious to the indignant Arthur Horner who was still stood at the speaker's podium, 'it is clear that events beyond the control of this body have moved past a point of no return. I move that Congress be adjourned for the day, and that the Central Bureau accompany myself and Comrade General Secretary Horner to the meeting rooms to assess the situation.' There were mutters of dissent and cries of 'shame!' from some corners of the room, but the mostly disoriented and largely pro-Maximist Congress relented quickly. 'Nobody really had any idea what was going on – the wireless and *The Chartist* had made no mention of the Iceland situation. I was one of those who wearily raised my hand to support the adjournment. It wasn't clear at all what would happen next,' wrote Margaret Cole.[94] As the Central Bureau moved to the meeting rooms, someone noticed that Harold Wilson, the fateful messenger, had passed out. He was not alone.

'The fear in everyone's eyes as we brushed past them to head to the meeting rooms was evident,' wrote Eric Blair, on his way to join Mosley in his capacity as Commissary Without Portfolio, 'and we suddenly all felt very small, like children. Our little revolution seemed somehow trivial. The Catholic Wars and the conflict of the American Brigades (who had arrived home to a shower of praise a few months before) had not ever threatened our existence. We were a young, socialist nation with few friends, and this had never been clearer than now. I passed Niclas y Glais – he had aged terribly since 1936. He looked at me with a distant fear in his eyes. Everything – the Agricultural Revolution, the redevelopments, the squabbles over the Transportations – had become irrelevant in the space of twenty minutes. The Royalists threatened us with total destruction, and we apparently had no place to which to turn. If we acquiesced to their blockade, they would surely seize Iceland and quash the revolution there, then use the bases to stage an invasion of Britain. If we tried to break the blockade, we would be plunged into war immediately and nobody apart from Oswald, the Chiefs of Staff on the Defence Committee and perhaps Clem had any idea whether our forces were ready for that. Our armies had some strong, experienced units thanks to the various entanglements we had involved ourselves with since 1936, but the Navy was still a highly confidential matter and the Republican Air Force had an impressive array of new fighter aircraft but a deficit of well-trained pilots. But the Canadians had played their hand now, and surely were therefore ready to go to war now – if we appeased them to gain more time for ourselves, we would surely be granting them all the time they would need to refine their invasion force. With all these thoughts flying around my head, along with those

---

[94] Margaret Cole, *Our Darkest Hour: Memoirs from the War* (London: Penguin Publishing Cpv., 1951) p.9.

usual fears a man has for his family – Eileen had told me she was with child earlier that week – I approached Meeting Room 7A.'[95]

Blair, along with the rest of the Bureau, was surprised by what he found in his Chairman's behaviour when his comrades had assembled. Standing with his back to the group and his hands folded behind him, Mosley spoke calmly and apparently rationally while looking out of the window into the street. 'It will be necessary, I feel, to invite those members of Comrade Horner's… faction into this meeting. Unity is vital in a time like this. Comrade Horner, perhaps you could fetch them from the Congress floor. I have already asked my personal secretary to contact some other figures whose presence I feel will be useful.' The medium-sized meeting room quickly became an exceptionally awkward place to be, with Commissaries milling around making small-talk and, very quietly, discussing what on earth would happen next. Bevan was deep in thought, muttering to himself every so often, while Attlee cornered Blair and began an uncharacteristically testy rant regarding the state of 'the books' (Attlee's preferred shorthand for the country's economy). Ernest Bevin stood alone in a corner, flabbergasted at what he had permitted to happen. Others steered well clear. Edwin Gooch lit a cigarette and puffed furiously. Annie Kenney wrung her hands and paced in silence, while William Gallacher and Tom Wintringham spoke feverishly about the suspected strength of the Canadian and Royalist armed forces – Gallacher's spy networks had failed to make particularly significant inroads across the Atlantic. Within an hour, Horner's party had arrived. G.D.H. Cole, Harry Pollitt, Niclas y Glais, J.B. Priestley, Lewis Jones and newcomer Christabel Pankhurst sat with the General Secretary at one end of the lengthy conference table. The rest of the meeting congregated around them and, eventually moving from the spot to which he had seemed rooted since he entered the room, Mosley sat at the head of the table.

'Welcome, Comrades. I am sure none of you wish to delay our decision-making process any further, so I would like to—' Mosley was interrupted by a rap at the door and the appearance of his secretary,

---

[95] Eric Blair, *Keeping The Red Flag Flying* (London: Onward Books, 1955) p.42.

Mrs Hardie. She informed him that the guests he had invited had arrived at Congress House. Mosley took this in stride and continued speaking. 'Comrades,' he began once more, 'many of you have scoffed at my appeals for unity in the past. I will admit that they have, in these divided times, sounded often hollow and insincere. But gentlemen,' he said, reverting for a moment to his unfortunate habit of using pre-revolutionary language in high-pressure situations, 'I ask you now to accept my word that as our Union teeters on the brink of war, I am prepared to do everything that is necessary to preserve it. Comrade Horner, I hope you will be by my side in this. Comrade Blair, I know that Britain may rely on you in whatever role you take.

'Comrade Attlee, your management abilities might just save millions of British lives. Comrade Bevan, your construction of Britain's infrastructure has thus far been impeccable. You may now have the honour of fighting for what you and your fellow workers have built. To those of you from our armed forces – Comrades Wintringham, Wedgwood-Benn, Kirke and Chatfield – I say that I need not personal loyalty from you, or anything quite so reactionary. But our country needs its finest men ready, armed and willing. I have every belief that this can be accomplished with you at the helm. To the rest of you,' he continued, gesturing to Annie Kenney and the various members of Horner's party, 'I know your skills and revolutionary fervor will serve our country well in the coming time. But, Comrades, I hope that you will permit me one last unilateral decision.' There was a ripple of disapproval from the table, starting with Cole, but Horner quietened them down, his eyes fixed on Mosley.

'Thank you, Arthur,' Mosley began. 'Comrades, you will no doubt agree with me that what this Bureau lacks is a Commissary for War. If we are to find ourselves embroiled in a conflict for our very survival, we will need someone with fire in his belly, the cause of labour in his heart and the machinations of a genius in his brain. I hope that you will therefore agree with my choice for this position, even those of you who, like me, have had more than your fair share of troubles involving him. Mrs Hardie,' he called, 'please send in the Commissary for War.' All eyes turned to the door. It opened, and the silence that fell was deafening. The tall, dishevelled man in the doorway looked Mosley in the eye.

'Alright, you bastard. What do you want?' said James Maxton.[96]

The situation was quickly explained to Maxton, who had already only agreed to enter the building housing his greatest political enemies when he had been informed by Mrs Hardie of the Canadian blockade. Maxton sat, almost crumpled, in a chair at the end of the room while Mosley calmly laid out his proposal for the size, remit and responsibilities of the Commissariat for War. Blair noted that Maxton had not aged well since he had last seen him in person. His cheeks seemed more hollow and he was significantly thinner. Years of marginalisation and arrest (but never quite imprisonment) had damaged the man's body but not, as would become evident, his mind. As the man he hated spoke, Maxton's eyes widened as he took in all of what was being said. The two great rivals stared at each other throughout Mosley's short speech outlining the situation and what was expected of him. When the Chairman had finished, the Clydeside firebrand removed his hat. With an infinitesimal nod, he agreed with the proposal, with one condition. 'I pick my own people,' he said, 'no point having me if you hamstring me with your lackeys. No offense intended, Eric.' Blair took none, or so he wrote. With the Commissary for War now on board, Mosley turned, once more in his unnervingly soft 'administration voice' as Blair called it, to the matter of internal security. 'We doubtless have many spies in the country,' he asserted, 'as well as many portions of the mercantilist classes that would easily back the Royalists over the Revolution. Comrade Beckett has made excellent headway in building an internal security department that is able to monitor these elements to some degree. However, Comrade Beckett's military experience suggests to me that he should be appointed as a member of the Forces Committee – Comrade Wedgwood-Benn, as the current Chair, do you have any objection to this?' No objection was received, but Tom Wintringham was notably fuming. The rotating chair system for the Chiefs of Staff meant that even though

---

[96] This section is based on primary accounts of the meeting, mainly the Blair book referenced in the previous footnote.

Wintringham was in overall command of the Armed Forces, decisions about the makeup of their structure were presided over by himself or Kirke, Chatfield or Wedgwood-Benn, depending on the time of year. The move was almost certainly a means for Mosley to marginalise Wintringham even further.

With Beckett also satisfied, Mosley introduced the meeting to his other 'guest' who had been waiting outside – Clive 'Jack' Lewis, an occasional novelist who had become fascinated with the concept of purging reactionary elements from the Union of Britain and had called for such in short stories distributed in pamphlet form. His most famous work, *The Lion, The Witch and the Wardrobe* was about 'the witch' (Queen Victoria) and her lion (the Empire) stalking four children forced to work in horrid conditions in a Victorian dystopia until they hid in a wardrobe, only to find it a portal to the Union of the 1930s. An apparently jolly man from his appearance, he entered the room in a characteristically ill-fitting suit and with what was left of his hair somewhat out of place. Mosley had come into contact with him through Beckett (who had made him his deputy after he broke up a Royalist sabotage network that had been operating near Bristol) and had been impressed by the latter's recommendations that the quirky novelist be his replacement. Blair noted at the time that 'although it was the first time I laid eyes on him, something about him unnerved me. He seemed outwardly pleasant, much like a popular uncle, but his eyes were slightly too large for his head, and always seemed to be wide open as if taking in every detail on one's face. I was instantly without doubt that this man was capable of a frightening amount of cruelty.' His words were more prophetic than he knew.

Nevertheless, the appointment was passed by the assembled men without much difficulty. The men and women at the table who did not have official positions waited to see what would happen next. Some thought they would be asked to leave. However Mosley, magnanimous as he was on this fateful day, offered each and every one of them a job in the new or existing departments. Christabel Pankhurst was flabbergasted to be offered the post of Deputy Commissary for Foreign Affairs – the first woman to reach such a diplomatic height in Europe.

Lewis Jones joined Maxton at the Commissariat for War, while Niclas y Glais and J.B. Priestley were offered the roles of Undersecretary for Particulars and Commissary for Information respectively. Only G.D.H. Cole and Harry Pollitt were left out of this process, but Mosley insisted that this was merely because they would be offered new positions as the meeting went on. Glancing at Arthur Horner to receive his approval, Mosley put forward his final motion for this stage of the meeting before the Iceland matter was to be tackled by those assembled. In light of the circumstances, this new, expanded Central Bureau was to be termed 'the Emergency Executive' and would act in accordance with the wartime powers granted to such an executive in the Constitution of the Union of Britain. Maxton, who had himself played a part in writing those provisions, supported the move, as did Horner. With the three powerbrokers of the meeting in agreement, it seemed inevitable that the motion would pass, and pass it did, but not before an amendment calling for 'some provision of democracy' to be instated had been tabled and passed by y Glais, Cole and, interestingly, Blair. As the clock struck eleven, Mosley banged a small gavel and called the first meeting of the Emergency Executive, with himself as its Chair and Horner as its General Secretary, to order.

The first priority of the new Executive was to achieve détente between the parties involved on the subject of agricultural reform. Horner and his faction made it clear after Mosley welcomed them to the meeting that threat of war or no threat of war, they would have no part in any body that was not prepared to rectify the 'gross mistakes' committed in the preceding fifteen months, and duly tabled their immediate resignations if the meeting proceeded without any agreement on the topic. Rhetoric against the Second Revolution had been stepped up, with Cole's Guild Socialist League giving out reams of pamphlets criticising the nationalisation of the land as 'Enclosure all over again' and, most recently, a group named 'The Heirs Of Winstanley' had begun taking violent action to seize control of state farms and live on them in early-Revolutionary-concept (or indeed Civil War-era) communes. John Beckett, the now-former Interim Head of Internal Security, gave a testy report of the latest actions of these 'terrorists' when Cole attempted to rationalise their behavior. 'Is it "understandable", Comrade,' he asked, 'that two Land Officers would be taken from their homes in the dead of night and shot in the middle of a wood? That fourteen women and children died in the burning of a labourers' compound just last night?' Cole was shocked by the second figure and quickly backpedalled, but insisted that the way to prevent this discontent was to moderate the policies of Comrade Gooch's department and seek compromise. All eyes turned to Mosley to see if he agreed with this prognosis. After a long pause, during which Mosley seemed to search the ceiling for an answer, he gave a slow reply in which he agreed to 'reconsider' elements of the Second Agricultural Revolution.

Three hours later, an exhausted Arthur Horner was feverishly writing down the decisions that had been taken. The general consensus was simple and two-layered: Mosley's claim that he had only intended to make Britain as self-sufficient as possible because of the risk of a blockade by Canada or Germany was accepted. So, too, was his logic that if 'Fortress Britain' was to succeed as a strategy, 'the fortress will need more than a kitchen garden'. Nevertheless, as a concession to Horner, Cole and Maxton (whose talent he and the country desperately needed), nationalised agriculture was accepted to be 'not viable at this time'. The protests of Edwin Gooch were diminished by an assurance that although the Second Agricultural Revolution programme was to be halted 'for the duration', existing state farms would continue to be expanded in size and the recently-formed Land Army would be presented as an option to conscientious objectors if conscription was introduced at any point during the war that was now, it seemed, coming sooner rather than later. This would serve as a suitable replacement for the steady flow of Transported individuals from the cities. As a further concession to the Guild Socialist League, Cole was to become an undersecretary in the Commissariat for Agriculture and liaise with y Glais at the Particulars Division (a thinly-veiled propaganda department) to develop the so-called 'Dig For Victory' campaign. Britons would be encouraged to 'take the mantle of the Levellers' and turn swathes of public land, be it parks, Downs or even one's own garden, over to agriculture and form farming co-operatives to gain as much food as possible from 'every square inch of our green and pleasant land'. It was a sign that Cole had become happy with the situation – happier than he had been for months, in fact – when he took Mosley aback with an apparently nonnegotiable demand. When Mosley cautiously enquired as to what the demand was, Cole broke into a smile and laughed, 'We shall need a great many potatoes.'[97]

Finally, the matter of democratic accountability for the Executive resurfaced as part of the agricultural détente negotiations. As Horner and y Glais expressed particular discomfort with the present image of a 'cabal' running the country 'from some bunker, out of touch with our fellow workers who will soon be suffering', it was Eric Blair who, after four years on the peripheries of Mosleyite rule, finally played his hand. Proposing that, to combat the limitations and unwieldy scale of the Congress of Trade Unions when it came to governing during a lengthy crisis, a more regularly-assembled body be formed 'for the duration'. Suggesting, seemingly off the top of his head, that it be named the 'Council of British Workers' and that it could be made up of one representative from each of the Syndicates represented in the CTU (which would amount to approximately one hundred and sixty members), he concluded that in order to avoid associations with reaction and the sordid local governments of the old regime, the term 'Councillors' was inappropriate. After a stunned silence at what was surely the longest outburst Blair had ever given out in such a large meeting, Mosley asked what he believed *would* be appropriate. After a moment's consideration, Blair put forward that, in keeping with British Revolutionary history, these representatives could be termed 'Agitators'.

And so it came to pass that out of a debate on agricultural reform, an indirectly elected body of consultation (legislation was out of the question, as ever) was born. To be housed temporarily in the former House of Lords (paradoxically, the hypocrisy of the name 'House of

---

[97] G.D.H. Cole, *The Hammer, Torch and Spade* (Peterborough: Orchid Publications, 1961) p.14.

Commons' had disgraced the chamber more than the unabashed name of the former upper house, red leather was deemed more suitable than green, and besides the Commons had been turned into the main hall of the Museum of the Old Regime in 1927 and the Royal Carriage now hung from its ceiling) and overseen by Agitator-in-Chief Blair (the ever-modest Blair had put forward the ailing Tom Mann for the position, but had been quick to agree that Comrade Mann was too old to take on such a position now – suspiciously quick, in Horner's eyes), the Council of British Workers was to be proclaimed to the CTU the following day, and elections carried out immediately among the delegations from the Syndicates present.

With détente achieved with regards to agriculture, the Emergency Executive turned to the matter of the general situation regarding foreign relations. There was a long, poignant silence in which all eyes fell on Ernest Bevin, and it was in a low, controlled voice that Mosley 'suggested' that it would be most appropriate, in light of the unchecked escalation of the Iceland Crisis, for the Commissary for Foreign Affairs to offer the Committee his resignation. Bevin, who had been in a stunned silence since Harold Wilson first staggered onto the Congress floor, gave a muted murmur of agreement and asked if he might therefore be excused from the meeting. Arthur Horner, however, raised a hand and signaled for the burly Gloucestershire dockworker to keep his seat. 'I think that, in light of the Commissary's years of service and clear ability, it would be a great shame to lose him at this trying time,' he said, suggesting Bevin remain in the meeting in case a 'more appropriate use' for his talents as an organiser of labour could be found. This was met with agreement and the elephant in the room of Bevin's incompetence in failing to properly engage with the Crisis was somewhat diminished in size. Mosley quickly seized control of the discussion and handed out documents outlining his plans for a 'Commissariat for Solidarity', a sort of consultative bureau that helped Trade Union leaders with any problems or suggestions regarding quotas. Mosley had planned to introduce it during the next Three-Year Plan, but matters had taken an unexpected turn and it seemed only right to encourage more co-operation immediately, given the circumstances. After assuring Annie Kenney that her position as Commissary for Female Workers would remain unchanged and inviting Harry Pollitt to head the new Commissariat for Solidarity, Mosley turned with a smile to Ernest Bevin and told him he would be intensely valuable in a Deputy role answerable only to Pollitt and Mosley himself. Bevin accepted in a fluster, presumably still terrified that he was going to be shot the moment he got home, but it was clear to all present now that the matter was resolved.

The matter of Bevin's replacement was a more complex one. G.D.H. Cole, though begrudgingly present and a former holder of the position, declared himself uncomfortable with foreign affairs and said the Dig For Victory campaign would take all this energy. Bevin's deputies were all young, with his chief undersecretary Harold Wilson barely into his twenties (he had got the job through, Bevin admitted, admirable brilliance). Ambassador[98] to Bengal R.H. Tawney was suggested by Eric Blair as a candidate, but Mosley vetoed the idea as he suspected (correctly) that Britain would soon need a respected and longstanding voice on the subcontinent, and Tawney was much-beloved by the Bengali people and their government. It was after a quick discussion and quicker rejection of the then-ambassador to France, Herbert Henry Elvin, that a decision was reached. Elvin was, in any case, highly involved in the growing maelstrom of the Third Moroccan Crisis, and had to give platitudes on a daily basis to the French government as it stepped up its support for the Syndicalist rebels in Marrakech.

In retrospect, Stafford Cripps, British ambassador to the Socialist Republic of Italy, was an inspired choice to define Britain's foreign policy. Well-spoken and of aristocratic stock, he was also a committed orthodox Marxist who had refused to involve himself with the various factions that had dominated Union politics since 1925. Thanks to these two qualities he was perfectly domestically acceptable while being not inappropriate for the various dealings with the Royalists, Imperialists and, if it should come to it, Russians that Mosley

---

[98] British Special Representatives abroad had been formally re-designated as Ambassadors in one of the first acts of the Maximist administration in 1936.

anticipated. He arrived at Congress House a day after receiving news of his promotion via telegram, and left instructions for his deputy, Samuel Miliband,[99] to succeed him in Rome.

Cripps being incommunicado until he arrived in London on 28 September, it was left to the members of the Emergency Executive to formulate the British response to the Canadian blockade of Iceland themselves. The situation was alarming – over eight hundred British citizens, more than half of them civilians, were posted in the island nation and the government had recently fallen to the newly-formed Congress of Icelandic Trade Unions after riots over food prices. The Canadians had sent a blunt telegram to London declaring that Britain's obvious attempt to gain a 'new Atlantic base' against the rights of self-government desired by Icelanders was unacceptable and that the blockade would send freighters ashore at 0600 local time the next day to collect all British personnel and take them as far as Scapa Flow. If British personnel did not board at this time, the Canadian government accepted no responsibility for what would happen to them during its planned 'restoration of the democratic government' which it intended to perform 'with all necessary force'. Bevan quipped that it was nothing more than 'the most violent eviction notice in history', and it was agreed by all parties that the real intention of the Canadians (and their 'Exile' puppetmasters) was to gain the base of Reykjavik for themselves for possible future operations against Britain. Bevin sheepishly informed the committee that one benefit he had agreed to when keeping half an eye on the agitation operations that Britons had undertaken in the Icelandic capital had been basing rights that the Union would have enjoyed for the directly inverted reason. Mosley cut through the ensuing chatter by saying that, while he had no desire to take the country to war, this was a clear violation of British rights to the sea and international solidarity. In addition, over eight hundred

---

[99] An émigré from the German client state of Flanders-Wallonia, Miliband had arrived with his family shortly after Britain's ports re-opened in 1927. An excellent grasp of Marxist theory and knowledge of six European languages had seen him quickly adopted into the diplomatic service after he gained British citizenship in 1931.

British lives had been put at risk and held hostage by a foreign power. There could be no alternative but to reply to the Canadian telegram with an ultimatum, published in *The Chartist* and forwarded to the Canadian equivalent newspapers, that demanded the lifting of the blockade and the withdrawal of all Canadian military units from Icelandic waters.

As the couriers left the room and made their way to Broadcasting House to make the ultimatum public to both the Canadian and British peoples, there was still much to discuss. Determining the state of the armed forces was established as the paramount priority. As this vote passed, Clem Attlee raised a hand and noted that it was now three o'clock in the morning, and suggested an adjournment of the meeting. Mosley agreed, but declared he himself would meet with the members of the Defence Committee to determine the strength of the Union and, if the situation ended as feared, how best to relieve the Britons on Iceland by force.

And so, as the most transformative twenty-four hours in the Union's history came to an end, and the sun rose over the twenty-seventh of September 1940, the telegraph wires of Europe and the Atlantic became wild with traffic. Around Britain, men and women slept peacefully in their beds, unaware of the changes that their leader would announce via the wireless at eleven o'clock the next day. In the pews of Congress House, Trade Union leaders and their fellow delegates stretched out to a far less easy sleep, but most of them found themselves unable to rest fully before doing at least a brief set of calculations regarding how to ready their workers, their families and their communities for the inevitable. In meeting room 7A, Eric Blair requested leave from the meeting to plan his speech to the Congress floor the following day in which he would establish the Council of British Workers. Bevan and Attlee retired to Britain House to prepare their departments. Pollitt and Bevin followed to begin building their department. J.B. Priestley took a cab to Broadcasting House and requested a small office in the basement, which by February 1941 would become the nerve centre of Britain's Commissariat for Information.

James Maxton remained with Mosley and Horner as the meeting with the Defence Committee began, but asked to be excused for a few minutes to contact his wife. According to his diaries, he did not in fact contact his wife, but went straight to the John Maclean memorial outside Congress House. 'I know you'll think me a fool, a traitor and a sellout for getting into bed with that bloody Baronet, John,' he said, allegedly quite audibly, 'but I know that if you were here now, in these shoes, facing a choice between siding with *him* and fighting to keep this republic alive, or doing nothing while the bastards tear down everything we and the people of this country built, you'd be in that meeting too. So I don't want you turning up in my bedroom like some Red Jacob Marley, d'you hear me, you old bastard?'. He returned to the meeting fresh-faced and sharp-witted, and together he, Horner and Mosley worked through the night, none of the three giving off the slightest indication of tiredness.

The members of the Emergency Executive continued to go their separate ways for the time being. Commissary for the Intelligence Bureau William Gallacher scheduled a meeting with T.E. Lawrence and his adjutant Ian Fleming about readying their Revolutionary Exportation Directive for immediate deployment in Iceland. Annie Kenney sat down at her typewriter and began to write well over a hundred letters, each one beginning with the word 'Sisters—'. G.D.H. Cole jotted down some designs for the Dig For Victory campaign's posters in his notebook as the night's last train on the Northern Line pulled out of Congress House station. A few carriages behind him, Jack Lewis leant back in his hard seat and made a mental note to do something about the two loudmouthed servicemen sitting nearby who had clearly had too much to drink. Careless talk cost lives, after all. Christabel Pankhurst couldn't quite believe the size of her office as she sat down in a chair behind the desk of the Deputy Commissary for Foreign Affairs in Britain House. Meanwhile, on a train hurtling across southern France, Stafford Cripps put aside a newspaper calling for war with Germany over 'the Moroccan insult' and turned his mind to the notes he had begun to make about securing French support against Canada.

Tomorrow was going to be a thoroughly interesting day.

International Interlude

1936-1940

The Storm before the Tempest

A selection of articles and extracts which provide a cultural and political cross-section of affairs outside Britain during the time period covered in the preceding volume.

Extract from 'To Kill A Mockingbird' by Harper Lee

This is an extract from one of the most popular books of all time. Harper Lee's To Kill a Mockingbird is a powerful tale of racism and power politics in the Deep South in the months leading up to the Second American Civil War and, ultimately, the Civil War itself. Although published in 1960, it uses many of Harper Lee's own personal experiences from the time in which it is set to weave an engaging tale for all ages. Told in first person by the innocent Scout Finch, it provides a child's insight into the wild politics of the period, personified by her father, the apolitical Atticus Finch, spurred to join a so-called 'Red Cell' – one of the many independently-built outposts of the Combined Syndicates of America deep in American Union State territory that refused to bow to corporatism. Finch joins with the militiamen, teachers and local working men who formed this cell after Huey Long's thugs murder a number of his colleagues in law, as well as a black rape suspect he was preparing to defend in court. This segment sees Atticus approached by the local militia leader with the task of shooting dead a Union State scout before he can report the Syndicalist positions.

*

Nothing is more deadly than a deserted, waiting street. The trees were still, the mockingbirds were silent, the carpenters at the barricade had vanished. I heard Mr. Tate sniff, then blow his nose. I saw him shift his gun to the crook of his arm. I saw Miss Stephanie Crawford's face framed in the glass window of her front door – she hadn't come out for days, not since they came for her boy. Miss Maudie appeared and stood beside her. Atticus put his foot on the rung of a chair and rubbed his hand slowly down the side of his thigh.

"There he is," he said softly.

Tim Johnson came into sight, walking dazedly in the inner rim of the curve parallel to the Radley house. He was no bigger than the fingertip on my pinky. "Look at him," whispered Jem. "He's trying to hide behind the piles of garbage."

It was true. Tim Johnson – I couldn't call him "The Enemy" like everyone said to – was creeping up the road. If it wasn't for the barricade he would have had as good a view of us as we had of him. The street was now longer and flatter than it had ever seemed before.

Mr. Tate put his eyeglasses to his forehead and leaned forward. "It's him all right, Mr. Finch. He's wearing the blue armband."

Tim Johnson was advancing at a snail's pace, but he seemed dedicated to one course and motivated by an invisible force that was inching him toward us. Perhaps he'd seen us before, at night. Or perhaps his Minutemen Chaplain told him that this neighborhood was full of red bookworms, like the man who had been shouting in the street a week before. Atticus had told us not to listen to chatter like that. "Some people don't like that we don't agree with them, and so they tell us that what we think comes from foreigners and isn't American. Mr Marx is one of those foreigners. It's no better than the way they treated Tom because he wasn't like them." He'd given Jem a copy of the Manifesto and sent us both to bed. I stole it from Jem that night and tried to read it under the covers, but there were too many long words and I couldn't understand it. The next day, I asked Atticus why Mr Marx couldn't write more simple, like when Mr Reed was on the radio. Atticus told me off for reading what I couldn't understand yet, but before he went outside he promised me he'd 'explain everything' on my birthday.

"He's lookin' for a tree to climb," said Jem. Mr. Tate turned around. "You're right, son, the bourgeois sonovabitch is trying to find an angle to sketch out where we've put our guns."

Tim Johnson reached the side street that ran in front of the Radley Place, and what remained of his poor mind made him pause and seem to consider which road he would take. He made a few hesitant steps and stopped in front of the Radley gate; then he tried to turn around, but was having difficulty.

Atticus said, "He's within range, Heck. You better get him before he goes down the side street – Lord knows he's seen enough now to bolt back to his people and sight their mortars. Go inside, Cal."

Calpurnia opened the screen door, latched it behind her, then unlatched it and held onto the hook. She tried to block Jem and me with her body, but we looked out from beneath her arms.

"Take him, Mr. Finch." Mr. Tate handed the rifle to Atticus; Jem and I nearly fainted.

"Don't waste time, Heck," said Atticus. "Go on."

"Mr. Finch, this is a one-shot job."

Atticus shook his head vehemently: "Then don't just stand there, Heck! Take him now!"

"For God's sake, Mr. Finch, look where he is! A miss and he runs all the way home and tells them what he's already seen. You know how fast that boy is. I can't shoot that well and you know it!"

"I haven't shot a gun in thirty years—"

Mr. Tate almost threw the rifle at Atticus. "I'd feel mighty comfortable if you did now," he said.

In a fog, Jem and I watched our father take the gun and carefully move toward one of the firing posts at the top of the barricade. He climbed quickly, but I thought he moved like an underwater swimmer; time had slowed to a nauseating crawl.

When Atticus raised his glasses, Calpurnia murmured "Sweet Jesus help him," and put her hands to her cheeks.

Atticus pushed his glasses to his forehead; they slipped down, and he dropped them in the street. In the silence, I heard them crack. Atticus rubbed his eyes and chin; we saw him blink hard.

In front of the Radley gate, Tim Johnson had made up his mind. He had fixed his eyes on an old tree with a thick knot in its bark. Jem and I knew from experience that it was easy enough to climb. He made two steps forward, then stopped and raised his head. I pictured his eyes narrowing. We saw his body go rigid.

"He's seen the gun!" Jem hissed.

With movements so swift they seemed simultaneous, Atticus's hand yanked a ball- tipped lever as he brought the gun to his shoulder.

The rifle cracked. Tim Johnson flopped over and crumpled on the sidewalk in a heap. He didn't know what hit him.

Mr. Tate and two of his men vaulted the barricade and ran to the Radley Place. He stopped in front of the body, squatted, turned around and tapped his finger on his forehead above his right eye.

"You were a little to the left, Mr. Finch," he called.

"Always was," answered Atticus.

*

The end of the book, in which the town of Maycomb, Alabama (renamed Maclean-Paine, Alabama in the penultimate chapter) is overrun by Union State troops and abandoned by its Syndicalist leaders, was voted the most powerful ending in literary history in a British poll in 1999. The image of Scout and her brother looking back on the burning town as their father mumbles prayers about not running out of fuel until they reach the units of the Combined Syndicates of America that are said to be trying to break through in Tennessee is unquestionably a very powerful one, as is the apparently obvious sense of an inevitable end for the Finch family. Meera Syal said, during the polling, that 'we know they aren't going to make it to the militia in Tennessee. There's hundreds of miles and a whole corporatist army between them and freedom. But Atticus drives on, and the last thing we hear of Scout is that she knows, in that way that only children can when all is so lost, that they will make it to safety and to liberty. That's why I cry each time I read it.'

The book was banned in the Combined Syndicates of America between 1972 and 1984.

Front page of 'Golos', published March 1937

This editorial front page from the Russian newspaper 'Golos' (meaning 'Voice'), celebrates the 'merits' of Wrangel's first year in charge of the country.

ALL GLORY TO THE VOZHD

RUSSIANS,

It is impossible to comprehend that a year ago we mourned the loss of the great unifier Kerensky. A great man capable of ruling Russia as one but constrained by petty democracy and the forces of sedition was finally struck down by the bullets of the cowardly intelligentsia. How grateful we are to brave, noble Pyotr Nikolayevich Wrangel for his diligent actions during that black time for our nation. In just one year, he has welded our fragile state into a corporatist behemoth, free of meddling bureaucrats and the plague of famine that rocked our fragile economy under 'democracy'. In forming the Council of State for Industrialisation, Modernisation and Centralisation our leader showed the mettle and genius required to rescue our motherland from this quagmire.

WHO can forget the blissful summer of peace, stability and reconstruction that we as Russians enjoyed after the violence and agitation that threatened to overturn the new corporate order? The Bolshevik remnants are smashed and the Kadets driven out of the towns and cities because of their stubbornness and limp-wristed ideas of 'democracy'. Only true, Russian statists are free to govern our land,

and we may all sleep more easily in our beds now that we have this assurance.

WHEN have Russians ever enjoyed a greater sense of security than now, thanks to the re-organisation of the armed forces under brave General Kornilov and the internal reforms enacted by Pyotr Wrangel's able deputy, Felix Yusupov? The social classes of Russia are at peace with one another and know the world will once again look on Russia with the fear and respect our land deserves.

WHERE were you on Saturday of last week when our leader was officially proclaimed Vozhd, the new, forward-looking and unquestionable autocrat of all the Russias? That is something we shall all remember and proudly tell our children, grandchildren and great-grandchildren.

And so, brave Russians, Golos today salutes the Vozhd for his spirit, his spine and his steel. He is truly the personification of the force needed to pull Russia from her age of stagnation – he is not backward-looking like the reactionary Tsarists, but nor is he mindlessly futuristic and with no regard for tradition like the Bolsheviks, Mensheviks or other dangerous leftists. As Europe plunges into chaos because of decadent, uncontrolled capitalism, the welding of the Russian state to her corporations, factories and businessmen stands as a beacon for the East and as an example to be followed or shared.

All Glory To The Vozhd!

GOLOS

Personal Diary of Mohandas Gandhi, 1938

In 1938, the man who would dominate the Indian subcontinent for a quarter of a century was the up-and-coming Colleague for Internal Development and Security. Recently granted a seat on the 'Supreme Council of the Bharitya Commune' (the governmental core of the People's Republic of Bengal) by Prasad, he had led the moderate faction of Bengal's Marxists in their calls for collectivism as a means of ending the caste system. The militant 'Bosists' (named after their leader Bose) opposed Gandhi's appointment and objected to his 'soft' approach to displeased peasants. This opposition dominated Gandhi's first six months in office almost as much as the task of 'selling' collectivisation, but he would eventually succeed, with Mosley himself envying that he had 'not a Gandhi, but a Gooch' attempting to convince the public of the necessity of the Second Agricultural Revolution.

*

11 January 1938

Another exhausting day. As I write, the train is steaming across the country for more of the same tomorrow. Giving speeches, distributing pamphlets and meeting local leaders is hard enough without the Bosists jeering me wherever I go. They stand on the sidelines with their clubs and blades and demand a stronger line from my department against those who dissent. Do they not know that honest disagreement is usually a good sign of progress? I do not have the energy to write much more tonight. I have, I will confess, been working at my desk since we returned to the train. I have decided to call my intentions the NIP – the New Industrial Plan. From what I am hearing every day from the people, it is direly needed – they all lost so much from collectivisation, and while it is undeniable that their grandchildren will benefit from its economic consequences that will not keep dissent from reaching dangerous levels. They need more support, a looser set of regulations and – there I go again. I am terrible at knowing when to stop writing. I will write more tomorrow, diary. Until then, goodnight.

25 February 1938

My dear, dear diary. Today, Bengal entered a new stage in her development as a nation. The New Industrial Plan was accepted by the Supreme Council and will be put into action immediately. The state factories standing idle or hardly in use will begin producing farming machinery in great quantities next month. I hope it does not make me arrogant to wish to report the standing ovation I received for the crown jewel of my proposals. The Fertiliser Distribution Initiative was, according to my colleagues at the Bureau for Public Planning, 'a stroke of genius' that should see agricultural yield increase while imposing no further controls on the peasants. This was, of course, what I had already calculated, but it was pleasing to have it ratified in such a public manner. The free fertiliser should also serve as a 'carrot' as opposed to the 'stick' still favoured by Bose and his hardliners – though some of them defected at the Commune meeting today, voting for my proposal. I have never been more proud of anything I have done. Thanks to my work, a Democratic Socialist future is at last secure for the people of Bengal.

6 August 1938

Bliss! My arms are sore from embraces, handshakes and the receipt of gifts. It is said the local people throw flowers on the line when 'the Gandhi Train' is on its way. The NIP has all but solved urban unemployment thanks to the re-opening of the factories. To think that they lay empty for so long after Mr. Attlee's railway programme came to its end. The tractors pouring from them as of last month are of a good standard, and are given heavenly nicknames among the peasants. The fertiliser is popular beyond imagination, and the farmers tell me it is working. There is even a story of children standing on a field of corn so thick it supports their weight. Nonsense, of course, but such things are good for morale. It is difficult to believe, dear diary, that I, little Mohandas, with my 'western, bourgeois education' and 'stupid idealism' have managed to turn our country's darkest hour into her finest. To think the Bosists called me a moron. Could a moron do *this*? To echo our British friends, we must go onwards! Onwards, diary, onwards!

19 October 1938

Yet another frustrating day with the Commune, dearest diary. The old men of the revolution refused to support the expansion of the NIP which the country needs if we are to compete with the Delhi Raj or the corrupt Princes in the south. The world knows that I am a man of peace, and I will take no part in building an army, but if our economy remains unprepared for the aggressive war we know we can expect from our reactionary neighbours, it is tantamount to treason to allow it to go on and risk the starvation of our blockaded peoples. There is too much industry in our border regions, I say, we must build in the safer areas – no, they reply, we do not have the funds and the people's army will defend us. The people's army, while vastly improved since the arrival of those advisers the Internationale sent, is not large enough to protect the length of our border from any possible incursion. But my attempts to open their eyes are in vain. That fool Prasad is the worst. He appointed me to fix the problems his policies had created. His stubbornness and ignorance now is enough to make one think that he, in fact, is the problem himself.

Does it not seem, therefore, dear diary, that I have one problem left to solve?

'Red, White, or Blue', Irish Folk Song, c.1939

After de Valera's return from Ottawa, Irish public opinion reached a higher state of politicisation than any time since 1925. The O'Duffy government struggled to control public outpourings of dismay over Ireland's perceived newfound love of the Royalists across the Atlantic. A country whose relationship with Britain transcended ideology, many Irish objected to being forced to align with one 'pack of Britons' over another. Through newspapers and radio broadcasts O'Duffy tried in vain to convey the seriousness of Ireland's situation. With the Vatican encircled, John XXIII little more than Mussolini's stooge and the Carlists rebuilding their own shattered Spain, Ireland found herself without friends in Europe. Her entanglement with the Catholic Wars had ended her détente with the Union of Britain and with Mitteleuropa recovering from the banking collapse of 1936, Canada was the only remaining obvious ally. Diplomatic realities apparently escaped the attention of the Irish people, however, for songs such as this could be heard in the pubs and streets of Dublin, Cork and Derry (and the parts of Belfast not still under martial law) long into the night.

*

In nineteen hundred and twenty-two
Irishmen vanquished the red, white and blue
We showed them we were sick of their King
And the people of Britain found they agreed.
They drove him away to the ends of the earth
(And we gained more trouble than Ulster was worth)[100]
Our friends were the Fathers, our brothers in God
The Red menace came and he mangled the lot
'We need new friends,' says O'Duffy, the clown

---

[100] The continued need for conscription caused by the ongoing Irish 're-integration' of Ulster was continually unpopular throughout the interbellum.

And says we can find them in Ottawa town.

Chorus
But Ireland remembers
For how could we not?
Four hundred years
Are not quickly forgot.
And we know oppressors
Whatever their hue,
We'll share with no Britons
Red, White, or Blue.

The Blues are in Canada, the Reds are nearby
And ask old Jim Larkin, they're almost as sly!
They say, 'We're sorry, can we all just move on?
We'd like to make use of you, like at the Somme.'[101]
The Whites are the bastards who decided to stay
The Orangemen hear from them four times a day[102]
But even they'll promise the Irish the world
And all for a gallon of pure Gaelic blood.

Chorus

---

[101] A reference to the catastrophically ill-judged attempt by the British government to apologise for the old regime's treatment of Ireland. The timing (1939) made it obvious that the Union was doing so to lure Ireland into an alliance of convenience, which when married with the British Army's perceived use of Irish units as cannon fodder (most infamously at the Somme) explains the disquiet conveyed by this line.

[102] A reference to the oft-romanticised, much-exaggerated 'royalist underground' that was purported to be operating in the interbellum Union of Britain. The joke regarding 'four times a day' stems from an increasingly senile (some say drunk) Stanley Baldwin taking to the Canadian airwaves in late 1939 and boasting that said underground network was in 'near-constant communication' with Loyalist and Protestant paramilitaries in Belfast, the closest thing the British Isles had to an armed group wanting to preserve the old regime.

So Ireland remembers
For how could we not?
Four hundred years
Are not quickly forgot.
And we know oppressors
Whatever their hue,
We'll share with no Britons
Red, White, or Blue.

So if you are British, our message is clear
You'll find no assistance, no comradeship here
Your King is your business, and not none of ours
Quite frankly, we'd sooner join the Central Powers.

Chorus
For Ireland remembers
For how could we not?
Four hundred years
Are not quickly forgot.
And we know oppressors
Whatever their hue,
We'll share with no Britons
Red, White, or Blue.

Transcript of 'Die Deutsche Wochenschau', August 1939

The voice of the German state continued to thunder across the airwaves of the Reich, with this edition dealing with political machinations, rearmament and the seeds of fresh tension with France.

*

Die Wacht Am Rhein is played. Images of the Kaiser, his son, the Armed Forces and bright views of cities and farms flash across the screen. These fade away to a black card upon which, in white gothic writing, is written 'Die Deutsche Wochenschau'.

News from around the world! All the pictures and quotations that shaped this week in world affairs.

A montage of images of Chancellor von Papen meeting with the Kaiser and speaking in the Reichstag is played.

The Kaiser restated his support for Chancellor von Papen this week after a number of obstructionist factions in the Reichstag sought to depose him. The so-called 'Imperial Moderates', members of the Reichskanzler's own party Standischer Verbund led by Carl Goerdeler, have grown angry with the tariff-heavy economic response to the Berlin Crash that has defined von Papen's government. It is, however, undeniable that Germans are better off now than they were in the aftermath of September 1936. The Reichskanzler, together with Mr Schacht at the Finance Ministry, has worked to increase quality of life while making Germany's armed forces stronger. The Kaiser told the Reichstag of this himself on Tuesday, gracing it with a rare visit. His Highness was in good health and accompanied by his son, the Crown Prince.

A crude cartoon of a villainous-looking cockerel struts about in front of a fluttering tricolor before pecking at the Rhine on a map. Images of tanks and aircraft are displayed where appropriate.

Speaking of the armed forces, the need to defend ourselves was confirmed to be never greater when another outrageous demand for the secession of Alsace and Lothringen was received from the French embassy. German soldiers were ordered to partial mobilisation after the Syndicalists in Paris appeared to issue an ultimatum, but after a show of force was conducted along the border, including the deployment of the new Reichskampfwagen II, a hasty memorandum was delivered to the Kaiser informing him that the demand was 'no longer of concern'.

The French have once again shown that while they may hammer red to their banners, their true colour is the white of cowardice, spinelessness and surrender. Germany will never allow the good people, native or German, of Alsace and Lothringen to be oppressed under the yoke of Syndicalism. As the Kaiser himself said in his Christmas address: 'While there is a soldier left in Germany we shall fight. If he should fall, I will take up his rifle myself.' All Germans should take comfort in this, and men of viable age are reminded that the armed forces are always looking for new recruits. Who knows? Maybe a young man in your family could be lucky enough to end up in the Eagle Legion, the heroes of Burgos!

Obviously staged footage of caricatured Arab tribesmen charging at machine gun positions is played with drawn maps of Morocco overlaid. The scene fades into proud, tall German soldiers being inspected in Malta.

Georg von Brüchmuller, Chief of the Imperial General Staff, inspected Task Force Morocco on Friday as it took to sea. The agrarian rebellion in the country has, unfortunately, been intensified since the collapse of the nearby Spanish holdings and the driving out of their Syndicalist agitators. An unfortunate consequence of this has been a plague of Syndicalist rhetoric that is spreading across the country with violent speed, but the military intervention is firmly under control. We are, after all, the nation that quelled similar problems in Russia and China, Colonial Minister Von Lettow-Vorbeck reminded the Reichstag on the same day. 'What problems should we expect from our own tiny colony a fraction of the size and complexity of those behemoths?'

Footage of a football match is shown, with primitive cards displaying score where appropriate.

Finally, in sporting news, the Reich's football team defeated reigning Mitteleuropan champions Hungary in a tight contest on Saturday in Budapest. Captain Hermann Schleicher scored two, while Hungary looked set to win after a fine three thanks to impressive control. However, in the eighty-eighth minute the boys from Germany equalised with a strong header from Erich Höffer, and a free kick with just injury time remaining meant it all came down to midfielder Reinhard Heydrich, in the last game of his international career. With a beautifully curved ball, the retiring star secured a stunning victory over the champions. With a team of this calibre, there can be no doubt that Germany will take back the title properly at the next Mitteleuropa Cup in 1942!

Front page of *Le Temps*, 27 September 1940

Le Temps had been the paper of record for Frenchmen since before the Revolution and remained so after it. This extract deals with the beginning of the final stages of the Third Moroccan Crisis.

THE TIME HAS COME

We have watched Frenchmen oppressed.

We have watched fellow leftists murdered.

We have watched a Revolution be all but strangled in its cradle. It is time to stop watching and to take ***action***.

What free man has not heard of the terrible insult being forced upon France in Morocco? As if the suppression of the Moroccan worker's voice was not enough, the threat of war against any state that recognises the legitimate Casablanca government is a calculated attempt to provoke conflict with our labourers' republic. It is time for Frenchmen to stand up and, if the Germans long so for conflict, give it to them. Our liberating fire shall pour across their borders and not even the most terrifying of reactionary 'wunderwaffen' shall douse it. Our Moroccan brothers *shall* be freed. The German worker *shall* know the paradise of the Totalised state. The world *shall* see what we, the proud standard-bearers of the new France, are capable of.

We are ready. Our soldiers are ready. Our thousands of volunteers in Morocco are willing us on with one voice every day to take more direct action against the oppressive tyrant in Berlin. Each day the treatment of Moroccans, Chinese and – worst of all – our fellow Frenchmen in Alsace and Lorraine grows worse. Our fellow workers in Italy took action to free their brethren from the Papist yoke. Our

Comrades in Britain know that all that is necessary for evil to triumph is for good men to do nothing.[103] For too long the people of France have watched as evil occurs before our very eyes.

The time has come for action. The time has come for war.

---

[103] It is amusing to ponder what Edmund Burke would think of his quotation being appropriated by French Revolutionaries.

Volume III

1940-1945

The Second Great War

'The lamps are going out again.'
Stafford Cripps, December 1940

The Iceland Campaign

Mark Wintringham

'It is warmer than I expected.'
Lieutenant General John Vereker on landing at Höfn, 9 October 1940

It seems most appallingly reactionary to be required by scholarship to assess one's father's legacy. One need only read the numerous biographies written by the junior members of the Churchill, de Gaulle and Hohenzollern families to be convinced of the right's self-flagellating obsession with the strengths and weaknesses of their forefathers. But here I sit, a letter from John Durham by my side, asked to write several chapters about the Second Great War, a subject which for years I have refused to do any more but lecture on. To claim the entire war to be my father's legacy would be, of course, arrogant folly, and so my task of paternal assessment is made considerably easier by the millions of Britons who shared the burden he faced. He may have been Tom Wintringham, Chairman of the Home Defence Committee, but the trials and tribulations he went through in organising our great national struggle were no more or less challenging than those of Clem Attlee at the Exchequer, T.E. Lawrence in the arms factories of the Ruhr, or Private Joseph Bloggs of the 2nd Warwickshire Front. Whether the men and women of the Union of Britain 'did their bit' in the bunkers of Whitehall, at the front at home or abroad or in the fields and factories that fuelled the righteous victory of the workers, every single one of them played their part.

And so, to begin. John Durham's excellent preceding chapter has painted an all-too-clear picture of Europe in October 1940. Diplomatic trains and aircraft hurtled across the continent, delivering memoranda and ultimata that would shape the rest of the 20th century. Within a month, the great powers of Europe would be at each other's throats. The dual causes of the Second Great War – the Iceland

Blockade and the Third Moroccan Crisis – meant that the conflict became, almost immediately, intercontinental in its scope. From the farthest corners of the Atlantic to the streets of Rabat, the righteous fire of Revolution blazed from the muzzles of rifles, pistols, artillery and naval guns, and was answered by the frantic flashes of an old order that, like a wounded predator, was at its most dangerous when at its most desperate. War was declared on Britain by Canada at 1100 GMT on 1 October[104] and a state of war came into being between France and Germany three days later on 4 October due to an expired ultimatum demanding a complete withdrawal of the latter's forces from Morocco. It was upon this backdrop that the men of the first expedition to Iceland (or rather, the first expedition in wartime) boarded the ships of the Home Fleet and set sail for the most unlikely of battlefields. The average age of those men was 23 – relatively high – and a third of the enlisted men had degrees or similar qualifications. They were Britain's best and Britain's brightest, and they were off to fight the Royalist menace.

In their way stood a navy that would become so great a scourge to British livelihood and freedom that Mosley himself called it 'the only thing that ever truly frightened me.' The Royal Navy, still defiantly flying the flag of the old regime and bearing all its old hallmarks,[105] was, unlike much of the Royalist war effort, a force to be reckoned with.

In many ways, the British Army that disembarked at Höfn was unrecognisable compared to that which it would later become. Wintringham's sweeping 'People's Army' conscriptions had only just begun, and many of the men and units involved were veterans of Italy or America. To use a blunt turn of phrase, they were a tough bunch,

---

[104] The British Government-in-Exile, in what is surely an amusing historical footnote, declined (appropriately) to declare war, even though that was among its constitutional 'rights' as set out in the Canadian Parliament's British Government Act of 1927. This was in part due to its members' belief that to declare war on Britain would give the wrong impression, and equally due to the potential absurdity of the alleged British Government declaring war on itself.
[105] The largest Battleship to leave Britain during the Exodus, the aptly-named HMS *Revenge*, was rechristened HMS *King George V*.

and they knew it. Facing them were untested elements of the Royal Canadian Army and the 3rd Division of the 'British Army'. Here a common problem of semantics will be addressed. With two armies – indeed, nations – stressing that they were the rightful claimants to the name 'British', is it inevitable that confusion will arise when narrating battles between the two. For this reason, my chapters in this book will describe those units loyal to Edward VIII, Churchill and reaction as Royalist, while units of the Union will be referred to as British. These means of distinction have been selected in part due to their being the method of choice of Army Popular Command (APC) during the War itself.

Alongside this mixture of Royalist forces were a section of the Icelandic armed forces, itself an exceptionally irregular force armed with antiquated Danish rifles and comprising barely a division in size. Iceland had barely been independent long enough to formally organise an army before the Reykjavik Riots had forced any able-bodied man loyal to the government onto the streets. To these militias now fell the unenviable task of pacifying a country torn apart by extremes on the left and right while two great powers fought their war in its streets and on its mountainsides.[106] The remainder of the Icelandic Army was, more often than not, loyal to the nearest bread supply. The troops that did not desert and head for their families were fighting partly out of a sense of adventure and partly to ensure the 'invaders' – both British and Canadian – did not damage their green and pleasant young republic too heavily. There were, of course, reactionaries and socialists in Iceland, too. Some men would welcome the British forces with open arms, while others fled to the path of the Canadian advance out of fear or cynicism.

The British advance would be coming from the south of the country, while the Canadians aimed to meet them from the west. Admiral Chatfield's decision that the Republican Navy would not seek decisive battle against the Royal Navy was a *de facto* acceptance that the

---

[106] For more on this matter, I recommend Sprøgoe's seminal *A Country Almost Stillborn: Iceland 1938-1941*, which, as of the time of publication, has recently been translated from the original Danish.

Canadians would have unmolested access to the port of Reykjavik, far and away the only harbour suitable for disembarking the army of a major power. But Chatfield had a plan to bring an end to this unmolested status as soon as possible. She sailed in the middle of the Home Fleet, she carried 60 aircraft on her decks, and her name was RNS *Land and Labour*.

Lieutenant General John Vereker, tasked by APC with commanding British forces in Iceland, understood that each day the enemy controlled Reykjavik, their position became less assailable. Having learned the lessons of failed amphibious operations thanks to the criminal Churchill's folly at Gallipoli, he ordered an immediate breakout from the peacefully-secured port of Höfn by the end of the first day of disembarkation. The combination of Icelandic terrain and British equipment meant the only option was to snake along the southern coast of the country, inevitably meeting the Canadian and Royalist forces, but planning to do so on British terms. The initial phase of the offensive was successful but understated, as then-Colonel Alex McDade of the 4th Infantry Column wrote:

> 'We found ourselves in a defensible position with guns and ammunition necessary to hold for a number of days, perhaps a week. Food and water were in plentiful supply. Enemy artillery had been sighted some miles west so efforts were made to camouflage ourselves against the hillside. My Comrades and I ate well on the first night and looked forward to challenging the enemy to take back what we had taken from him. He would not succeed.'

McDade was a veteran of the Catholic Wars, and his battle-honed instincts proved correct. On the morning of 18 October, Canadian units and some 'Government' Icelandic units attacked the 4th's position. A skirmish lasting some four-and-a-half hours ensued, with the reactionaries retreating at 1130. The 4th took only light casualties while the Canadian and local troops fell in droves. Although it was not realised at the time, the defence of Hill 12 had seen the first shots fired in anger not only of the Iceland Campaign, but the first exchange of fire between Canadian and British troops in history.

On the Royalist side, Field Marshall Ironside knew he and his Canadian allies had the simpler task: push on to Höfn and drive the enemy back into the sea. Höfn was little more than a village, its harbour exposed. He was thus content to continually unload further reinforcements from the grandly (and prematurely) named 'Liberation Fleet' while using his forward units to halt the British counter-advance towards Reykjavik. Two days of inconclusive skirmishes followed, with neither side gaining much of an advantage. The rocky coastal roads left little room for manoeuvre, so fearing a stalemate, Vereker gave the codeword 'Naseby' to Admiral Chatfield. and RNS *Land and Labour* began steaming towards the agreed location.

The Reykjavik Raid was the first test of a purely carrier-launched force of aircraft bombing a harbour. Poor weather made this a difficult task, and three Roundhay Skua dive bombers crashed when attempting to land thanks to low visibility. Though ostensibly less modern, Ringway Syndicate Swordfish biplanes proved more capable of hitting their targets in the event, while two-winged Royal Canadian Air Force and Royal Air Force Gladiators duelled them in the skies above the harbour. The sight was one of several ways in which the opening weeks of the Second Great War resembled the First.

The bombing having killed more Icelandic civilians than enemy personnel, and disembarkation visibly still taking place, it was decided that another approach would be pursued to interfere with the Canadian landings. With Chatfield still reluctant to deploy the Home Fleet against the Royal Navy, trepidation apparently shared by the equally timid Royalist Admiral North, a dossier marked 'Most Secret' and bearing the name Operation Copenhagen was opened by Vereker. Contact with London was established, and Mosley gave the necessary order.

The Revolutionary Exportation Directive had shipped to Iceland with the second wave of British troops. Unlike their Army counterparts, the eighty commandos had not disembarked at Höfn, and remained on board the cruiser RNS *Gramsci*. Lawrence was not with them, having drawn lots with Ian Fleming over being allowed to accompany their men to Iceland. Fleming's more naval background made him the more suitable candidate regardless, but neither man would be going into battle as part of the RED's first deployment.

Operation Copenhagen is today best-remembered as the opening sequence of the 1961 film *Europe Ablaze*, in which it is presented as a heroic but ill-fated assault by plucky socialists let down by poor weather and bad luck, some of whom survive and go on to form the core cast of the rest of the film. This is inaccurate on a number of counts. The weather, while cold and wet, was no worse than would be expected for Iceland in October, and did not suddenly turn to a storm mid-firefight. 'Bad luck', as was so often the case in pre-1976 films about the War, was code for incompetence and under-preparedness in the upper ranks. More morbidly, the characters in the scene who go on to fight in the Ruhr with Lawrence of Germania could not have done so in real life, for all the RED commandos who took part in the raid were captured or killed.

The failure of limpet mines to work in icy North Atlantic conditions could, perhaps, have been foreseen through proper testing. Mosley's order for Lawrence to be shot at dawn was nevertheless the height of unreason, and had Horner not intercepted it in time, it is likely the firing squad would have held an immediate vote on whether to carry out the execution.[107] Lawrence only learned of the order some months later, at which point he was in the Ruhr and having no trouble making explosives successfully detonate.

The RED's first outing had been a near-complete failure, and Fleming would return to London able to successfully argue that his original plan – to spend five days recruiting Icelandic socialists to assist in the attack before going ahead – should form the blueprint for future RED actions. This would not help operations on Iceland in the here-

---

[107] Though now illegal, soldiers' ballots regarding decisions taken by officers took place sporadically in the opening months of the War. They went unpunished until a section of the Alsace Front was encircled thanks to a lengthy balloting process over orders to advance. A sympathetic Wintringham successfully had the death sentence commuted to hard labour for the organisers, but the example was set. Only a handful further such actions took place during the War, usually over moral questions. See *Crises of Conscience: RAF Terror Bombing Ballots 1942-1943* by Shirley McKitterick.

and-now, however, and Vereker liaised with Chatfield to assess the situation and possible ways forward.

On the front line, the stalemate continued. Colonel McDade and the 4th Column had led an assault on 14 October which seized a naturally-defensible point on the banks of an inlet of the Atlantic. The nearby village of Grafarkirkja became the forward HQ for British forces. The 4th's position remained the furthest point of advance by British troops, and was successfully held against lacklustre probing attacks by Royalists. Identification proved a problem in the field – the British Army, the Royalists, and the Canadians all wore the Brodie tin hat with its distinctive flared rim, and the armies' greatcoats were virtually indistinguishable from one another, being based on the same First Great War counterpart. Incidents of friendly fire claimed more lives than enemy action on two separate days of the stalemate, and the Central Bureau was informed. Wintringham began working immediately with Eric Blair and veterans of the Catholic Wars to make recommendations on changing the Army's uniform. The shift to the flatter, rimless helmet that would enter production in 1941 would mark the biggest change. The wider changes to the British uniform would largely rely on information from the field in Iceland, mainly Major Bill Alexander's detailed report on the use of strips of red cloth, as in Spain, to create armbands. On the Royalist side, the Brodie helmet would be maintained, but uniforms would shift to a dark shade of blue, akin to the blue of the Canadian flag (red having been expunged from it in 1930 because of the new connotations of that colour, and possible confusion with the banner of the Union of Britain). But during the Iceland Campaign, all of this was in the future. Friendly fire remained an issue, and reports of summary executions of captured trench raiders made the front line even less merry a place.

British and wider Internationale respect for the laws of war remained broadly intact on the Alsace Front and throughout the conflict with Germany and Mitteleuropa. This was not the case in the battle against the Entente, the alliance of old powers trying to 'take back' their countries from 'revolution'. With both sides believing that the war would end with the execution of the entire enemy high command for either treason or counter-revolutionary activity, the usual element of self-preservation involved in giving orders that respected the Geneva Convention was removed. For this early stage of the conflict, records are hard to come by, having been deliberately destroyed in many cases. We know that as the war went on, particularly after the Nantwich Massacre, agreements were put in place and some respect for enemy prisoners was restored. Whether Vereker or Ironside personally gave orders akin to Brigadier Warrington's infamous 'No Quarter' instruction at Stafford[108] is unproven and broadly unsuspected. But the Iceland Campaign set the tone for British clashes with Royalist forces, and it was a grim one.

By the middle of the second week of the campaign, there looked to be only one remaining option. Royalist and Canadian numerical and material advantage meant Vereker would not countenance a frontal assault, and he would likely faced elected mutiny if he did. The lessons of the last war had at least been learned. The RED had fallen flat, the terrain negated any other form of unconventional assault, and air superiority was either with the enemy or an irrelevance due to the weather. Chatfield reluctantly began to move the fleet towards Reykjavik.

The Battle of Surtsey began when, in the morning mist of 20 October 1940, destroyer RNS *Portsmouth Combined Works* opened fire on HMS *Echo*. By the time the smoke cleared eight hours later, the Royal Navy had decisively seen off the assault by the Home Fleet, and the only saving grace the Republican Navy could cling to was the destruction of battleship HMS *George V* by aircraft, the first time this feat would be achieved during the War. Intelligence failures were further blamed, Station X at Horse Guards having fallen for false communications in a cipher the enemy knew had been cracked. The Royalist fleet was underestimated in size, and it was realised too late that the Republican Navy was simply stretched too thin. The Home Fleet comprised only two-fifths of Britain's naval strength, with Channel, Irish, and North Sea fleets all protecting their vital waterways

---

[108] See *But Lose His Soul: British War Crimes during The Defence*, Eric Dutt (London: Combined Press, 1965)

for fear of surprise invasions or raids. The Royal Navy, by contrast, had set out in strength from Canada and brought the majority of the Royal Canadian Navy with it. The scale of the forces arranged against the Home Fleet only became clear when HMS *Ajax* led a force of light cruisers into view from the south, the initial broadsides devastating Chatfield's destroyer screen. A more aggressive Royalist admiral than North might have done even more damage.

The battle formally ended when RNS *Land and Labour*, the Union's oldest carrier, was holed below the waterline and went down with four hundred hands. Chatfield ordered a full retreat and the cautious North only pursued for two miles. The Royal Navy contented itself with the victory it has secured. And why not?

RNS *Tolpuddle* was forced to limp back to port, carrying Ernle Chatfield and his staff. Chatfield would be dismissed within days, and Rear Admiral Fred Copeman, the first admiral born in a workhouse and a veteran of the Catholic Wars who had been in command of RNS *Winstanley*, received a hefty promotion. Vereker suffered the same fate, being demoted to Brigadier and threatened with a Popular Tribunal. Colonel McDade, having led the successful evacuation of the fraction of British forces that made it off Iceland and back onto their troop ships, became Lieutenant General McDade within the month. Mosley's paranoia had begun to show itself, and widely-held suspicions of the old order appeared vindicated by what is now regarded by historians as an unwinnable situation for even the most brilliant commanders. Nevertheless, the class profile of the upper ranks of the British Army had begun to shift.

The Iceland Campaign was a dismal failure for virtually all branches of our Union's armed forces. I said at the start of this essay that I would not hold back in my assessment of my father's role in this failure. It is true that his recommendations, particularly regarding more post-Revolution personnel, would have altered the progress of the campaign, but perhaps not its outcome. But as Chairman of the Home Defence Committee, particularly one who had been warning of the threat of an assault on Iceland for some years, he must shoulder some blame for the failure to properly anticipate the enemy's level of commitment. The decision not to bring any armoured divisions to Iceland based on flawed assumptions about terrain ought to be condemned, but it is probable that doing so spared Britain's Ironsides, veterans of America, from being left behind in Iceland if the campaign was still a failure. And in the week following the evacuation, Wintringham's decision to sack Walter Kirke as Army chief-of-staff of Army Popular Command and assume that role himself would have far-reaching consequences for the War, and for domestic politics.

The evacuated troops had barely reached Scapa Flow when reports reached the Central Bureau that suggested there would be no respite for the British war effort. On 30 October, Chairman Mosley called an emergency meeting of the Central Bureau to discuss the latest news from the British Co-operative Force on the Alsace Front.

To be continued?

The story of *The People's Flag* ends here. The vast majority of it was written in 2010-11, and I have only recently revisited it. If this published release proves to generate appetite for a continuation of the story, I will endeavour to publish the volumes dealing with the Second Great War and its aftermath with Sea Lion Press.

If you liked this book and don't want to wait until then, a number of my other works are available with Sea Lion Press. *Agent Lavender* is a comic novel, written with Jack Tindale, telling the story of Harold Wilson being outed as a KGB spy and the chaos that ensues. *Meet the New Boss* chronicles the history of a very different far-left Britain: a state of vassalage imposed by Moscow after it is liberated by the Red Army in 1946. *Zonen* is a simple short story about Denmark occupying northern Germany after the War, told as a series of interviews.

All these and more can be found on the Sea Lion Press website, under 'Our Books'.

Thank you for reading *The People's Flag*. Perhaps one day John Durham and his fellow academics will return to continue the tale.

Tom Black
July 2019

Sea Lion Press

Sea Lion Press is the world's first publishing house dedicated to alternate history. To find out more, and to see our full catalogue, visit **sealionpress.co.uk.**

Sign up for our mailing list at **sealionpress.co.uk/contact** to be informed of all future releases.

To support Sea Lion Press, visit **patreon.com/sealionpress**

Printed in Great Britain
by Amazon